Big Lake
Snowdaze

By Nick Russell

Nick Russell
1400 Colorado Street C-16
Boulder City, NV 89005
E-mail Editor@gypsyjournal.net

Also By Nick Russell

Fiction

Big Lake Mystery Series

Big Lake
Big Lake Lynching
Crazy Days In Big Lake
Big Lake Blizzard
Big Lake Scandal
Big Lake Burning
Big Lake Honeymoon
Big Lake Reckoning
Big Lake Brewpub
Big Lake Abduction
Big Lake Celebration
Big Lake Tragedy
Big Lake Snowdaze

Dog's Run Series

Dog's Run
Return To Dog's Run

John Lee Quarrels Series

Stillborn Armadillos
The Gecko In The Corner
Badge Bunny

Standalone Mystery Novels

Black Friday

Nonfiction

Highway History and Back Road Mystery
Highway History and Back Road Mystery II
Meandering Down The Highway; A Year On The Road
With Fulltime RVers
The Frugal RVer
Work Your Way Across The USA; You Can Travel And
Earn A Living Too!
Overlooked Florida
Overlooked Arizona
The Gun Shop Manual

Keep up with Nick Russell's latest books at
www.NickRussellBooks.com

Author's Note

While there is a body of water named Big Lake in the White Mountains of Arizona, the community of Big Lake and all persons in this book live only in the author's imagination. Any resemblance in this story to actual persons, living or dead, is purely coincidental.

Chapter 1

"Oh, Jimmy. On the long list of crazy things we've done since I met you, this one tops them all. Let's just forget about this whole thing while we can."

"Stop being such a wuss, Parks. How bad could it possibly be?"

"Bad, Robyn. Real bad."

"I'm going to do it, too."

"Yeah, but you've already got internal plumbing. When my junk hits that cold water, it's gonna go places it was never intended to be!"

"Well, if you're going to act like a little girl, you might as well be one."

"When I was stationed in Alaska I fell through the ice on a little creek," Deputy Ted "Coop" Cooper said. "It was only knee deep, but that was enough for me. I can't believe I'm doing this."

"I swear, Marsha," Parks warned, "if you do something like locking the doors when we try to get back in, or driving away and leaving us standing there, I'm going to hunt you down if it's the last thing I ever do."

"Relax, will you? I promise I'll have all the doors unlocked and the heater going full blast. And here," the woman behind the steering wheel of the Chrysler Pacifica held up a big stainless steel thermos and said, "this hot buttered rum will be right here waiting for you."

"It's so damn cold out there that I just farted snowflakes! Whose idea was this, anyway?"

"It damn sure wasn't mine," Sheriff Jim Weber said. "You can blame Juliette Murdoch at the Chamber of Commerce for this one. She's the one that dreamed up the challenge between us and the volunteer fire department."

1

"Yeah, but that was between the Sheriff's Department and the fire guys. How the hell did I get roped into it?"

"When the FBI gave you this cushy job up here, part of it was to assist the local police agencies, right? That's what you're doing. Besides, I had to keep one deputy dressed and on-duty to hold back the crowd when they see that good-looking body of yours."

"No, man," Parks said, shaking his head. "They never covered this in training at Quantico."

"Just quit your sniveling," Robyn said. "Okay guys, get ready, they're going to start the countdown!"

Outside the minivan Town Councilman Kirby Templeton, wearing a heavy parka with a fur-lined hood, was using a bullhorn to address the gathered crowd.

"Okay folks, are you ready?"

There was applause from the crowd, and Kirby shook his head.

"No, that's not going to cut it. I asked, *are you ready*?"

This time there were hoots and hollers and cheers from the audience.

"That's more like it," Kirby said. "Now, you all heard the rules, right? When Councilman Gauger fires the shotgun, ten representatives from the Big Lake Fire Department, over here on the left, and ten representatives from the Sheriff's Department, there on the right, are all going to run down the boat ramp and into that icy water. They have to get at least chest deep and they all have to duck themselves under at least once. This is an endurance contest folks, and whichever department has somebody stay in the water the longest is the winner. Will it be the big brawny men of the Fire Department?"

There were loud cheers from the crowd.

"Or will it be those brave men and one daring lady from the Sheriff's Department?"

More cheers and applause as fans of the Sheriff's Department showed their support.

"Okay then, I guess we'll all know pretty soon, won't we?"

More cheers from the crowd.

"Chief Harper, if your firemen are ready, honk your horns."

Horns blasted on the two vehicles holding the firemen, signifying they were ready to go.

"Sheriff Weber, how about you?"

Marsha held her hand down on the Pacifica's horn, and next to them Meghan Northcutt, wife of Deputy Jordan Northcutt, blew her SUV's horn.

"All right! Councilman Gauger, are you ready?"

Standing on the shore of the lake, Frank Gauger nodded and shouldered his Ithaca 20 gauge over and under shotgun, aiming it out over the ice covered lake. "Okay, on three. Everybody help me count it down," Kirby said over the bullhorn.

"One," shouted the crowd.

"Oh, this is crazy," Parks said.

"Two."

"I don't want to do this!"

"Three!"

Gauger pulled the trigger and the shotgun roared. Car doors flew open and nineteen men, along with Deputy Robyn Fuchette, poured out of their vehicles and ran the few feet to the concrete boat ramp, slipping and sliding as they made their way down to the ice cold water. There were hoots and hollers from the crowd, and whistles at Robyn in her one piece bathing suit.

Those were quickly followed by shrieks from the contestants as they plunged into the icy water.

"Oh-My-God! I'm gonna die!"

"Damn, it's cold!"

"No way!"

"I think my nuts just fell off!"

"Stop being such sissies. Get those heads under!"

The water was so cold that it burned, and Weber felt his whole body clench by the time it had reached his knees. He knew he had to go out further and duck under, but there was nothing he wanted more than to turn tail and run back to the warmth of Marsha's van. As it turned out, he didn't have to force himself to go on, because Dale Portwood, a string bean of a man who spent his working hours mowing grass and laying sod in the summer for a landscaping company and driving a snowplow in the wintertime when he wasn't answering calls as a volunteer fireman, slipped on the icy ramp. He landed on his rear end and slid into the water, knocking four or five people off their feet like some kind of human scythe as he went.

With his back turned away from shore, Weber hadn't seen that coming and swallowed a mouthful of cold water on the way down. He bobbed to the surface, coughing and choking, and managed to get his feet under him. The water was up to his armpits and he was surprised that once he had been totally immersed it didn't feel nearly as bad as the cold air did. All around him people were yelling and shouting, and at least half of the contestants had already admitted defeat and run for the warmth of the waiting cars.

Weber looked over at Steve Harper, Big Lake's Fire Chief, who was standing in the water chastising his men as they fled. "You're all a bunch of chickens. You gonna let these guys beat us?"

"Not me, I quit," Robyn yelled as she pushed past him and ran up the ramp.

"Traitor!" Weber yelled after her.

"You gonna follow your girlfriend, Jimmy?"

"Not until you're outta here," Weber told him.

"Hell, son, I plan on staying here until the spring thaw so I'll be the first person to catch a fish next year!"

There was a yell from over his shoulder, and Weber turned to see if it was one of his deputies giving up, or a fireman who had had enough. He was surprised to discover that it was Kevin Upchurch, Harper's best friend. While Upchurch, who worked as a maintenance man for the school system and stood head and shoulders above his shorter friend, had always been unerringly loyal to Harper, it looked like he was about to betray the Fire Chief as he made his way toward the ramp. But then Weber realized there was something different about the tone of his voice. Upchurch had a look that was almost terror on his face,

4

and he was dragging something behind him. Weber looked again and realized it wasn't *something*, it was someone. At first he thought one of the participants in the Polar Bear plunge had collapsed, but then he realized it was a woman. A naked woman. A very obviously dead naked woman.

The sheriff looked at Steve Harper and said, "And I thought the worst thing that could possibly happen this weekend was when the mayor killed Santa Claus!"

Chapter 2

In the beginning everything had seemed to come together perfectly for Big Lake's first annual Snowdaze celebration. The summer before, when Chamber of Commerce Director Juliette Murdoch presented the idea to the Town Council as a way to kick off the winter tourist season, everybody on the Council had quickly climbed on board.

Paul Lewis, publisher of the *Big Lake Herald*, promised the newspaper's full support, including a front page story to announce the event's coming. Jennifer Kopman, the manager of Cat Mountain Ski Resort, pledged $5,000 to help cover initial marketing costs and said the resort would be promoting the event through emails and direct mail pieces to their customer lists. Mayor Chet Wingate, always stingy with a dollar, surprised everyone by putting a motion before the Council that they match Cat Mountain's contribution, and committees were formed to handle entertainment, transportation, food vendors, and all of the other things that go into making an event successful. Sheriff Jim Weber and Fire Chief Steve Harper were instructed to work together to handle details of things like safety, parking, and security.

Of course, not everybody was thrilled.

"Ain't it bad enough we got all these summer people parading around up here? Used to be, back before the ski lodge opened up, we could at least get a break from them in the wintertime," Arnold Foster had groused from the audience. Arnold was a curmudgeon who spent a lot of time complaining when he wasn't otherwise occupied in his ongoing feud with his brother-in-law, Harley Willits.

"Shut your yap," Harley said. "You'd bitch if they hung you with a new rope."

"Well, it's true! There was a time around here when a man knew who his neighbors were. Now we got so damn many

7

flatlanders invading the place that we started locking the doors at night."

"*I'm* your neighbor, you idiot! Have been for over 25 years. And the only reason Margaret is locking the doors at night is to keep you from wandering off, now that you got senile."

"Who are you calling senile?"

"You, you senile old fart."

Mayor Chet Wingate had rapped his gavel and said, "That's enough! Do either of you two have something you want to contribute to the discussion at hand?"

"Yeah, I do," Arnold said, ignoring his brother-in-law. "Like I said, it's bad enough we got 'em here all summer. But ever since that damn ski lodge opened they're here in the wintertime, too!"

"You already said that. What's your point?"

"My point is, I don't like it! And all this damn Snowshoe festival you guys are talking about is going to do is bring more people we don't need up here."

"It's called Snowdaze," Juliette Murdoch had corrected him.

"I don't care what you call it, I don't like it!"

If Arnold didn't like something, there was no question that Harley was going to be all for it, no matter what it was. "I think we should do it. Sounds good to me."

"Nobody cares what you think," Arnold said before the mayor cut them off by rapping his gavel again.

"You two can take your argument someplace else. Does anybody else in the audience have something to say about this proposal?"

"Yeah," said Todd Norton, owner of the local auto parts shop. "I don't like it either. You're wasting taxpayer money on something that doesn't help the business community at all."

"Please stand up when you address the Council," the mayor had said.

"He *is* standing up," said Harley Willits, drawing snickers from the crowd and an angry look from Norton. At barely five feet tall, Norton had a strong case of little man's syndrome and walked around with a noticeable chip on his shoulder.

Rapping his gavel once again, the mayor shouted, "Silence! Stop interrupting, Harley." Turning to Juliette Murdoch, he asked, "Would you care to address that issue, Ms. Murdoch?"

"Certainly," she said, standing up. "Yes, this will help the business community, Todd. More people in town means more dollars are being spent in our local businesses. That's a no-brainer."

"Sure, they're going to spend money in the restaurants and bars, and motels, and probably out at the ski lodge, too. But how does that help me? Do you think folks coming to town for this stupid festival are going to stop at my place and buy a fan belt or an oil filter?"

"Not necessarily. But more outside money coming into town benefits all of us. You're right, maybe a visitor isn't going to come into your shop. But if he spends money at the restaurant and tips the waitress, maybe that gives her the money she needs to buy that fan belt or a filter for her car. That's what I mean when I say we all stand to gain from this."

"Yeah, right. I'll believe that when I see it," Todd said sarcastically.

Even given those objections, the Town Council had voted unanimously in support of Snowdaze, and a few months later it was a reality.

Even Mother Nature seemed to be cooperating with the event planners; a cold front had brought a heavy snowfall to the White Mountains of Arizona, dumping over a foot of the white stuff at the higher elevations just two days before Snowdaze weekend began in early December. The little mountain town looked like something out of a Norman Rockwell painting, with Christmas decorations strung from the light poles on Main Street, kids building snowmen in their yards, and smoke rising from chimneys all over Big Lake.

Yes, it looked like Snowdaze was going to come off without a hitch. Everybody was saying so. Well, almost everybody.

Maybe Sheriff Weber was a natural born grinch, as his fiancée, Deputy Robyn Fuchette, sometimes implied. Or maybe his years wearing a badge had made him cynical. But he had a bad feeling the moment Mayor Chet Wingate had come up with the whole Santa Claus idea.

~***~

"You want to jump out of an airplane? Have you lost your mind, Chet?"

"No, I haven't lost my mind. Just listen to me. This is going to be great. The kids are going to love it!"

"Okay," Weber said skeptically, folding his arms across his chest and leaning back in his chair.

"Think about it," the mayor said. "Santa Claus parachuting down onto Main Street. Can you think of a better way to kick off Snowdaze? Why, I'm telling you, this is going to put Big Lake on the map! What other town does that?"

"None that I know of," the sheriff replied. "Maybe there's a reason why."

"There *is* a reason. It's because their mayors aren't visionaries like me."

"Chet, aren't you the person who is going to be playing Santa Claus?"

"Of course I am. Who's better suited for the job than me?"

While the round little man might have the shape for the job, Weber had never seen him display the temperament one would expect out of jolly old Saint Nick. Chet Wingate was a bossy, egotistical, bad tempered person who had never shown the slightest bit of kindness or generosity to anybody unless there was something in it for him. But apparently, the thought of playing Santa Claus appealed to his ego. After all, who was going to be the center of attention? That was something the mayor craved, and there was no way he was going to let some mythical character from the North Pole steal his thunder.

"Do you have any idea what's involved in jumping out of an airplane? It's not something you just do without a lot of training."

Weber wasn't sure how big a parachute it would take to hold Chet's weight, But he seemed to remember seeing videos of the Army dropping Jeeps on the battlefields with parachutes, so maybe it could be done. But it didn't sound like a good idea to him.

"I'm not actually going to be jumping out of the airplane," the mayor said. "We're going to dress up a mannequin like Santa Claus and put a parachute on it. Then, when the plane flies over Main Street, the pilot will push it out and have it land in that little park next to the Chamber of Commerce. I'll be hiding in the bushes, and once it lands behind them I'll come out in my Santa Claus suit. It will be an illusion, just like one of those magic tricks you see on television. I'm telling you, Sheriff Weber, this is going to work!"

Weber still wasn't convinced. "Why couldn't you just ride into town on the fire truck or something like that?"

"Because it's not dramatic enough! Any old Santa Claus can ride into town on a fire truck. But a parachuting Santa? Trust me, Sheriff. People are going to remember this for a long, long time!"

Weber thought the mayor's mental choo-choo had finally jumped the track, but as it turned out, Chet Wingate was right. People were definitely going to remember Big Lake's one and only parachuting Santa Claus forever.

Chapter 3

Larry Parks, Big Lake's resident FBI agent, wasn't any more enthusiastic about the mayor's scheme than the sheriff had been.

"Yeah, I guess it could be done. But it's not that easy."

"What's the problem? How hard is it to throw something out of an airplane? You fly over, you open the door, and you shove it out. Easy peasy, right?"

"No, that's not right. First of all, Mr. Mayor, you can't just open an airplane's door in flight. The force of the air going past is going to be pushing it shut. And my plane is a twenty year old Cessna 172 Skyhawk. It doesn't have autopilot, so I can't be flying the airplane and pushing this mannequin of yours out at the same time. I would need somebody up there with me."

"But it seats four, right? I know that you and your lady friend and Sheriff Weber and Deputy Fuchette have all four flown in it."

"Yes, sir. It seats four, under the proper conditions. But it doesn't have a side door somebody can just open to push something out of."

"But it can be done. You said so yourself!"

Parks sighed. "I guess if we had the mannequin in the right front seat, and if we took the door off, somebody sitting in back could manage to get it out of the airplane. But what about the parachute?"

"Don't they just open automatically?"

"They have what are called static lines that will pull the chute open, but I don't know the first thing about them. I'm just a weekend pilot."

"But it could be done?"

"There are so many factors. Like, I'd have to calculate my stall speed and..."

"Stall? No, keep the motor on. I don't want you stalling. That's all we would need, to have you crash right in the middle of Snowdaze. That could ruin the town's reputation!"

Park should have taken advantage of the mayor's ignorance of aerodynamics and used that as his excuse to abandon the project before it ever started. But, while he was an excellent investigator and all-around pleasant fellow, the FBI agent was sometimes cursed with too much curiosity. *Could* they really pull it off?

"I'm not talking about the engine stalling, Mr. Mayor, I'm talking about wing stall. When an airplane's wings move through the air it creates lift, which allows the plane to fly. But when it's moving too slow it doesn't have enough lift, and the wings stall. That's when the plane falls out of the sky. That's how you land, by coming in low and slow enough that you lose lift and you land on the runway."

"So how fast or slow does it have to be going?"

"Well, under optimal conditions my cruising speed is 140 miles per hour, and my stall speed is 33 knots, which is a little under 40 miles per hour. But to be safe, I would want to be somewhere around 40 knots, or 45 miles per hour."

"You can't be serious about this," Weber said. "Come on, Parks, don't even start thinking about doing this."

But his friend was already intrigued enough with the possibilities that he was doing mental calculations on airspeed, altitude, and weight and wasn't listening to the sheriff.

~***~

With Deputy Jordan Northcutt on board as his designated assistant, Parks made several practice runs in an open field near the airport in Springerville where he kept his Cessna. Of course they only had one mannequin and one parachute, which needed to be saved for the big event, so they used sandbags, which exploded very nicely on impact. Giggling like school boys playing hooky, they had a grand time of it and perfected their technique to where they were confident they could drop the mannequin exactly where it needed to land on the appointed day.

As it turned out, they should have practiced more.

~***~

On Saturday morning, the day of the Great Santa Drop, as it came to be known in local lore, Big Lake's Main Street was lined with residents and visitors who came out to see the Snowdaze Parade and to listen to welcoming speeches by the mayor and Juliette Murdoch. Then, at the appointed time, just as the speakers were wrapping up their spiels, the high wing Cessna flew over Main Street. People pointed and waved at Santa Claus, while Deputy Northcutt, crouched on the floor behind the passenger seat, reached around to throw candy out to the crowd. Children and adults alike scrambled to pick up the treats as the plane flew out of sight, climbed, and made a turn and then descended to fly back down Main Street in the opposite direction, more candy coming out the door. While everybody was distracted, Mayor Chet Wingate had slipped out of sight and quickly pulled on his Santa Claus suit and white beard. As the plane turned and made ready for its third and final pass down the street, everyone was ushered back to the sidewalks as loudspeakers in stores and on light poles all began playing *Here Comes Santa Claus.*

Maybe it was the difference in weight between sandbags and a mannequin, maybe it was because they had no idea how to deploy a parachute from a static line in spite of the You Tube videos they had watched, or just maybe, as Weber secretly suspected but Larry Parks never admitted to, he had known from the start it wouldn't work and it had all been just one more of his diabolical schemes.

But whatever the reason, when he banked the Cessna to the right and Jordan pushed the mannequin out the airplane's door, it had plummeted headfirst straight to earth, the unopened parachute streaming behind it. And, of course, they missed the park completely. Santa Claus smashed into the pavement right in front of the Chamber of Commerce building and exploded into a thousand pieces. Children screamed as their mothers grabbed them and tried to cover their eyes to shield them from the sight, which only got worse when Arnold Foster's Saint Bernard,

Freckles, bounded into the street, grabbed one of the mannequin's arms, and walked away with it in his mouth.

Unaware of what had happened because getting into his costume took longer than he had anticipated, Chet finally got the damned fake beard to stay in place, pulled on his red and white Santa cap and ran out into the street, shouting "Ho, Ho Ho, Merry Christmas!" The first clue he had that there was a problem was when he stumbled on the mannequin's head, kicking it across the street, where it landed at the feet of an overweight lady from Tucson named Hazel Whitcomb. She promptly passed out, the first of many terrible reactions she would have to the horrible scene she had witnessed. At least that's what her lawyer claimed in the lawsuit he filed against the town on her behalf a week later. And forever afterward, Big Lake's Mayor Chet Wingate was known as The Man Who Killed Santa Claus.

Chapter 4

Obviously, an exploding Santa Claus one day and a dead woman the next put a bit of a damper on Snowdaze. While Juliette Murdoch worked hard to keep a smile on her face as she reassured everybody that things were fine and the rest of the event would go on as planned, anyone could tell the smile was forced. After the discovery of the body, quite a few people left. But not before one summer resident remarked within earshot of Juliet and the mayor, "A guy got murdered at the Fourth of July celebration, and now this. I sure as hell don't want to be around here for Halloween!"

"This is just terrible," the mayor said. "How could you let this happen?"

"How could *I* let it happen," Juliet asked, incredulously. "You're going to try to lay the blame for this on *me*, Chet?"

"Well, the whole thing was your idea in the first place."

"Oh, no," Juliet said, shaking her head. "No, no, no. *Snowdaze* was my idea. That crazy stunt with the parachuting Santa Claus, that was all you, Chet. I had nothing to do with that. And as for this," she said, gesturing to where Weber and several deputies were crouched around the blanket covered body at the boat ramp, "this has nothing to do with Snowdaze at all. You need to find somebody else to blame for that."

Realizing she wasn't going to be buffaloed, Chet left the Chamber of Commerce Director to her fake smiles and platitudes as she tried to keep the event afloat and made his way over to the boat ramp.

"Stay back behind the crime scene tape," Weber ordered, but the mayor ignored him.

"Why? There have been people trampling all over this place for two days now. How soon can you wrap this up and get her out of here? This whole weekend is turning into a disaster."

"Yeah, Chet. Because the weekend is what it's all about, right? It doesn't matter that somebody's dead. The show must go on."

"All I'm saying is..."

"Deputy Reed, get this man out of here. And if he gives you any trouble, arrest him for interfering with a police investigation."

The mayor started to protest, but Dolan Reed took him by the arm and led him back to the crime scene tape. Lifting it, Dolan pushed him onto the other side.

"You can't treat me this way. I'm the mayor!"

Dolan, a balding, fortyish man who wore heavy framed eyeglasses and had just the beginnings of a potbelly that he fought hard to keep from growing, was a veteran deputy and not the least bit impressed with the mayor's protests.

"Sorry, sir. I work for Jimmy. He says you have to stay over here with everybody else, so that's where you're staying. Deputy Wingate, get over here."

Archer Wingate, the mayor's overweight son, had been trying to be inconspicuous, which was hard to do for a man his size. Reluctantly, he walked up to where his father and Dolan stood on opposite sides of the crime scene tape.

"Deputy, the sheriff says he does not want the mayor, or anybody else, coming through that tape. If anybody tries, it's your job to keep them out. Got it?"

"Yeah, but..."

"No butts about it. Those are the sheriff's orders."

Dolan left Archer there to deal with the issue and went back to the body.

"It's Jill Cotter isn't it?"

"Yeah, Jimmy, it's Jill."

Jill's husband Tom, seven years older than her, was a long-haul trucker who was sometimes gone for two weeks or more at a time. Early in their marriage she had accompanied Tom on a few runs, but it didn't take her long to decide that being on the road wasn't for her. Jill didn't enjoy the long days staring out at the world through a windshield, and she couldn't sleep in the tiny compartment behind the truck's cab with the noise of idling diesel engines parked next to them in truck stops and highway rest areas.

It didn't help that Jill was a people person, and brief interactions with truck stop waitresses and conversations with other drivers who only wanted to talk about how to dodge the weigh stations or the best way to fudge their logbooks wasn't enough for her. And let's face it, Tom never had been much for conversation to start with.

She had tried reading books to pass the time, but was prone to motion sickness when she did. After a particularly miserable trip through Kansas, Jill had climbed down out of the Kenworth on shaky legs and made Tom buy her an airplane ticket home. She had vowed never to get back in the truck again and she never had.

But as much as she hated being with her husband in the truck, staying home alone was no picnic either for an attractive young woman like Jill. Anyone with half a brain could only watch so many daytime soap operas and tell-all reality shows, and before long the boredom was killing her. She tried several jobs, including waiting tables at the Frontier Cafe and working behind the front desk at the Sky-Hi Retreat Motor Lodge, but none of them really interested her and she didn't last long, either being told her services were no longer needed, or simply not returning if she overslept one morning and decided she didn't want to go to work anyway. Besides, Tom was only home a few days a month and he wanted her to be there when he was.

She had also immersed herself in a variety of craft projects before she realized she had no talent for creating things. She didn't have any close female friends to hang out with, and with no children, she was lonely. Jill needed something to help fill her long, empty days. And her long, empty nights, too.

She found just what she was looking for in Brian Spangler, a dark haired wannabe country singer who was long on looks but short on talent. That lasted a few months, until Brian moved on down the road looking for greener pastures and new stages to play on. Next had come Grady Holmes, a rodeo cowboy who proved to be just as good at riding women as broncos. Jill was sure she was in love with him and had even snuck away one weekend to go to a rodeo down in Wilcox with Grady. But that was enough for her. There were too many cute little cowgirls in their tight Levis and western shirts stretched tightly across their chests for Grady to focus on just her. When he brought a sassy redheaded barrel racer named Tanya back to their motel room to party with them, Jill had slapped his face, grabbed the keys to his Dodge pickup from the nightstand, and driven back to Big Lake. There had been other men after that, among them a Forest Service volunteer who manned the fire lookout tower outside of town last summer, and a hitchhiker named Frankie she had picked up coming home from Show Low one afternoon.

Weber liked Tom Cotter, and he had long wondered if the man had heard any of the rumors about his wife's extracurricular activities while he was on the road. Now he couldn't help but wonder just where Tom was, and how his wife managed to turn up naked and dead under the ice of Big Lake.

"What do you think?"

"Hard to tell at this point," Deputy Chad Summers said. "I don't see any obvious trauma, like a gunshot or bruising on her neck from being strangled. I think we're going to have to wait for an autopsy to tell us the cause of death."

"Any idea how long she's been in the water?"

"I wish I could say. What do you think, Dolan?"

"If it were summer I could tell you better, but the cold water really slows decomposition. Could be a few hours, could be a week or more."

"He's right," Buz Carelton said. One of Weber's most experienced deputies, Buz had earned his nickname during his high school days, a result of his skinny neck and hawk-like nose that his classmates said made him look like he was part buzzard. Buz and Dolan were the two best crime scene techs in the Sheriff's Department. "Even in summertime this water stays pretty damn cold. But this time of year, it's a crapshoot trying to estimate that, Jimmy."

"Well, we're not accomplishing anything here," Weber said. "Do you guys have everything you need at this point?"

"Yeah," Buz said. "We've taken pictures and looked over the scene as best we could. But like the mayor said, there have been people tramping all over here for days now. The chances are slim to none that we're going to find any evidence around here. And that's assuming she went into the water here, which we don't know. It's a big lake and she could have gone in anywhere."

"Let's get her out of here," Weber said, whistling and waving to the two paramedics who were waiting inside the cab of the ambulance with the motor running to keep warm.

He stood up and looked down at the dead woman. "Such a shame for a pretty girl like that to wind up like this."

The sheriff and his deputies watched as the paramedics put the dead woman onto a stretcher and loaded it into the back of the ambulance, then drove away.

"What do you want us to do now, Jimmy?"

"First I want you to go home and take long hot showers. I don't know about you guys, but drying off inside a vehicle and then getting dressed and coming back out here in the cold isn't the most comfortable thing I've ever done."

"Yeah, I'm chilled to the bone," Dolan said. "You need to do the same thing, Jimmy."

"I will. How about you guys meet up at the medical center and see if the doctor there can come up with any ideas as to time and cause of death. And call the Medical Examiner's office down in Tucson and tell them we're sending one down to them. Chad, how about you and Coop start asking questions around town. Does anybody know if Tom is here or on the road?"

"I have no idea," Chad said. "If he's home, his truck will be parked in the side yard. If not, he could be anyplace."

"I guess I'll drive by and take a look," Weber replied. "I don't know which is worse, finding the guy at home and telling him his wife is dead, or having to call him someplace and giving him the news that way."

"That's assuming he doesn't already know," Dolan said.

21

Weber didn't want to believe that a hard-working, good man like Tom Cotter might be responsible for his wife's death, but the sheriff knew that if he was, he wouldn't be the first cuckolded husband that had reacted with violent passion when faced with the truth of his wife's infidelity.

"Yeah, assuming he doesn't already know." Weber watched as the ambulance drove away, wishing, as he did sometimes, that he had gone into another line of work.

Chapter 5

Tom Cotter's Kenworth was not at the house, but there was an old Chevy Silverado 4 x 4 pickup in the driveway. The driveway had not been shoveled and Weber had to wade through the snow to get to the front porch. He rang the doorbell, and when no one answered he rapped on the door. Still no response. He went around the house, looking in the windows, but couldn't see much. Obviously, nobody was home.

"James Weber, don't tell me you have been reduced to becoming a Peeping Tom? I had higher expectations of you."

He turned to see a tall woman as broad shouldered as a football fullback standing on the front porch of the house next door with her hands on her hips, looking at him reproachfully.

"Hello there, Mrs. Zimmerman. I'm looking for Tom Cotter. Have you seen him around?"

"Do you normally look for people by peering in their windows? Have you not heard of a doorbell before?"

"Yes, ma'am, I rang the doorbell. Nobody answered."

"Technically, you pushed the button to make the electrical connection that caused the doorbell to ring. You didn't actually ring it yourself."

Obviously, Mrs. Zimmerman had not mellowed any since the days when she taught high school English. A stickler for accuracy, the longtime teacher always acted like a misplaced comma or semicolon was on a par with truancy, or robbing a convenience store. Her size and her snappish attitude had intimidated generations of students and other faculty members alike.

"No, ma'am, I guess you're right."

"Of course I'm right! I'm always right."

Weber didn't doubt that, but didn't want to prolong the conversation any longer than he had to, either.

"At any rate, have you seen your neighbors lately?"

"I try very hard to avoid them whenever possible," Mrs. Zimmerman said disdainfully.

"Oh? Why is that?"

"Because they are not worth my time."

"So you don't much care for them? Why is that?"

"Much? What has much got to do with it?"

"What?"

"You said much. Much means a large amount. Are you asking if I largely did not care for them? If that is your ill-phrased question, I just told you that I try to avoid them whenever possible."

Sheriff Weber took a deep breath. "My apologies, Mrs. Zimmerman. I didn't mean to confuse you."

She looked at him imperiously. "I am not the one who is confused, James Weber. You are. Maybe if you paid more attention when others were speaking you wouldn't be. Although I don't know why that surprises me. You were the same in my English class. You didn't listen then, and you are not listening now."

"Yes, ma'am. Again, I apologize. But back to the Cotters. You don't care for them, is that correct?"

"You are making an assumption. I did not say I don't care for them."

"Well, do you or don't you care for them?"

"I don't give them any thought one way or the other," she told him.

"Really? You said you go out of your way to avoid them as much as... whenever possible. How come?"

"Is there a reason you're asking me so many impertinent questions?"

"I wasn't trying to be impertinent," Weber said. "But yes, the reason I'm asking is because I need to locate Tom as soon as possible."

"Have you asked his wife where he is? I would assume she would know."

"No, I haven't spoken to her." Weber didn't want to say too much, although he knew it wouldn't take long for the news of Jill Cotter's death to be all over town once the gossip train fired up.

"And why not? I would think that she would be the first person you would ask."

"Well, here's the thing..."

But before he could finish the sentence, Mrs. Zimmerman interrupted him. "He finally killed her, didn't he?"

~***~

Mrs. Zimmerman kept him waiting for twenty minutes until Robyn could make her way through the crowd watching the start of the snowmobile race at Snowdaze and drive to their location. "Some women might not see anything wrong with letting a gentleman into their home without someone else being there," the old schoolteacher had said haughtily. "But I believe in standards and morals. It is what separates us from the animals."

Weber couldn't help but notice that she looked toward the Cotter house when she said that.

When Robyn pulled in behind his Explorer he got out to greet her.

"So, what's up? She thinks you're some kind of rapist or something and won't talk to you unless you have a chaperone?"

"That's right, you didn't go to school here, did you? You haven't met Mrs. Zimmerman yet?"

"No," Robyn said, "and why is it that I'm thinking this isn't going to be the most pleasant part of my day?"

"Let me put it to you this way," Weber said, as they walked to her door, "if you thought that lake water was cold, you ain't seen nothing yet."

The house was dark. Heavy, dark furniture. Heavy, dark drapes at the windows that held the sunlight at bay. Lamps with low wattage bulbs in them. There was a large couch covered with some type of thick fabric that felt stiff when they sat down on it. Weber couldn't help but wonder if they were the first visitors to ever sit on the thing. There was no television, no stereo, nothing that would let the world of entertainment intrude. But there were bookcases. Large, heavy bookcases filled with thick tomes that stretched from floor-to-ceiling covered three walls of the room. The house had a stale smell to it and Weber wondered if Mrs. Zimmerman ever opened the windows during the summertime. Probably not, he decided. He wouldn't be surprised if she considered fresh air frivolous.

Mrs. Zimmerman sat in an old French Provincial armchair with some type of dark blue upholstery that looked almost black. She didn't offer them coffee or tea, or exert any effort to make them feel welcome. Weber was pretty sure she had very few visitors, if any, and he thought that was probably fine with her. He didn't see Mrs. Zimmerman as being much of a hostess.

"I'm very busy, so please ask your questions and go on about your business."

"Thank you for making time for us," Weber said.

"I didn't really have any choice in the matter, did I? If you remember correctly, you insisted on this interview."

"Yes, ma'am, I did. This here is Deputy Robyn Fuchette, and ..."

"*This is*, Deputy Robyn Fuchette," Mrs. Zimmerman corrected him. "It's obvious that she is *here*."

"Yes, ma'am," Weber said, feeling chastised and like he was back in her classroom. "At any rate, why did you ask me if Tom Cotter killed his wife?"

"Isn't it obvious?"

"No, ma'am, it's not. At least not to us."

"We wouldn't be having this conversation if she was still alive. And if she is dead, who else but her husband would kill her?"

Weber knew that it was common knowledge that the spouse is always the first suspect when somebody is murdered. Any television crime drama could tell you that. But since Mrs. Zimmerman didn't have a television that he could see, and the books on her shelves seemed to lean toward the classics and great literature, not mysteries or true crime stories. And while it might be obvious to her that Jill Cotter was dead, that didn't mean she had been murdered.

"You said earlier that you didn't care for the Cotters. Why is that, Mrs. Zimmerman?"

"You are making assumptions again. I believe I corrected you about that in our earlier conversation. You are the one that said I did not care for them, not me. That is *your* assumption. Jumping to conclusions. It is lazy thinking. Life has no shortcuts, James Weber."

"No, ma'am, I guess it doesn't," he said, wishing there was some way to shortcut this conversation. "Let me ask you, how *did* you feel about them?"

"You ask a lot of questions, don't you?"

"Yes, ma'am, I do. That's my job."

"I remember you as a student. You were lazy then, too. I had hoped to inspire you to make something of yourself, but you didn't, did you? You could have gone to college if you would have applied yourself. But that would have taken too much effort on your part, wouldn't it?"

Weber knew that in the former teacher's eyes, anyone without a college degree, anyone who worked with his hands, anyone who dedicated their life to public service, would never measure up to her standards. In truth, even those who did further their education would not make the grade with Rita Zimmerman.

"I'm sorry I disappointed you."

"I doubt that very much. But you did not disappoint me. I never expected you to accomplish anything in your life, given your performance as a student."

Robyn came to his aid, asking, "Had you had any problems with the people next door, Mrs. Zimmerman?"

"No. As I said before, I avoided them. We had nothing in common and no reason to interact. It's bad enough that he parks that big truck of his right there in the side yard. It's an eyesore. I call the Sheriff's Office to report it, but they keep telling me it's perfectly legal for him to do so. Apparently you and the other deputies are too lazy to come out and actually look for yourselves. But I'm sure that attitude starts at the top," Mrs.

Zimmerman said, giving Weber a baleful look. "And lately, whenever he is home, all they do is argue. Argue very loudly, I might add."

"I see. May I ask, why do you think Mrs. Cotter has been murdered? And why do you think her husband did it?"

"Didn't I just say they were arguing a lot? It was only a matter of time before he caught her."

"Caught her doing what?"

Mrs. Zimmerman screwed her face up and said, with an expression one might make after biting into a lemon, "Fornicating with every Tom, Dick and Harry who came her way, that's what!"

Chapter 6

"You were right about her being colder than the lake," Robyn said when they left the schoolteacher's house.

"Don't let her hear you talking like that. I'm sure she would tell you that the proper thing to say is I was *correct*, not right."

"Can we go someplace warm to talk about this? I'm still cold."

"I need to go by the medical center and see if they figured out anything, and then check in at the park again," Weber said. "Why don't you go home and take a long hot shower, then run back to the office and see if you can find any kind of contact information for Tom Cotter?"

"Or, you could come home and take a long hot shower with me. A loooong, hottt shower." She gave him a lascivious look that sent additional shivers down his spine, but of a much more pleasant type than those Weber had been having since he plunged into the lake's cold water.

"I wish I could, but there's too much going on."

"Okay," Robyn said with an exaggerated pout on her face as she got into her car. "Are we still on for dinner tonight with Parks and Marsha?"

Weber pulled his phone out of his jacket pocket and checked the time. "Six o'clock, right?"

"Right. At Ming House."

"If I don't get back to the office before then, I'll meet you there."

Robyn drove off in one direction, toward her house, while Weber went the other, to Big Lake's small medical center.

~***~

Buz and Dolan were waiting for him in the lobby when he arrived, sipping coffee and trying to ignore the young boy with a snotty nose who kept pointing his finger at them and shouting "bang-bang" gleefully as he climbed over furniture, using it for cover. The boy's mother ignored him as she read an old magazine, or at least stared at the pictures so she wouldn't have to exert any effort in parenting.

"Anything?"

Dolan nodded his head sideways and Weber followed him and Buz through a pair of double doors and down a hallway. They went into a room where Jill Cotter lay on an examination table, covered with a light sheet.

"Doc Johnson couldn't find anything either, Jimmy. But I did notice one thing."

"What's that?"

Dolan moved the sheet enough to expose the dead woman's left arm and hand.

"She's not wearing a wedding ring."

"Did she ever wear one?"

"I don't know. Normally, if a person wears a ring for a long time there will be some indication on their finger. If it's summertime, it might be a lighter band of skin that didn't tan. If they just took it off, the skin might be indented where the ring was. But with her being in the water for who knows how long, it's hard to say."

"So what does that mean? Assuming that she did normally wear a ring and it's missing."

"It could mean any of several things," Dolan said. "I imagine by now you've heard the rumors about her. "

"I'm pretty sure they're more than rumors," the sheriff replied. "She's been seen around town with different guys. I went to break up a fight at the Antler Inn a while back and it looked like she was getting pretty friendly with a couple of cowboys she was shooting pool with."

"Damn shame that a woman married to a guy as nice as Tom would be out fooling around while he's busting his ass trying to make a living," Buz said.

"Yeah. But guys, as much as we all like Tom, we have to consider the fact that if this wasn't an accidental death, he may have had something to do with it. He wouldn't be the first husband who was pushed too far."

"Anyway, getting back to the ring, let's assume that she did wear one," Dolan said. "Maybe she took it off when she was out playing."

"Could be."

"Or, assuming that she didn't make it into the lake under her own power, maybe whoever put her there has it."

"Okay. That could be, too."

"We're making a lot of assumptions here," Buz said, and Weber was reminded once again of what Mrs. Zimmerman had told him earlier about assumptions being lazy thinking. Damn, he needed to get that old biddy out of his head. It was bad enough dealing with her back in high school.

"You're right, Buz. And until we hear from the ME down in Tucson that's all we're doing is assuming. Hell, for all we know she could have fallen through the ice. "

"Were you able to find Tom?"

Weber shook his head. "There was a pickup in the driveway, but his big truck's not there. And it didn't look like anybody had been home recently. Robyn is trying to figure out how to get in contact with him. And I guess we need to find any other family members that need to be notified."

"Did you check with Mary?"

"Mary? No, why?"

"I'm not too sure about Jill, but I know Tom's got some kinfolk around here," Dolan said. I know his dad died a long time ago, but I think there's a brother and a sister, maybe more. If anybody would know who they are, it would be Mary. Maybe if you got hold of one of the family members they could point you in the right direction to find Tom."

Mary Caitlin, Weber's administrative assistant, was the wife of former sheriff Pete Caitlin. She had what seemed like an encyclopedic knowledge about everybody in town, their sometimes twisted family trees, who was married to who, who was raising a child that may not have been his, and who had a roving eye.

"Good idea," Weber said. "I remember the sister, but I haven't seen her in a long time. If anybody knows anything, it will be Mary."

He looked at the woman under the sheet one last time and asked, "did you get pictures of her tattoos?"

"We did," Dolan said.

"Forward them to my phone if you will."

"Got it."

"Anything else?"

"Nope. If I take off now I can get her down to Tucson before dark. Not that they can do anything with her until Monday, but still."

"You okay to do that, Dolan? It would be pretty late by the time you got back home." The deputy was a family man and Weber knew he cherished the time he had with them.

"Yeah, no problem. My wife's mother is here for three weeks, and I need an excuse to get away."

"Okay, make sure the van is gassed up. And what the hell, if it's too late, grab a motel down there for the night."

"Now there you go thinking like a single man again, Jimmy," Buz said. "We need to educate you before you and Robyn tie the knot next year. What Dolan needs to do is suggest that Grandma gets to spend some quality time with the two little ones at home while he and Wendy take Mrs. Cotter here down to Tucson. And of course, it's gonna be too late for them to drive all the way back up here in the dark. We wouldn't want them to hit an elk or something, would we? Think about it, Dolan, an overnight stay in a nice hotel, dinner, maybe a little romance without the kids around, and breakfast the next morning, all on the town's dime."

"It's fine with me," Weber said with a grin, "As long as Wendy doesn't mind a five hour trip in a van with a dead body."

"She's been sleeping next to Dolan all these years. Is it really that much of a difference, Jimmy?"

The sheriff chuckled and Dolan gave his friend the finger before pulling out his phone and pushing the button to call his house. "Hi, honey. How would you feel about taking a ride?"

~***~

There had been an exodus of people after the body was found, but apparently most folks had a short attention span, because by the time Weber got back to the park things were busy again. People were gathered around a huge bonfire drinking hot cider and roasting hotdogs on sticks, a large group of kids were having a snowball fight, the mayor was judging the first round of the snow sculpture contest, and a local musical trio called Rickie and the Rough Riders were on stage belting out country music. They seemed to subscribe to the theory that if you couldn't play well, at least play loud.

"What's going on?"

"All kinds of stuff," Deputy Tommy Frost said. "We had one kid get hit pretty hard in the eye by a snowball and the paramedics took him to the medical center to get checked out. His dad and the kid who threw the snowball's dad got into a shouting match over that and we had to break them up. Some lady was going on about carcinogens in the burned meat from the hotdogs. Jerry Pratt claimed somebody stole his snowmobile helmet just before the race started, but after he accused three or four different people of taking it, his wife found it in the back end of their SUV. So he had to go around and apologize to everybody. Oh, and I've had three or four people ask me what really happened to Santa Claus."

Weber looked at Jordan Northcutt and asked, "So?"

"So what, Sheriff?"

"So, what happened to Santa Claus? Did you and Parks plan it that way?"

The young deputy raised his right hand and said, "I swear, Sheriff, all I did was push the guy out of the airplane. Whatever happened after that isn't my fault."

Weber laughed and slapped him on the shoulder. "Plausible deniability. You just can't beat it, kid."

Chapter 7

Robyn had not been able to find out anything about where Tom Cotter might be, but Mary Caitlin had some useful information for them.

"Tom's mother, Joyce, is living in one of those retirement communities down around Green Valley," Mary told Weber when he got back to the Sheriff's Office. "She moved down there about ten years ago, after Vince died. His brother Don lives in Lakeside and runs a muffler shop, and his sister Kathy lives here in town. She's married to Greg Sterling, the man who runs that used furniture store on Third Street. Kathy has MS and is in a wheelchair."

"I remember her," Weber said. "And hearing something about her being sick. But I didn't know what was wrong with her or anything about the wheelchair. I don't remember Tom having a brother at all."

"I think he's two or three years older. Pete busted him for fighting a time or two, back when he was sheriff."

"Really? A troublemaker?"

"Not too bad. But he had a temper and he'd get to drinking in some bar and somebody would mouth off. Next thing you know, they're duking it out in the parking lot. You know how it goes."

Weber knew only too well, having broken up more alcohol-fueled fights than he could remember.

"How about Jill? What do you know about her?"

"Jill isn't from around here," Mary said. "I seem to recall that she came from somewhere over in California. Someplace out in the desert, like Barstow or Needles. I've only met her a time or two, and I wasn't impressed."

"Why was that?"

"She had shifty eyes," Mary replied. "She was at the library with a craft group taking a class on decoupage a couple of years ago when I was there doing some genealogy research. From where I was sitting I was looking right at them, and I noticed that instead of listening to the instructor and looking at what was going on, she was checking out every guy that walked into the place."

Big Lake's tiny public library was housed in a doublewide mobile home that had been gutted and remodeled to hold bookshelves, a few tables, and two computers for online research. "How many guys could she be checking out there? The place doesn't get that much business, does it?"

"More than you might think," Mary told him. "You know, Jimmy, it wouldn't hurt you to pop in there now and then. Learning doesn't stop when you leave high school."

"Have you been talking to Mrs. Zimmerman?"

"Who? Do you mean Rita Zimmerman?"

"Yeah. Robyn and I had a conversation with her earlier today."

"I'm sorry you had to experience that, dear," Mary said to Robyn. "Rita is a piece of work, isn't she?"

"I'll say she is! She had poor Jimmy stumbling over his tongue like he was the classroom dunce."

"She's older than me, but her younger sister Nancy and I were friends when we were growing up. Rita was always that way, even when she was a little girl," Mary said. "Bossy, a perfectionist. She never had any friends because nobody could tolerate her. But that was perfectly fine with her, because she always thought everybody and everything was beneath her."

"I remember when I was in her English class, we all had to choose a book by an American author and do a report on it," Weber said. "I chose *Travels With Charley* by John Steinbeck. When I got up in front of the class to give my report, she shut me down and told me that Steinbeck was nothing but a hack and a loser who spent his time hanging out with hobos and drunkards."

"She hates John Steinbeck, too?"

"Oh, yeah. Him, and Mark Twain, who she said was nothing but a buffoon. Hemingway was a drunken womanizer. Edgar Allan Poe was a deranged pervert who married his cousin. And the list went on and on. Not one book or author chosen by anybody in the class was worth the time to read, let alone to listen to our reviews. I sat there wondering why we bothered doing them in the first place."

Robyn shook her head in dismay. "I had some great teachers in school who inspired me. I'm sure glad I didn't have somebody like that."

"Getting back to the situation at hand, you weren't able to find out anything about where we can find Tom Cotter?"

"Not so far," Robyn said, checking a couple of other resources on her computer. "I show three vehicles registered in either his or Jill's names. One is a 2001 Chevrolet pickup, which I assume is the truck we saw at their house. The other is a 2012 Toyota Corolla. And then there's his semi, a 2010 Kenworth."

"Well, we know where the pickup is. So besides finding Tom, we need to locate the Kenworth and the Toyota. It's not like he can be driving both of them at once."

"It doesn't help that it's a weekend. How do truck drivers get their loads anyway? I mean, does he work for a company and they tell him where to go, or what?"

"I'm not really sure," Weber said. "I know Tom doesn't work for any one company, he owns his own rig. I remember him talking about hauling everything from tires to produce. Are there companies that act as a clearinghouse for loads like that?"

Robyn did a Google search and said, "Here we go. Freight brokers. They are the go-between that connects companies that have something to ship with trucking companies or independent truckers like what you're describing Tom might be."

Weber looked over her shoulder and said, "It looks like there are a bunch of them."

"I know. Where do we even start?"

"I have no idea," he told her. "I think the first thing we need to do is see if we can contact him directly." Weber looked at the clock on the wall and said, "If I hurry I've got time to run by the Sterling place before we meet Parks and Marsha for dinner. I think I'll go talk to Kathy real quick and see if she's got any contact information for her brother, or if she can tell me anything about any family Jill had."

"What you need to do is go home and take a shower," Robyn said.

"Why? Do I stink?"

"No, because you still haven't since you were freezing your butt off in the lake. You insisted everybody else take one."

"That's because I don't want everybody else catching pneumonia," he replied.

"Oh, so it's okay for you to catch pneumonia, but not the rest of us?"

"Here's how I look at it. All I really am around here is the eye candy. The rest of you do all the work. So yeah, if one of us has to be sick, it might as well be me. Besides, won't you be taking care of me and pampering me and all that?"

"No, because like you said, I'm part of the crew that does the real work around here."

"If it helps at all, I could probably break free long enough to come by and jam a thermometer up your ass every now and then," Mary Caitlin offered.

Mary was an attractive woman in her mid-60s with blue eyes that sparkled with mischief, a thick mane of graying hair, and a wild sense of humor. Weber had known her all his life and she was almost like a favorite aunt. The one who showed up late at night with fresh brownies and amazing stories to tell that kept kids up way past their bedtime.

"As entertaining as that sounds, Mary, I'll take a pass," Weber told her.

"Hey, cheat yourself out of a good time. I offered."

"Yes, you did," he replied, "and I'll be forever in your debt. And just a little bit creeped out, too."

"Whatever you decide to do, get a move on," Robyn said.

"I'm moving, I'm moving. Just keep Mary away from my hiney until I'm out the door."

"Don't be late," Robyn shouted after him as he left. "I'll meet you there."

Chapter 8

Weber had not seen Kathy Sterling in two or three years. She was younger than him and they did not move in the same circles when they were growing up, and he had not realized how long it had been since they had crossed paths. But he had remembered her as a vivacious, active young woman who liked cross-country skiing and singing karaoke. So he was not prepared for the woman who greeted him when he knocked on the front door of the Sterling home. She seemed to have aged 20 years.

"Jim Weber! It's been a long time."

"Yes, it has, Kathy. May I come in?"

"Sure," she said, moving a toggle switch on the arm of her powered wheelchair to roll it backward. "What brings you here?"

He stepped inside the house, where a pellet stove heated the large living room, and said, "I need to ask you a couple of questions about your brother, Tom."

"Tommy? Is he okay?"

"As far as I know, he is," Weber said. "But I need to get in touch with him. Do you know if he's out on the road?"

She shook her head. "I couldn't tell you. Tommy and I haven't spoken to each other in over three years."

"I'm sorry to hear that."

"Yeah, me, too."

There was a sadness about the woman, and Weber wasn't sure if it was simply because of her physical problems, or if there were other burdens weighing her down.

"You said you need to get hold of Tommy. Is something wrong?"

"I'm afraid there is," Weber said. "His wife is dead."

"Jill's dead?"

"We found her in the lake today."

"Well I'll be damned!"

He couldn't help noticing a wry smile on the woman's face.

"Not to be rude, but that doesn't seem to bother you very much," he said.

"Bother me? You just made my day, Jim!"

He didn't know what to say to that, and seeing his confusion, Kathy said, "I know I must sound horrible, but I can't help it. That woman tore our family apart. It's because of her that Tommy hasn't had anything to do with me or our brother Don in so long."

"What happened to cause the rift between you three?"

Kathy shifted slightly in her chair and said, "Jill happened. I knew she was trouble the first time I saw her. I mean, she could put on this fake act like she was your best friend and some kind of goody two shoes, but I saw right through that. I tried to be nice to her, for my brother's sake. I really did. But then she stepped over the line and there was no going back."

"Stepped over the line? How did she do that?"

"Do you know much about multiple sclerosis, Jim?"

"Not really," he admitted. "To be honest, not much at all, except that Jerry Lewis used to do a telethon for it."

"Actually, that was for muscular dystrophy."

"Now I really feel dumb. I'm sorry, Kathy."

"No problem, you're a cop, not a doctor. There are different kinds of MS. The kind I have is called Primary-Progressive MS, or PPMS for short. Only about 10 or 15% of the people who have MS have PPMS, and it usually occurs later in life. But not always. Lucky me, right?"

Weber didn't know what to say, so he didn't say anything.

"They call PPMS the equal opportunity MS," Kathy told him. "That's because most forms of MS victims are twice as likely to be women, but PPMS hits men and women about equally. Usually its progression is slow going, but not always. Again, lucky me, right?"

"I'm sorry, I don't know what to say," he admitted.

"There's nothing to say, it's not your fault," she told him matter-of-factly. "Shit happens. Anyway, among the many ways this disease affects somebody, besides the pain, and not being able to walk without somebody holding me up, and the fact that

40

I'm going to go blind before much longer, there are a lot of bladder and bowel issues. Yeah, gross, right?"

Weber really wanted to change the subject, but didn't know how to.

"I'm not telling you all of this to be disgusting," Kathy said, as if reading his mind. "But this is what led up to the problem between me and Tommy."

"Okay, I'm listening."

"Have you met my husband?"

"No, I don't think so. I'm sorry."

"Stop saying you're sorry! There are enough sorry people in the world."

Despite her physical problems, Weber couldn't help admiring the woman's openness and her matter of fact outlook on life. He didn't know if he could face the challenges she did on an everyday basis and not feel sorry for himself every waking moment.

"Anyway," Kathy continued, "Greg is just about the most wonderful man any woman could ever hope for. Not just a woman with all of my problems, but any woman. He's kind, he's patient, and he loves me to the moon and back. And to be honest with you Jim, I don't know how he does it. When we first got together we were always out doing something. Skiing the backcountry, fishing, hiking, camping, you name it and we did it. Then all of a sudden I get hit with this. It's bad enough I have to get MS, but I get what's supposed to be a slow moving version of it that came on like a freight train. Two years after my diagnosis I'm wearing diapers and in this damn chair. But did Greg ever act like I was anything less than what I always was? Not for a minute. I'll tell you the truth, Jim. Some people say they're impressed with the way I handle this, but Greg's the strong one. He works hard all day, he takes care of me, he changes my diapers, and there's not a day that goes by that he doesn't tell me a dozen times that he loves me."

She stopped talking for a moment and looked away. "Greg and I have only had one fight in all the time we've been together. It was when things started to go bad with me. I guess I was feeling sorry for myself and embarrassed that he had to clean me up. I told him he should just stick me in one of those homes where they put people who can't take care themselves and get a divorce and get on with his life. He got mad and told me he never wanted to hear me saying bullshit like that again. He said I was his wife and the only woman he had ever wanted. He said this disease didn't happen to just me, it happened to both of us, and we were going to stick it out together come hell or high water."

Weber had to swallow before he could reply. "He sounds like a hell of a man."

"He's all that and more," Kathy assured him. "So when Jill hit on him, I think he was more appalled than I was."

"She hit on him?"

"She sure did. She went over to the store one day and he said she was looking around and he didn't think anything about it. Then she started asking him about me and how I was doing, and how all of this was affecting our marriage, and again, he didn't think much about it. After all, she's family. Anyway, there was this little writing desk that she said she wanted but didn't have any way to get it home because it wouldn't fit in her car and she couldn't drive a stick shift, and Tommy's truck has one. So Greg said he would drop it off at their house on his way home after he closed the store. He's always doing that for customers and he didn't think anything about it."

"What happened, Kathy?"

"When he got to the house Jill hugged him, but he didn't think anything about that because she's always been real touchy-feely. He carried the desk in and put it where she said she wanted it, and she asked him to hang on for just a minute while she went and got the money to pay him. He told her that wasn't necessary, he didn't need any money for it. See, that's the way Greg is. Anyway, she had him wait while she went to the bedroom and he thought she was going to get some money. The next thing he knew, she came out wearing some little red négligée thing that he said you could see right through. Greg said he asked her what the hell she was doing and she told him how she gets lonely when Tommy's out on the road, and she knew that with my condition we probably weren't able to have sex anymore, so maybe they could help each other out. She said nobody ever had to know."

"You're kidding me!"

"I wish I was. Greg turned around and left and came home, and he was shaking so bad when he walked in the door I thought somebody had died or something. It took me a while to get it out of him because he didn't want to tell me what had happened."

"What happened after that?"

"I've got to be honest with you, Jim, if my legs still worked I would have probably gone over to their house and kicked her butt. Not just for coming on to Greg like she did, but because she's my brother's wife and she was cheating on him. Or at least trying to. But obviously that wasn't going to happen. I didn't know what to think at first, and Greg and I talked about it for a couple of weeks. He wanted to let the whole thing drop. I think he was pretty embarrassed by it. But I felt like I needed to tell Tommy about it. I felt he deserved to know the truth about her."

"And did you tell him?"

"No, I never got the chance to. Instead, I called our brother Don and asked for his advice about what to do. That's when Don hit the roof and said Jill had tried to put the make on him, too. Tommy and I have always been kind of laid-back, but Don can be a hothead at times. He called Tommy right then and told him all about it. Told him his wife was a no good cheating bitch and he needed to divorce her."

"How did that go over with Tommy?"

"About like a lead balloon. They got into an argument about it on the telephone, and then an hour or so later Tommy called Don back and said he had told Jill about their phone call, and she turned it around and put it all on Don and Greg. She said they were both always trying to get into her pants since the day they met her."

"And Tommy believed her?"

Tears were forming in Kathy's eyes. She wiped them away with a shaking hand as she nodded. "Yeah, he believed her. He hasn't said a word to either one of us, Don or me, since then. I tried, Jim. I called him three or four times and he wouldn't answer the phone. I know Don tried too, but he wouldn't answer for him, either. Then he changed his phone number and just shut us all out."

"That sucks."

Kathy looked down at her legs and the chair she was sitting in, then back up at him and nodded her head. "Yeah, it sucks. A lot of things in life suck."

Chapter 9

"Not to be rude, but you smell like lake water and dead woman," Marsha said, wrinkling her nose when Weber sat down at the table.

"So which one of these two clowns put you up to that, Robyn or Parks?"

"What? You don't think I have a mind of my own? You're not the only one who's eye candy around here, mister!"

"Well, I guess that answered my question," Weber said, looking reproachfully at Robyn, who stuck her tongue out at him. "Did you hassle Parks, too?"

"Hey, don't blame me for your fragrance," the FBI man said. "While you were out playing investigator, I was home soaking in a big tub of lavender scented water and playing with my rubber ducky."

"Is that what you're calling it now? I just call mine my willy."

"Really? We're having a nice dinner and you guys want to sit here and talk about your penises?"

"Hey, Robyn, that's my best friend you're talking about," Parks said. "We were so poor when I was growing up back on the farm in Oklahoma that it was the only playmate I had."

"Gross!"

"I guess we could talk about our lady parts," Marsha suggested.

"You don't have to do that," Parks told her. "When you two aren't around, Jimmy and me spend lots of time talking about your lady parts."

"Oh, really? I don't know if I should be flattered or concerned," Robyn said.

"I guess we should be flattered," Marsha told her. "If these two were sitting around talking about their tiny little boy toys when we weren't there, that's when we should be concerned."

"You've got a point," Robyn acknowledged.

"I can't believe you fools actually did it," Marsha said. "When they started talking about jumping in the lake, I was sure somebody would come to their senses and say "no way!""

"Don't blame me because Jimmy led me astray," Parks told her. "You know how susceptible I am to peer pressure."

"I know you're a fool, and your buddy here isn't much better. But I didn't think you'd go through with it, Robyn."

"I can't believe I did it either," she said. "It was so cold I had goose bumps bigger than my boobs."

"Well, in all fairness, your boobs aren't all that big," Parks said.

"Stop looking at my boobs, Parks."

"You just ignore him," Marsha said. "Any more than a mouthful just goes to waste anyway."

"Moving right along," Weber said, "I want the truth about that damn Santa Claus, Parks. You planned it that way right from the start, didn't you?"

"Who? Me? No, sir, Mr. Sheriff. I wouldn't do something like that," Parks said innocently. "If you don't believe me, just ask young Deputy Northcutt. He was up there in that plane with me."

"Yeah, that's another thing," Weber told him, "I don't appreciate you corrupting my deputies."

"I wasn't corrupting all of your deputies, Bubba, just that one."

"Aha! So you do admit you planned that whole thing the way it went down?"

"I admit nothing. No, sir, not one thing."

"Speaking of deputies, isn't that Coop coming in the door?"

"Yes, it is, Marsha."

"Who's that with him? I didn't know he had a girlfriend."

"I didn't either."

Seeing them, Coop smiled and nodded as the waitress, a small Asian woman dressed in black pants and a red blouse greeted them and started to show them to a table.

"Should we invite them to sit with us?" Robyn asked.

"I don't know," Weber said. "If they're on a date, maybe they don't want any company."

Parks, never one to worry about social protocols, called out, "Hey, Coop, we can add a couple chairs to our table if you want to join us."

The deputy said something to the woman, who nodded her head, and then to the waitress, who also nodded and escorted them to the table where the foursome was already seated.

"Hi, guys. Jimmy, I know you've met Roberta Jensen. Roberta, Robyn Fuchette is sitting next to Jimmy, and on the other side, closest to us, is Larry Parks, the FBI agent, and his lady friend, Marsha Perry. This is Roberta, everybody."

"It's nice to meet you," his date said as Coop helped her into a chair, then started to take her white cane to lean it against the wall before sitting down next to her.

"No, thanks, I'll keep it," Roberta said, holding onto the cane. "A blind woman never lets her white cane out of her control," she explained, setting it next to her chair. "It could get lost or even stolen, and I'd want it at hand in case of an emergency."

"I'm sorry," Coop said, "I never thought about that."

"No big deal. It's a learning process," she told him, then said to the rest of the group, "I hope we're not interrupting your dinner."

"No, ma'am," Weber said. "I just got here myself, and we haven't ordered yet."

Roberta was a short woman with long, naturally curly dark hair and an open, engaging smile. "I know I haven't met all of you, but I feel like I know you from what Coop has told me about you. Of course, I met you a while back, Sheriff Weber."

"Sheriff Weber? I thought we were past that, *Miss* Jensen."

She laughed and said, "That's right, *Jimmy*."

"There you go. That's better."

There was a moment of awkwardness, but Roberta managed it very well and soon the conversation was flowing like they had all been friends forever.

"So, call me nosy, but is this a first date or are you two an item?"

"Nosy," Parks said, and Marsha ignored him.

Roberta laughed and said, "We've been talking for a while."

"I see. And this is the first time he's brought you out in public."

Realizing how that might sound, she was at a loss for words, which was something that Weber had never seen before.

"Oh God, I'm sorry. I didn't mean that the way it sounded. I just meant he's been keeping you all to himself up until now."

Laughing, Roberta said, "It's not the way it sounded, don't worry about that. And we finally did have to come out because we ran out of food. The truth is, I've been kind of hesitant to be seen with a guy like him. I mean, after all, it's a small town and a girl has to worry about her reputation."

"I don't know why. I've never worried about mine," Marsha said, recovering nicely from her faux pas.

"You may not have worried about it, but your poor mother sure did," Weber said.

Everybody laughed, and then Coop said, "If you must know, Marsha..."

"Oh, I must," she said, interrupting him.

"Wait a minute," Roberta said. "You're the one that's not a cop, right? Jimmy, you may want to hire her. I think you're missing out on a good investigator."

"Or just a good snoop," Weber suggested.

Marsha laughed, then tore the end off of the paper wrapper from her drinking straw, put the straw to her mouth, and blew it at him.

"Anyway, as I was saying," Coop continued, "I met Roberta back during the investigation into George Duncan's death. I guess we kind of hit it off."

"Gee, you guess?" Roberta asked with a grin. "I thought you were a lot smarter than that."

"Oh, he's dense," Marsha said. "But it's not his fault, He's a man. They're all like that."

"Hey now," Parks objected, but she ignored him, leaning over closer to Roberta to ask, "So, have you had your way with him yet, girlfriend?"

"Marsha!"

"What?"

"You can't ask somebody questions like that the first time you meet them."

"Why not? Aren't you curious? You know you are."

But while Robyn may have been shocked by her friend's brashness, Roberta took it in stride, replying, "Let's just say things are progressing very nicely in that department."

Weber had never seen Coop blush before, but his deputy did then.

"You have to forgive Marsha," Robyn said. "She's our resident pervert."

"I prefer the term free spirit, if it's all the same to you," Marsha replied.

"Oh, I'm going to like hanging out with you two," Roberta said. Then she leaned in Marsha's direction and added, "My eyes may not work, but trust me, the rest of the parts are in top shape. And just to be sure, Coop's been inspecting everything and keeping it well-maintained, girlfriend."

The table broke up in laughter and the poor waitress had to wait for them to compose themselves enough to give her their orders.

Over dinner, Roberta told them about her life. How several generations of her family had lived in Big Lake, and how a childhood accident on her family's small farm had blinded her and she had been sent away to the Arizona State School for the Deaf and the Blind in Tucson for her basic education and to learn the skills a blind person needed to live independently. She didn't tell them, but Weber knew that she had thrived there, going on to graduate at the top of her class from the University of Arizona's Law School and establishing a successful family law practice in Tucson before growing tired of life in the big city. So, eventually she had returned to her roots, opening an office in the home she bought two blocks from Big Lake's Main Street.

Marsha and Parks both had a lot of questions about how a blind person operated a law practice, and Roberta explained that she employed a paralegal to do transcription work and used a computer program called JAWS to read what was on the screen.

"That seems strange when you say that you read something," Marsha said. "I think of reading as being something that sighted people do."

"I actually read quite a bit," Roberta replied. "Besides stuff for work, I've always got an audiobook that I read when I'm relaxing in my chair at night, or when I go to bed." Then she turned her head toward Coop and smiled and added, "Well, maybe I don't read in bed quite so much anymore."

For the second time that evening, Weber saw his deputy blush while everyone laughed at his expense.

Their dinner was pleasant, and Roberta fit right in with the crowd, giving back as much as she got. When the group finally broke up Weber walked Robyn to her car and said, "I'm going to stop by the office and check in before I head home."

"You know what they say about all work and no play, Jimmy."

"Yeah, I heard something about that. I just want to see if anything's come up I need to know about."

"That's why you have a telephone in your pocket," Robyn said. "If something was going on that they needed you for, Kate Copley would have called you. That's why we have dispatchers, remember?"

"I guess," Weber said. "But with all this Snowdaze stuff going on, and that woman turning up dead, I just feel like..."

Robyn glanced around to see if anybody was close enough to observe them in the winter darkness, then grabbed his coat collar and pulled him close. She kissed him, her tongue darting into his mouth before she pulled away and said, "Coop may be inspecting everything and keeping it well-maintained for Roberta, but this girl needs some preventive maintenance, too."

"I see. And apparently I've been falling down on the job?"

Robyn grinned impishly at him and said, "Let's just say I'm not a do-it-yourself kind of girl, okay?"

He smiled back at her and said, "I just may throw this damn telephone in the snow bank so Kate *doesn't* call me."

"That's not the worst idea you've ever had," she told him. She got in her car, started it, and drove away, with Weber right behind her.

Chapter 10

Weber spent his first two hours Monday morning going over his deputies' reports from Snowdaze and the other weekend activities. Aside from the catastrophic Santa Claus drop and the discovery of Jill Cotter's body in the lake, there had been the usual number of incidents one would expect on a busy weekend in Big Lake. A few fender benders as people from Tucson and Phoenix learned the hard lesson that just because their SUVs had four-wheel-drive that would get them going in snow, it didn't mean they could maneuver or stop any better. There had also been one single car accident where a vehicle had gone off the road on a curve and overturned. Fortunately the driver and his two passengers had only sustained minor injuries. Deputies had responded to two bar fights, as well as calls about three different couples who had ended their evenings with domestic disputes. There was also a report of a stolen Nissan crew cab pickup, but further investigation revealed that the owner's estranged wife had taken it from the parking lot of one of the local watering holes. Deputy Chad Summers had determined that since both of their names were on the truck's registration it was a civil matter, and advised the husband to consult with an attorney to help get the matter resolved.

With that done, the sheriff drove to Second Time Around, Greg Sterling's used furniture store. He found the man showing a young couple a set of bunk beds and browsed through the store until he was free. Weber had been expecting some kind of musty junk shop but he was wrong. All of the merchandise was clean and of good quality, and was arranged to present an eye-appealing display. He was admiring an oak coat rack when the customers left and Greg approached him.

"Sorry about that. Thanks for waiting. How can I help you?"

Greg was a solidly built man with collar length black hair and a thick, bushy mustache.

"No problem. You've got a nice store here."

"Thank you. You must be Sheriff Weber. Kathy said you were at the house yesterday and told her about Jill. I'm sorry I wasn't there. I had to go over to Nutrioso to make a bid on a houseful of furniture."

"Is that how you get your inventory?"

"Some of it. I buy out estates, I go to some furniture auctions in Phoenix and Tucson and even over in Albuquerque sometimes. And I advertise a lot. You'd be surprised how many people buy something and use it for a season or two and get rid of it. Especially up here."

In the last few years Big Lake had seen a lot of growth, with summer cabins and condos going up everywhere, it seemed. While the influx of summer people had helped the local economy, which had never thrived, they had also brought a lot of changes that many of the old-timers resented.

"Greg, when I was talking to your wife yesterday, she told me about the thing that happened between you and Jill."

"Nothing happened," the man said defensively. "I wouldn't touch that bitch with a ten foot pole."

"Poor choice of words on my part," Weber said, "my apologies. I should have said that Kathy told me what Jill did."

He could tell the man was still upset by the encounter with his sister-in-law.

"I'll tell you what, Sheriff, Jill may be a good-looking woman and all that, but she really destroyed our family. Tommy and Kathy used to be really close. Don, too, but with him living over in Lakeside we didn't see him quite as much. But whenever Tommy came in off the road he'd hang out with us. Or at least he would until he got mixed up with her."

"What do you know about Jill? I mean, besides the obvious. Do you know where your brother-in-law met her, or where she was from, anything like that?"

"Barstow, California," Greg told him. "She was working the front desk at a motel there where he had to stay for most of a week when the transmission went out on his truck. He came home and told us all about this beautiful woman he met and how great she was, and we were both thrilled for him. Well, that is, until we met her."

"She didn't make a good first impression?"

"She tried, I guess. But it didn't take very long to figure out that Tommy was just a meal ticket for her and a way out of Barstow. I don't know what she was expecting here, but if it was bright lights and big city, she was in for a shocker."

"What was their marriage like, do you know?"

"I don't know if you know Tommy very well or not, Sheriff, but he's a good guy. There's no question he was head over heels in love with her. Jill could do no wrong in his eyes. But it didn't take long for her to start complaining."

"About him?"

"About him, about him being gone all the time, about how boring this town is, about how the people here are all hicks. She talked like Barstow was some big fancy place and so much better than here. Have you been to Barstow?"

"Just to pass through," Weber admitted.

"That's about all I'd ever want to do," Greg replied. "There were a few times when I wanted to ask her why she didn't just go back there, if it was so wonderful. But I wanted to keep peace in the family so I kept my mouth shut. So did Kathy, until Jill pulled that crap she did, coming out of the bedroom half naked. But that was the last straw."

"Kathy told me Tom hasn't talked to either one of you since then?"

He shook his head. "Nope, not a word. Not to us, and not to Don. And it really broke Kathy's heart. I'll be honest with you, Sheriff, if I knew then what I know now, I would have just kept my mouth shut about the whole thing. I feel responsible for all the bad feelings everybody has."

"There's no reason for that," Weber said. "If you hadn't said something, Tom would have found out sooner or later. It's a small town and people talk."

"I know that," Greg said with a sigh. "But I just hate the fact that I had a part in the whole thing. Kathy has lost so much already, and then she lost Tommy, too."

Weber considered himself a pretty fair judge of people, and even if Kathy hadn't already told him what a good husband Greg was to her, he would have been impressed with the man. There was a basic kindness and integrity to his character that showed through.

"Don't beat yourself up about it," Weber told him. "Like I said, it was only a matter of time before he found out. Let me ask you this, Greg. Do you know anything about Jill's family back in Barstow?"

"Not a lot. I think she said her dad was dead, and I got the impression her mom was on her third or fourth husband. To be honest, it didn't take long before I started tuning her out. It got pretty tiresome hearing how great her life was before she came here and how much she sacrificed to be with Tommy. Like I said, sometimes I wanted to tell her that she should go back where she came from, since she was always so miserable here."

Two women came into the store and Greg excused himself to go greet them. They told him they were just browsing, so he left them and returned to the sheriff.

"I know you're busy and I don't want to keep you any longer that I have to," Weber said. "Just one more thing. There are a lot of rumors about Jill fooling around behind her husband's back. Do you have any idea who any of those men might have been?"

"Yeah, I know one of them. You probably know him, too. Scott Welch."

"The guy who runs the western wear store?"

"Yeah, him."

"Isn't he married, too?"

"Yep. To Darcy. Pretty girl with the long hair that works at the Thriftway."

"I know her," Weber said.

"I was making a delivery out at a place on Echo Lane a few months ago. As I was unloading my truck I happened to look across the street and there was Jill coming out the door of a house, and she turned around and kissed the guy before she left. And I'm not talking about a quick peck, I'm talking about a serious lip lock. Then, when she started down off the porch to get in her car she saw me and gave me this mocking look. Like she was daring me to say something. I didn't, but I sure wanted to."

"And the guy was Scott Welch?"

"It was him. It wasn't but two weeks later that he was in here with Darcy looking for stools for their breakfast nook. He was holding her hand and acting like he was the most devoted husband in the world. I'll tell you what, Sheriff, I'm a pretty easy-going guy, but I wanted to grab him by the throat and shake some sense into him. He's got a good woman like Darcy, smart and pretty, and there he is fooling around behind her back with Jill. What makes a man do that?"

"I wish I could tell you," Weber said. "I thought Scott was a better man than that."

"Yeah, me, too. I don't know him well, but I've seen him at a couple of Chamber of Commerce meetings and he always seemed like a good guy. Now it's all I can do to hold my tongue when I see him."

One of the women who were browsing in the shop asked, "Excuse me. Does this sofa pull out to make into a bed?"

"Yes, it does," Greg told her, then looked back at Weber to see if the sheriff had any more questions for him.

"Thank you for your time, Greg. And thank you for being the kind of man you are. The world needs more people like you."

They shook hands and Greg went to assist his customers as Weber was leaving.

Nick Russell

Chapter 11

Back at the office, Robyn still hadn't had any success in locating Tom Cotter. "I put in a request to get his cell phone number, but they don't want to give it to me without a court order," she said. "They started giving me all this nonsense about privacy laws and all that."

"Keep trying, okay?"

"I'm on it. What do you think about putting out a BOLO for him and his truck?"

Weber knew that if they issued a Be On The Lookout alert for Tom they might get some results, but he was hoping to be able to contact the man directly to tell him his wife was dead. Then again, if Cotter had anything to do with her demise, he might be trying to avoid any type of law enforcement.

"Let's hold off on that just now, okay?"

"I did find out a little bit more about how independent truckers get their loads," Robyn told him. "Besides the freight brokers, a lot of truck stops have kiosks where a driver can log in and search for nearby loads that are available. Apparently some companies bypass the middleman freight brokers, and instead they post their loads on these kiosk networks. And then there are websites where companies can post their loads directly, and drivers can check in and find them. I guess with today's technology, a trucker can run his own business from the cab of his semi."

"Don't those big trucks have some kind of GPS locator system or something? I would think their companies must have some way of keeping track of where they are, how long they are parked to be sure they are getting their mandatory rest hours, and all that," Deputy Dan Wright said.

"They do for the company drivers," Robyn replied. "But with Tom Cotter being an independent driver, I don't know if his truck has one. And if it does, how we would access that information? Let me keep looking around."

"While you're doing that, I'm going to call the brother in Lakeside," Weber said.

But before he could go into his private office, the door opened and Mayor Chet Wingate came in, stomping snow off his feet.

"Sheriff Weber, what's the status on that dead woman?"

"I haven't heard back from the Medical Examiner's office down in Tucson yet. But I assume she's still dead."

The mayor frowned at him and asked. "Why do you always go out of your way to be rude and disrespectful to me?"

"I don't know, Chet," Weber said, "I've never given it a lot of thought. I guess I just always figured you were the kind of person that everybody was rude and disrespectful to."

"It gets very old. I was hoping we could someday mend our fences and become friends."

"Naaa, we've got a good thing going the way it is. Why upset the apple cart?"

"Very well. I just wanted you to know that I've spoken to every member of the Town Council by telephone or in person, sharing my displeasure with the way you handled things at Snowdaze."

"And tell me, Chet, what was wrong with the way I handled things?"

"What was wrong? What do you think was wrong?"

"This is your story. You tell me."

"You roped off the area where we had planned to have children making snow angels and we had to find a different place for that to happen at the last minute. "

"So I did something wrong by keeping people from trespassing onto a crime scene, is that what you're telling me?"

"Crime? What crime? Are you telling me that woman was murdered? Why haven't I heard about this until now?"

"No, Chet, we don't know if she was murdered or not. I'm still waiting to hear from the ME about her cause of death. But she got under that ice some way."

"So you're saying it wasn't a crime scene?"

"Technically, no it wasn't."

"But yet you still blocked that whole area off and disrupted the activities we had planned there."

"Christ, Chet, there was a dead woman laying there, naked! Should we have just let the kids walk around her body? If it wasn't a crime scene, it was the scene of a police investigation."

"And how do you think that looked to all those people who came here for Snowdaze? Would you be in a hurry to return to some place where something like that was going on right in the middle of the biggest event of the winter?"

"You're right, Chet. That was damned inconsiderate of that woman to pick that weekend to turn up dead. How about I write her a ticket for disturbing the peace or something and we can stick it in her casket when they bury her? Better yet, should we have just pushed her back under the ice and waited for the spring thaw?"

The mayor gasped at his comment. "How can you be so cold and heartless? What kind of man are you to say something like that?"

"I'm a man who is about to kick your chubby little butt out the door, that's the kind of man I am," Weber said. "You come in here saying all this crap about us mending fences and being friends, and in the next breath you tell me that you've already been talking to the other town council members and trying to throw me under the bus? Yeah, that's real friendly of you. Get the hell out of here, I've got work to do!"

Weber turned and went into his office, slamming the door behind him hard enough to rattle an aerial picture of Big Lake on the wall. Mary, Robyn, Dan, and Judy Troutman at the dispatcher's desk all looked at the closed door, and then at the mayor.

"Well, what are you all doing, sitting around wasting the Town's time? Get to work," Chet ordered, then went out the door.

"I think I liked him more last summer when he was pretending to be an invalid, riding around on that handicapped cart of his and sucking on that oxygen bottle all the time," Robyn said as the door closed on a gust of cold air.

~***~

"Yeah, Kathy called and told me about what happened to Jill," Don Cotter said when Weber phoned him at his shop in Lakeside. "I figured I'd be hearing from you."

"Do you have any idea how we can get in touch with your brother?"

"Nope. Haven't talked to him in a long time and his phone number's changed."

"Do you think your mother would have it?"

"If she did, she wouldn't know who she was calling," Don told him. "Mom's got dementia and she doesn't know her own name half the time, let alone any of us."

"I'm sorry to hear that," Weber said. "I knew she had moved down south quite a while ago, but I thought she was in some kind of retirement community."

"She was for a while before she started going downhill. We tried having a caregiver come in to help her out, but none of us have very much money. At least, not enough to pay for anybody decent. We tried two or three of them that answered ads we had in the paper down there. One showed up about half the time, and when she did she spent most of her time texting or watching TV instead of taking care of Mom. Another one ripped off her TV and DVD player, and some jewelry and a bunch of other stuff. We couldn't prove it, but she was the only one that was in and out of there. Mom was getting worse all along, and we finally decided that putting her in the care home was the best option. Between selling her house and using that money, and her Social Security and dad's retirement, we got enough to keep her in a decent place. I used to go down and see her, but it was damned hard. Half the time she didn't know who I was, or if she did, she would sit and cry and beg me to take her home. I know it sounds cold, but I just stopped going. That probably makes me sound like a real jerk, doesn't it?"

"Not to me it doesn't," Weber told him. "I can't imagine how rough that must be."

"Anyway, as far as getting hold of Tommy, I don't know what to tell you. We used to be real close, but after that stuff with Jill, that put a stop to it."

"Kathy told me what happened between Jill and Greg, and she said when she told you about it, you told her the same thing had happened with you? Can you tell me more about that?"

"Nothing to tell, really. Tommy was out on a run someplace and Jill showed up here at my shop one day out of the blue. Said something was wrong with her car. She said the motor was running rough and acting funny. I asked her why she came all the way over here and she said because she didn't know any of the mechanics in Big Lake and knew she could trust me not to rip her off because we're family. Hell, I didn't think anything about it. So we got in the car and drove around a little bit and it seemed just fine to me. I told her I'm a radiator guy, I'm not really into engines, Especially this modern stuff with all the computers and electronics they have on them. I told her that Randy Laird there in Big Lake is pretty sharp and he's as honest as the day is long, and suggested she go see him. He's got the test equipment to plug it in and find out what it was doing."

"Then what happened?"

"She made some comment about how plugging things in sounded fun to her, and I really didn't pick up on it. Then the next thing I know, she's right in my face and reached down and grabbed hold of my junk. I asked her what the hell she thought she was doing, and she said she was just thanking me for my time. I kind of pushed her away and told her I didn't appreciate bullshit like that from my brother's wife."

"How did she react to that?"

"She told me that what Tommy didn't know wouldn't hurt him. That it could just be between me and her and nobody else had to ever know about it. I told her *I* would know, and to get her ass out of here."

"Did she leave?"

"Yeah, she left. But not before she told me that she was tired of going without while Tommy was out running around the country in that damn truck of his. Said if I wasn't going to take care of business, there are plenty of other guys who would."

"She sounds like a real piece of work," Weber said.

"I should have called Tommy right then and told him about it. I wanted to, but I didn't want to break the poor guy's heart, either. Now I wish I would have. Maybe it wouldn't have changed anything between us, but at least maybe Greg wouldn't have gotten drawn into the mess. He's got enough on his plate taking care of Kathy as it is."

"You don't know that. From what I've heard about Jill, I think she got around and wasn't looking for anything exclusive, anyway."

"I don't know, Sheriff. Sometimes I think she was getting off on the fact of making it with one of Tommy's family members. There's one thing I do know, though. It might break his heart losing Jill like this, but he's better off without her."

Chapter 12

Weber was drinking a cup of coffee and chewing on a cigar when Mary knocked on his office door and stuck her head inside. Seeing him, she said, "Don't you dare light up that nasty stogie in here, Jim Weber!"

"Relax, you old witch. I haven't smoked a cigar in two years. I'm just reminiscing."

Though he knew smoking was bad for his health, as well as being socially unacceptable, Weber loved cigars. And not just any cigars. He had favored vile, evil looking black cheroots that produced toxic clouds of blue smoke that drove ladies away and could make the stomachs of even strong men queasy after a night of heavy drinking. But his physician, and then Robyn, had convinced him that it was time he put his favorite vice aside in the best interest of his health and his love life.

For a while he had cut back on his consumption, lighting one up only when he was alone in his Explorer or relaxing at the end of a long day's work. Or occasionally, when the pressures of the job got to be too much and he wanted to punish the world around him. But they say that the love of a good woman can change a man, and while Weber wasn't sure if it was Robyn's love or the fact that she had threatened to insert one of his cigars into a portion of his body where no cigar should ever go, but for whatever reason, he had stopped smoking them. Even so, he still kept an old box of cigars in his bottom desk drawer and occasionally chewed on an unlit one just to keep himself in practice.

"Well, see that you don't start again."

"Yes, my Commandant," he promised. "Did you come in here just to hassle me about cigars, or did you have some other way to make my life miserable, too?"

"I came to tell you that Kathy Sterling is on the phone and she said she needs to talk to you. But take that stinky thing out of your mouth before you do so she can understand what you're saying."

Weber used the cigar as an extension of his middle finger when he shot Mary the bird, then picked up the telephone on his desk and pushed the blinking button.

"Hi. Kathy. Jim Weber."

"Have you had any luck tracking down Tommy yet?"

"No, I'm afraid not. I talked to your brother Don, and I was hoping that maybe your mother might have some kind of contact information for him. Do you think the nursing home where she's at might have it?"

"I don't know. They usually call me or Don if there's a problem with Mom's meds or anything we need to know about."

"Okay. What's the name of the place? I'll give them a call anyway, just to ask."

"Desert Aire Convalescent Center, down in Green Valley."

"Do you have a phone number for them?"

"I do," Kathy told him and gave him the number. He wrote it down on a Post-it note, then asked, "What can I do for you today, Kathy?"

"Well, I got to thinking, I don't know if this is legal or not, but if you need to get into Tommy's house, I have a key. That is, assuming he never changed the locks. Before he married Jill and I got sick, me or Greg would go by and check up on it and take in the mail when he was out on a run. Would that be trespassing or anything if you went in there without his permission?"

Weber didn't really know the legalities, but as far as he was concerned, with Jill dead, that made Kathy her brother's next of kin. He would like to get inside the house and see what kind of information it might hold. Besides hopefully helping them locate Tom, it might reveal some clues to help them find out what happened to his wife.

~***~

Weber half expected Mrs. Zimmerman to accost him again when he returned to the Cotter house and he wasn't looking forward to another meeting with her. Fortunately, if she did see his vehicle in the driveway, she chose to remain inside. He unlocked the door with the key Kathy had given him and stepped inside.

"Hello. Anybody here? Sheriff's Department. Anybody home?"

He didn't expect any response, but at the same time, it was part of the routine. If there was someone in the house, he didn't want them to think a burglar had invaded the place. When nobody answered, he and Robyn did a quick walk-through to be sure that the place was empty.

"Somebody's not much of a housekeeper," Weber said. He had been in worse places. Far worse. The Cotter home wasn't filthy, just untidy. The bed was unmade in the master bedroom, there were dirty plates, silverware, and glasses in the kitchen sink, and a trashcan near the back door was nearly overflowing.

"Somebody's not much of a cook, either," Robyn said when she saw the fast food wrappers, and boxes for microwave pizza and frozen foods in the trashcan.

"If I couldn't get it through a drive-through window or stick it in a microwave, I didn't eat before you came along," Weber replied.

"Yeah, right. I bet every single woman on this mountain was standing in line waiting to invite you over for a home-cooked meal."

"Not so many as you might think."

"So, how many were there?"

"A few, not many."

"How many is a few?" Robyn teased.

Weber had to tread lightly here. In the past Robyn had been overly jealous at times, a flaw in her character that he didn't like, and something that had almost ended their relationship a time or two. They seemed to have moved past that, but he was still cautious.

"Let's just say a few and leave it at that, okay?"

Robyn surveyed the living room, looking for anything out of place. "The place may not be ready for Sunday visitors, but it doesn't look like a crime scene, either. Do you see any evidence of a struggle, blood splatter, anything at all?"

"No, I don't, "Weber said. "Where do you think we might find Tom's phone number?"

"There was a desk in the spare bedroom," Robyn said. "Let me look there and see if I can find anything while you snoop around the rest of the place."

Weber always felt like a voyeur when he was going through someone's home, but he knew at times it was necessary. A gun cabinet in the living room held two Remington high-powered hunting rifles, a Marlin semiautomatic .22, an old single shot Winchester 20 gauge shotgun, and a newer Mossberg 12 gauge pump. There was a big screen TV mounted on the wall, a pair of recliners, and a couch. None of them new.

The master bedroom held a king size four poster bed, as well as a mismatched dresser and nightstands. An open door led to a bathroom. The only things that might look out of place were a towel discarded on the floor and a tube of Crest toothpaste without the cap on it on the vanity. That and splotches and spots on the mirror above the vanity reinforced his earlier comment about somebody not being much of a housekeeper.

He went back into the bedroom and opened a second door to reveal a closet full of clothing, most of it women's. The nightstands looked to be made from some kind of pine that had been painted a deep green. One held a flashlight, a Taurus .38 revolver with a four inch barrel, an old pocket watch, and some folded road maps, along with a few other mundane items. Obviously this was Tom's side of the bed. Weber picked up the revolver and opened the cylinder. Fully loaded. Replacing it, he closed the drawer and moved to the other side of the bed. Jill's nightstand contained a hairbrush, a Samsung Galaxy tablet, an old flip style cell phone that looked like it had seen better days, some candy wrappers, and a small packet of Kleenex. Some sort of scented candle sat in a porcelain holder, melted wax dripped down the side. He bent over and sniffed the candle, not sure what it was. Maybe sandalwood, he thought.

There was a jewelry box on top of the dresser, along with a framed photograph of Tom and Jill. Weber opened the box and saw a cheap assortment of costume jewelry, along with a gold wedding band and an engagement ring with a small diamond that could have come from any chain jewelry store in any shopping mall in the country.

Two drawers of the six drawer dresser held men's underwear and socks and a couple of flannel shirts. The others were all full of women's clothes. One drawer had a selection of négligées and other sexy bedroom wear. Weber noticed that two of them were red, and wondered if one might be the same outfit Jill had worn when she had tried to lure Greg Sterling into bed.

"I found it," Robyn called from the other bedroom. Weber pushed the dresser drawer closed and went to where she stood holding an envelope in her hand.

"What have you got?"

"Cell phone bill. There are two numbers. If you look at the breakdown of calls, one of them is all local, or at least in this region. Big Lake, Show Low, Springerville. But the other number shows calls from all over the country, including a lot of them back here to the first number. That's got to be Tom's, right?"

"Yeah, that makes sense." He pulled out his cell phone and dialed the number Robyn had pointed out on the phone bill. It rang three times and then a man answered.

"Hello. Tom here."

Weber could hear the sound of an engine and other noises, indicating the man was on the road. "Tom Cotter?"

"Yeah? Who's this?"

"Tom, it's Jim Weber in Big Lake."

The other man's voice was guarded when he asked, "Yeah?"

"Are you driving right now?"

"No, I just fueled up at the Flying J in Albuquerque. Getting ready to get back on the road now. What's wrong? Did something happen to my sister?"

"No, Kathy's okay. But I'm afraid I've got some bad news for you," the sheriff said.

Nick Russell

Chapter 13

Weber knew there was no easy way to deliver this kind of news, especially over the telephone, so he tried to keep it as brief as possible. "I'm afraid your wife has passed away, Tom. I'm sorry."

"What? Jill's dead?"

"I'm afraid so."

"No. No, she can't be. There's got to be some kind of mistake."

"I wish it was a mistake," Weber told him. "But it's her."

"Why? I mean, how? She's not sick or anything. Was there some kind of traffic accident?"

"We don't know yet," Weber told him. "She was found in the lake Sunday morning."

"In the lake? That doesn't make any sense at all. What the hell would she be doing in the lake?"

"Again, we don't know much of anything at this point."

"It must be somebody else. Maybe somebody who looks like her or something."

"I'm sorry, Tom, but there's no mistake. It's Jill."

There was silence on the other end of the line for a moment, and Weber thought maybe they had lost the connection. "Tom? Are you there?"

"Yeah, I'm here," Tom Cotter said in a ragged voice. "I can't believe this. How can Jill be dead?"

"That's what we're trying to figure out. When was the last time you talked to her?"

"Let me think. Tuesday. Or maybe Wednesday. Shit, I can't think straight. No, it was Tuesday. Tuesday morning. I had just dropped a load in Oklahoma City and was making a pick up for a short run up to Tulsa. I called to tell her I wasn't going to make it home by the weekend like I planned because there was a split load I could take from there, some of it going to Wichita and the rest to Denver. From there I was hoping to get a load headed south toward home. She got mad at me because I'd promised to be back in time for that winter festival or whatever was going on. But it's hard making a buck out here these days, and you've got to take the loads when you find them and take them where they need to be."

"When you talked to her then did she say anything about being sick or not feeling well?"

"No. Jill never got sick. Do you think that's what happened? Do you think she got sick and something happened to her?"

"I wish I could tell you, Tom, but I just don't know. We sent her down to Tucson for an autopsy."

"An autopsy? They're going to cut her up?"

"I'm sorry, but when we have an unexplained death of a young person, it's standard procedure."

There was no reply, but Weber could hear the man sobbing and he waited a long moment to give him time to compose himself. Finally, he said, "I hate to have to tell you about it this way, but we didn't have any way to get a hold of you and didn't know when you'd be home."

"That's okay. I just can't believe any of this. It's like I'm stuck in some nightmare and can't wake up."

"You said you're in Albuquerque now?"

"Yeah. I just got some fuel and a little bit of rest and I was going to deadhead home."

"Are you going to be okay to drive here on your own?"

"Yeah. I'll make it. I'll head out right now and get there as fast as I can."

"There's nothing you can do to change anything at this point," Weber said. "So please don't go rushing and put yourself or anybody else on the road in danger. Okay, Tom?"

"Yeah. Yeah, okay. I'm on my way. Should I go to the house or to your office, or what?"

"If you don't mind, I would prefer you not come to the house. Until we know what happened to Jill, I'd like to preserve any evidence there might be here."

"Evidence? What kind of evidence? Wait a minute. Do you think somebody did something to Jill? Like somebody killed her?"

"Like I said, we just don't know. Tom, do I have your permission to look around here in the house, so we can see if there's any indication here of what happened to Jill?"

"Sure, whatever. Damn, Jimmy. I just don't believe this. I wish I could wake up and this was all a bad dream."

"I wish it was a bad dream, too. I really do, Tom. Why don't you call me when you get close to town, okay?"

"Okay. I'm on my way."

"What do you think?" Robyn asked when the call ended.

"It's hard to say. When you're looking at someone and giving them that kind of news you can read their body language and get something, sometimes. But over the telephone, who knows? He sounded pretty broke up about it, like he couldn't believe what I was telling him. I guess we'll know more when he gets back to town. Meanwhile, let's keep looking around here."

"Can we do that without a warrant?"

"He gave us verbal permission."

"Is that enough? What if we find something incriminating and he claims he never gave us permission?"

"Like what?"

"I don't know," Robyn said. "We could find a bloody ax that he murdered his wife with and the whole case would get thrown out of court?"

"Well, if we find an ax, we'd better find a damn good makeup kit to go along with it, too. Because I sure didn't see anything that looked like a wound on her body, did you?"

~***~

It was 225 miles from Albuquerque to Big Lake, and Tom Cotter made it home in just under four hours. Weber and Robyn were back at the sheriff's office, having spent half of that time at the trucker's house and finding no evidence of any foul play there. With nothing else to do, Weber had called the Medical

Examiner's office down in Tucson, even though he knew they would not have had time to do Jill's autopsy yet.

"It's a Monday, Sheriff Weber," Doctor Hurtado said when Weber got him on the line. "Do you know how many ways people down here find to get themselves killed over the weekend?"

"I would imagine there's quite a variety," Weber replied.

"Oh, yeah. Besides the usual car wrecks, and shootings, and stabbings, and overdoses, I've got a 20 year old frat boy who jumped off the third floor balcony of his hotel room on a bet. He thought he could make it all the way to the swimming pool. That didn't work out too well for him. He landed headfirst six feet from the water."

"Ouch."

"Yeah, ouch. His fraternity brothers all hauled ass, leaving a mess in the room for housekeeping to clean up, and a mess out by the pool for us to deal with."

"It's always good to know your bro's have your back," Weber said.

"Then there's the lady who went hiking on Mount Lemmon and got lost in the dark and fell over 200 feet. Took Search and Rescue six hours to find her and get her out of the canyon where she ended up. And let's not forget the idiot who decided his barbecue wasn't heating up fast enough, so he threw a cup of gasoline onto the charcoal briquettes."

"Some would say that's just natural selection," Weber suggested.

Doctor Hurtado laughed at the dark humor and said, "Hey, it keeps us in business. Anyway, looking at the notes, you sent us a floater? Isn't it wintertime up there in the mountains?"

"Yes, it is."

"So was she ice fishing or something?"

"Not unless she was doing it buck naked," Weber told him.

"Okay, now you've got my attention."

"If you think that's interesting," Weber said, "wait until I tell you about the exploding Santa Claus."

~***~

The call ended with Doctor Hurtado promising to get to Jill Cotter's autopsy as soon as possible, hopefully late that afternoon or first thing in the morning. When Weber got off the phone he thought about retrieving the cigar from the wastebasket next to his desk, and decided that if he had reached that point he might as well just smoke the damn thing and be done with it. Fortunately, he was spared from making that decision when Mary knocked on his door and told him that Tom Cotter was on the telephone.

"I just left Springerville and thought I'd give you a call before I lose the signal coming up the hill. Do you want me to come to the Sheriff's Office?"

"Do you have a trailer hooked on the back?"

"No. Like I said, I was dead heading home before I got your call."

"Then why don't you come here to the office? There's room in the parking lot."

"Okay, I'll see you soon."

When the call ended, the sheriff stared at the phone in silence, not looking forward to the conversation he was going to have with Cotter when he got back to Big Lake.

Chapter 14

"I keep going over it in my head, over and over, and I still can't believe it's true." The trucker was sitting red eyed and shaky in the chair next to Weber's desk. "I know you said it was her, but maybe you're wrong. You must have found somebody else. Someone who looks like her."

"No, Tom, it's her."

"You said she was naked, right? So if she was naked she didn't have any identification on her. Maybe it's like I said, somebody who looks like her."

Weber knew Cotter was grasping at straws, holding onto any possibility that there had been a terrible mistake, a misidentification. The sheriff had seen it many times when somebody was faced with news they couldn't accept. He pulled his phone from his pocket and showed the man pictures of the rose tattooed on the dead woman's left breast, and the tattoo from the small of her back. Cotter's lips trembled and tears rolled down his cheeks as the photographs proved once and for all what he had been trying to deny on his long drive home.

"What happened to her, Jimmy?"

"I wish I knew," Weber told him. "I talked to the medical examiner's office down in Tucson a little while ago and they're going to try to get her autopsy done this afternoon or first thing in the morning. That should tell us something."

"Man, just thinking about them cutting her up turns my stomach. I wish they didn't have to do that. I understand it's necessary, but still..."

Trying to keep the man from thinking about the gruesome details of what was going to happen to his wife's body, Weber asked him, "Did Jill have any kind of medical issues at all that you know of?"

Cotter shrugged his shoulders. "Not really. I mean she used to complain about her back hurting once in a while, and she'd get kind of short of breath. Usually when I wanted her help stacking firewood or something like that. To be honest with you, I thought she was just saying that to get out of work. I love Jill, but she isn't the most energetic person in the world."

"How about a family history of anything like heart disease or that type of thing?"

The bereaved man shook his head. "Not that I know of. But I really don't know much about her family. She wasn't close to them at all. I met her mother twice, and both times they got into an argument and we left. And her dad's been dead for a long time."

"Any other family members that you know of?"

"She's got a half-brother somewhere in the Pacific Northwest, but I couldn't tell you where. From what I was able to piece together, after her dad died, her mom, Claire, married a couple of different guys, and lived with a couple more. It wasn't exactly the best situation to grow up in. As soon as Jill was old enough to get out on her own, she did."

"I see. And her mother's still in Barstow?"

"No, she never did live there. That's just where I met Jill. Her mom was living in Las Vegas the first time we went to see her. I think she was on husband number three then. Or maybe boyfriend twelve. I really don't know. Then, a year or two later she was living in a trailer park in Temecula, California and working as a barmaid."

"Do you have any idea how to get in touch with her?"

"Sorry, I don't, Jimmy. Like I said, they never got along. I don't know when the last time Jill talked to her, but it's been a while."

"How about you, Tom? The last time you talked to Jill was on Tuesday?"

"Yeah, sometime in the middle of the day."

"Did she seem okay then?"

"Yeah, fine. Well, she was pissed off because I told her I wasn't going to be able to make it back in time for that snow festival or whatever they called it. Jill doesn't understand that sometimes loads come up that you have to take. I couldn't turn around and deadhead all the way back from Oklahoma. That truck of mine isn't exactly one of those little smart cars you see everybody driving these days. It sucks up a lot of diesel."

"And that's the last time you talked to her?"

He nodded his head. "Yeah. We got into a fight about that and she hung up on me. I tried to call her back a couple of hours later, hoping she had cooled down. But she didn't answer. And I called two or three more times over the next couple of days but she wouldn't answer then, either."

"Was that like her? To get mad and not answer when you called?"

"Yeah, it was. It wasn't the first time this happened. To be honest with you, Jimmy, I just figured she was pouting and she'd get over it." His voice broke when he added, "I hate to think that the last time we talked, we argued and it ended this way."

Weber wanted to tell him not to beat himself up over the incident. Things like that happened. Instead, he said, "Tom, I have to ask you some difficult questions. "

"All right. What do you need to know?"

"You told me about that argument. How were things between you and Jill?"

"How were things? Do you mean how did we get along, something like that?"

"Yeah, that's what I mean."

"Jimmy, you can't believe I would do anything to hurt Jill. My God, I love her!"

"These are just routine questions, Tom. But we have to get through them."

Cotter shook his head in frustration, then said, "I understand. Let's get it over with. In answer to your question, we got along okay."

"Okay?"

"Yeah, okay. I mean, we had our ups and downs like any couple does. But I'd never do anything to hurt her."

"Did you argue a lot?"

"We argued, sure. Doesn't every couple?"

"Of course they do," Weber said. "I guess that's just part of life. What did you two argue about, Tom?"

"I don't know. Mostly about me being gone so much. Jill was always complaining about being alone and not having any friends. I tried to get her to go with me on some of my runs, but that didn't work out. She'd get carsick."

"So you argued about you being gone so much. Anything else?"

"Not really. Money, I guess. Yeah, we argued about that. Jill could never seem to understand that just because I brought in a lot of money sometimes, didn't mean we could just go spend it. It costs a lot of money to keep a truck on the road, between fuel and maintenance and fees and all that. We had some pretty bad arguments about that."

"Because she didn't understand the business side of things?"

"Yeah. A couple of times she put me in a pretty bad position."

"What do you mean by that, Tom?"

"See, Jimmy, the way it works is, I work with three or four different freight brokers most of the time. There's one down in Phoenix, and he might have me pick up a load of brick down there and take it to Las Vegas, just as an example. Then when I get there I take a picture of the delivery receipt with my phone and I send it to him. And he makes a direct deposit into my bank account to pay me. Then, he might have me pick up a load somewhere in Nevada and take it to Montana or wherever, and he makes another direct deposit into my account. Or sometimes, if there are several short runs I'll have him wait and deposit everything at once. So I might get three or four or five thousand bucks deposited at one time. But that's not all profit. I've got to pay for the fuel I use making those runs, or tires, or whatever. A couple of times Jill saw all that money and just took it out of the bank and spent it. That left me sitting high and dry, my credit cards maxed out on fuel purchases, and no way to get more."

"That's got to be a bad position to be in. What happened then?"

"Fortunately, the one broker I use in Phoenix is a pretty good friend and he knows he can depend on me. So he advanced me the money. But instead of putting it in the account like normal, he gave me a receipt showing the money was coming and I was able to go to a factor to get the cash."

"I don't know what that means," Weber told him. "What's a factor?"

"Think of it as a bank that loans money to a trucker, based on what he has coming from a freight broker. So let's say I had $800 coming to me. I can email that receipt to a factor, and he will give me about $650. He keeps the rest as his fee."

"That takes a big chunk out of your profit, doesn't it?"

"Yes, it does. It's kind of like one of those payday loan places. It's easy to get caught up in that cycle and the next thing you know, you're working for them because as soon as you get some money in and pay them off you have to get another advance and you're right back where you started "

"So how do you break that cycle, Tom?"

"In my case, I set up a different bank account that Jill didn't know about, and I had a debit card for it. I had a couple of freight brokers deposit money into that account when they paid me, so I would have operating cash. The rest of it went into the regular account, so Jill didn't know what was going on. All she knew was that less money was coming in, and she didn't like that. But I always made sure there was plenty of money to pay the bills and take care of things here at home."

"Besides the finances and you being gone so much, did you two argue about anything else?"

"What's this all about, Jimmy?"

"Like I said, it's just routine."

"No," Cotter said shaking his head, his voice starting to rise. "If Jill died in some accident or because of a medical problem you wouldn't be asking these kind of questions. What the hell happened to my wife? I've got a right to know."

"Look, Tom, you know me. You know I wouldn't bullshit you. We truly don't know what happened. That's why we have to cover every base. This isn't personal, I'm not accusing you of anything, I just need to get the overall picture of your lives. That will give me some ideas of what might have happened to Jill."

Cotter took in a deep breath and held it for a second, his eyes closed, and it seemed to help him compose himself. He nodded his head and opened his eyes again.

"Okay, yeah, we argued about money, and we argued about me being gone, and... damn, I don't want to get into all this."

"What else was it you argued about?"

From the man's reluctance, Weber had an idea what Cotter was so reluctant to say. Very few men want to admit their wives had been unfaithful to them. But Weber had to know, and he gently said. "It's okay, Tom, whatever it is, you can tell me. I'm your friend."

Cotter's eyes were closed and he shook his head and said, "We argued a lot about cheating."

There, it was out in the open. Weber knew it had been difficult for his friend to approach the subject and he was glad they were over that hurdle. At least he thought so, until Cotter said, "Every time I turned around, Jill was accusing me of cheating on her. She was convinced I was screwing every truck stop waitress, lot lizard, or skanky woman hitchhiker in the country."

Chapter 15

Weber hadn't expected that, and before he could respond Cotter said, "Jimmy, as God is my witness, I never laid a finger on another woman since the day I met Jill. Never even looked. I wasn't interested in anyone else but her. Not one little bit. I don't know where she got that idea, but she just latched onto it like a dog to a bone and wouldn't let go. No matter how many times I told her that would never happen, she was always convinced I was messing around behind her back. She said she knew how easy it is to get laid out there, and I guess that's true if a guy was looking for it. But I wasn't!"

Weber wasn't totally surprised. He knew that a lot of cheaters believe that the best defense is a good offense. If they can keep the other person busy denying the things they are accused of doing, their partner never has the time to wonder what they themselves might be up to.

"I believe you, Tom. I know the kind of man you are, and I don't believe you were cheating, either."

"I wasn't! And I never could figure out why she seemed so convinced I was. But she kept saying that's why I wanted to be out on the road in the truck. So I could pick up women and cheat on her."

It was obvious the man had been hurt by his wife's accusations, and Weber knew he had to proceed cautiously.

"Tom, let me ask you this. Do you think Jill ever cheated on you?"

"No way! Nope, don't even go there, Jimmy!"

He shook his head adamantly, folding his arms across his chest defensively. Obviously he hadn't heard any of the rumors about his wife's activities when he was out of town, or if he did, he chose not to believe them. They say love is blind, and apparently it was true in Tom Cotter's case.

"I didn't mean any disrespect, Tom. Believe me, it's just as uncomfortable for me to ask some of these questions as it is for you to answer them."

"You've been talking to my sister, haven't you? That's where this bullshit's coming from, isn't it?"

"I have talked to Kathy," Weber told him. "And to her husband. And to your brother, Don, too."

"And those lying bastards are talking all kind of bullshit about my Jill, aren't they? Well none of it's true!"

"Tom, I know there's a big division in your family over accusations that were made. I can't fix that, but we do have to talk about..."

"No," Cotter said, standing up and shaking his head. "We're done here, Jimmy. I'm not gonna sit here and listen to lies about my wife."

"Tom, sit down."

"Forget it! I've told you everything I know. You're not telling me a damn thing, just repeating bullshit you heard from people who couldn't stand Jill."

"Why do you think that is, Tom? Why do you think your own brother, and your sister, and Greg would all lie about Jill?"

Cotter's face was red and he was shaking with rage at that point. He pointed his finger at Weber and said, "You back off, Jimmy. You back off right now. I don't care if we are friends, and I don't care if you are wearing that badge. You say one more thing about my Jill and we're going to go at it right here and right now!"

Weber held up his hands in an attempt to calm the man, "Tom, please sit down."

"Am I under arrest for something?"

"No, you're not."

"Then I'm out of here. Unless you're going to try to stop me."

"Nobody's stopping you, Tom. But I really do wish you would sit back down so we can talk."

"I'm done talking to you. Where can I see my wife?"

"You can't see her right now," Weber told him gently. "Like I said, she's down at the Medical Examiner's office in Tucson.

Once they are done with her, you can make your funeral arrangements. I've already given them your name and phone number."

Cotter walked to the door of his office and started to open it, then turned back to Weber and said, "You son of a bitch. I always thought you were my friend, Jimmy."

"I am your friend."

Cotter shook his head, looked at the sheriff one last time, then opened the door and left.

~***~

"It just breaks my heart to see Tom hurting so bad," Mary Caitlin said. "The look on his face when he went out the door was like his whole world had ended."

"It has ended, from his perspective," Weber said. "I didn't see any point in upsetting him any worse than he already was. Poor guy's going through hell as it is, and then me asking him questions like that."

"It had to be done, Jimmy."

"I know. But that doesn't make it any easier."

"You know what really sucks? That wife of his doing what she did behind his back, then putting this big guilt trip on him, accusing him of being the one that was cheating. I don't get that. It's bad enough that *she* was doing it, but then she makes him the bad guy?"

"I know. And from the way he acted, I don't think Tom had any clue what was going on when he was out on the road. He really believes that his brother and Greg Sterling made up all that stuff about Jill to cover the fact that they were both trying to get something going with her."

"He always impressed me as a pretty smart guy," Deputy Tommy Frost said. "It's hard to believe he would think that both his brother and his brother-in-law did the same thing."

"Well, when you love somebody that much, you believe what you want to believe," Mary said.

"So, what now?"

"I don't know that we can do much else right now," Weber said. "Until we hear from the ME's office we don't even know what we're dealing with."

"I was thinking about something," Robyn said. "Where did she go into the lake?"

"Hard to say," Weber told her.

"Is it, Jimmy? I mean, didn't they have a guy from the county use that big bucket loader or whatever it was to break up the ice at the boat ramp when we all went in for that plunge thing?"

"Yeah."

"So doesn't there have to be a hole someplace where Jill's body went in? Like, could she have fallen through a weak point in the ice and left a hole?"

"Not necessarily," Weber said. "The ice was thick there by the boat ramp, but there are other places where it doesn't even reach all the way to shore."

"Not to mention the fact that Coyote Creek feeds into the lake all year long, so you've got open water there," Chad Summers said.

"But you may be on to something, Robyn. It might not hurt to have Parks fly over the lake and see if he can find any holes where she might have fallen through. It's been cold, but I don't think a hole big enough to fall through would have frozen over already. What do you think, Chad?"

"I guess it's worth a shot. You could ask him."

Larry Parks was in the small park model trailer at the back of the Sheriff's Department parking lot that served as the FBI's field office in Big Lake. He looked up as Weber came in and asked, "What's up, Bubba?"

Weber told him about Robyn's question and asked if he would be willing to make a few low-level passes over the lake in his airplane.

"Let me see, I get to fly my plane and the Town pays for my fuel? When do we go?"

"Not we, you," Weber told him. "You know I hate getting in that damn thing."

86

That wasn't entirely true. Weber had flown with his friend half a dozen times, and while he was never entirely comfortable in the small airplane, Parks was a competent pilot and Weber admired his skills. Not that he would ever admit it.

"I can't fly the plane and look for this hole you think might be out there, too. I'm going to need a spotter."

"How about Northcutt? He seemed to like flying with you."

"Jordan's fine," Parks said.

"Okay, I'll have him get over here and hook up with you."

"Not today, Park said, shaking his head. "It's too late in the afternoon, Jimmy. By the time we got to Springerville and got the plane and came back, we would be running out of daylight. But we can be in the air at first light tomorrow morning, if that would help."

"Yeah, that's fine," Weber said. It got dark early in the mountains during the wintertime and he didn't want his friend or his deputy risking their lives in an effort that might prove futile, anyway.

He paused in the door of the trailer and said, "Just do me one favor, will you?"

"What's that, Jimmy?"

"Don't throw anything else out of the airplane. No Santa Claus, no elves, no flying reindeer, no Easter bunny. Is that too much to ask?"

Chapter 16

It was midmorning on Tuesday before Doctor Hurtado called from the Medical Examiner's office in Tucson.

"You're always sending me something interesting, Sheriff Weber. I'll say that for you."

"We do our best," Weber told him. "What have you got for me, Doc?"

"Well, to start with, we ran a toxicology screen on her, and Mrs. Cotter was intoxicated at the time of her death."

"Any idea what her blood alcohol level was?"

"Not knowing the exact time of death, I can only estimate. But I would say somewhere around 1.4 percent, possibly a bit higher."

"That's more than half again the legal limit for driving," Weber said.

"Again, this is an estimate. A lot of factors go into play here, Sheriff Weber. But it's an estimate I'm comfortable with. And there's something else. I detected traces of cocaine in her system."

"That's interesting. How much?"

"I can't give you an exact amount, due to her being in the cold water, but enough to make her high."

"Okay, can you give me any idea on her time of death? "

"I'm sure you've pulled some floaters out of the lake in your time, Sheriff. So as you know, bacterial action causes the body to bloat with gas and rise to the top. Hence the term, floaters. But in cold weather, that whole process is slowed down considerably. A body can stay on the bottom much longer."

Weber had indeed pulled his share of floaters out of Big Lake's deep waters, and shuddered at the memory.

"How long do you think she was in the water?"

"Under normal conditions, a good rule of thumb is that two weeks in the water equals one week on land when it comes to decomposition. The skin will absorb water and within a week or so it will start to peel away from the underlying tissue. Cold water like you have up there this time of year can produce the formation of something called adipocere. It's a waxy substance that is formed from the body's fatty tissue that protects it from decomposition. I've heard the texture described as soapy. When that process happens, bodies can stay pretty much intact for weeks. Given that I didn't see any decomposition nor any adipocere with your victim, I'm going to say she wasn't in there more than four days."

That fit in with Tom Cotter's timeline of saying he hadn't spoken with his wife since the previous Tuesday afternoon.

"Okay, now for the $64,000 question, Doc. What happened to her?"

"Well, not the obvious. She didn't drown."

"Really?"

"No, sir. No water in the lungs. She was dead when she went into the water."

"Do you know what killed her?"

"As I'm sure you saw when you examined the body, there were no outward signs of trauma."

"We didn't see any," Weber said.

"Neither did we," Doctor Hurtado told him.

"So what does that mean?"

"It could mean a lot of things, Sheriff. Obviously dead people don't make it into frozen lakes under their own power."

"So somebody killed her. How?"

"You're jumping to conclusions, Sheriff."

"I am? You like screwing with my head, don't you, Doc?"

"I'll admit I take a certain pleasure in it," the medical examiner admitted.

"We've got a drunk, stoned, naked woman in the lake, who didn't drown, and who you seem to be saying wasn't murdered. So what happened to her?"

"Mrs. Cotter died from a myocardial infarction."

"A heart attack?"

"That's correct. She suffered from hypertrophic cardiomyopathy, which is a condition that causes a portion of the heart to become thicker than normal. Quite often, including in Mrs. Cotter's case, it was the left ventricle. This keeps the heart from pumping blood effectively."

"What causes that?"

"In most cases it's genetic," Doctor Hurtado said. "If you look into your victim's background, I'm almost certain you'll find that one of her parents has the same condition, or had it if they are no longer living."

"Could there have been something that triggered this heart attack she had?"

"It's possible. Do you know if she was being treated for her condition?"

"Not according to her husband," Weber replied. "He said she was in good health overall."

Weber didn't recall seeing any prescription medications at the Cotter house.

"Many things can cause a heart attack, both internal and external. Judging by the thickness of the ventricle wall, and if she wasn't under a doctor's care, I would say it was only a matter of time before this woman had a cardiac episode. But I think what you're getting at is did something or someone cause it to happen when it did? And I think that's a reasonable expectation, given the conditions in which her body was discovered. Let's face it, Sheriff Weber, the odds that she walked down to the lake, took her clothes off, had a fatal heart attack, and then fell into the water are pretty astronomical."

"Let me get this straight," Weber said. "She died of natural causes. A heart attack, right?"

"That's correct."

"But some outside stimulus may have triggered that heart attack?"

"It's entirely possible."

"And what would that stimulus be?"

"That's impossible to say," the medical examiner replied. "Fear. Strong physical exertion. Some kind of drug."

"Like cocaine."

"Yes. As you know, cocaine increases heart rate and blood pressure. It could certainly have been a contributing factor."

"Can you tell if she had been using very long, Doc?"

"I don't think she was a heavy user or a long time user. I didn't see any indication of that in her organs, and believe me, I've autopsied a lot of drug users in my time."

"With her being naked, was there any sign of sexual assault?"

"A vaginal swab showed traces of semen, which we kept for DNA testing if you need it. Though, after that long in the water, I can't make any guarantees if it will still be viable or not. But there were no signs of trauma that would indicate rape," the medical examiner said.

"Is there anything else you can tell me?

"Only that I'm very curious about how she ended up in that lake. We both know that she had some help getting there. Let me know what you find out, Sheriff Weber."

~***~

"Did you see anything?"

"Lots of snow, lots of trees, and a bunch of elk. That's about it, Jimmy."

"No obvious holes in the lake?"

"Sorry," Parks said. "I wish I could be more helpful."

"Hey, you gave it your best shot. And you didn't bomb the town. I appreciate the effort."

"Did you hear from the ME's office down in Tucson?"

"I did," the sheriff said, and gave Parks and Deputy Northcutt a rundown on what the autopsy had revealed.

"Where do we go from here?" Jordan asked.

"We need to find Jill's Toyota. If we can locate it, it might give us a good idea of where she was right before she died. I'm going to go over to the Cotter house and have another talk with Tom. That's if he'll talk to me at all."

"How about I go with you?" Chad Summers suggested. "Tom and I have always gotten along pretty well."

"It can't hurt," Weber said. "He and I were always on good terms, too, before I asked him about Jill and the possibility of her cheating. That's when he flew off the handle."

"Let's give it a shot," Chad said. "I don't know what else we can do at this point."

Before they could leave the office the phone rang, and Mary Caitlin held up a finger to have them wait. She pushed a button to put the call on hold and said, "It's Kathy Sterling, Jimmy. She wants to talk to you."

Weber went back to his desk and answered the phone. "Hi, Kathy, what's up?"

"I was wondering if you have been able to get in touch with Tommy yet?"

"Yes, I did yesterday. When I called him he was at a truck stop in New Mexico and he got back to town a few hours later."

"How's he doing?"

"He's having a pretty rough time of it," Weber told her.

"I feel so bad for him, Jim. I want to talk to him, to let him know that we're here for him, all of us are, but I don't know how he'll react."

The sheriff saw a mental image of Tom Cotter's angry face when he talked about the accusations his brother and Greg had made about Jill and he knew that in the man's present state he probably would not be receptive to his family reaching out to him.

"I know you want to help him, Kathy. But I think it's best if you give him a little bit of time, okay?"

"He still hates us, doesn't he?"

"I won't say hate, but he's still pretty upset by what Don told him about Jill."

"But it's all true! None of us would make that up just to hurt him."

"I know you wouldn't," Weber assured her. "But right now he's not thinking rationally. I'll tell you what, I'll pass on your concerns for him, okay?"

"Thank you, Jim. Would you please tell him..." Weber could hear her voice breaking and then Kathy taking a deep breath, "would you please tell him that we love him. We all love him and we miss him. And we want to help him any way we can. We're family."

"I'll tell him that, Kathy," Weber said gently. "I promise."

Chapter 17

When he opened the door of his house, Tom Cotter looked like he had not eaten or bathed, or slept since Weber saw him the day before. His eyes were red and swollen, beard stubble covered his face, and his hair was mussed.

"What the hell do you want?"

"We need to talk to you, Tom."

"I told you yesterday, I'm done talking to you. And I'm done listening to lies about my wife."

"I spoke to the Medical Examiner this morning," Weber said. "I wanted to share some things with you that he told me."

Cotter looked at him for a long moment, then stepped aside so the sheriff and Chad could enter. He seemed to have aged overnight, and he shuffled his feet like an old man when he went back to his recliner and dropped down into it.

"What did you find out?"

"Tom, Jill died of a heart attack."

"A heart attack? No way! She was only 33 years old."

"Even kids die of heart attacks sometimes," Chad said.

"Do you remember her ever complaining of chest pains or anything like that?"

Cotter shook his head. "Like I told you the other day, sometimes she'd complain about being short of breath. When she first got here, she said it was because of the altitude. Then later on I just thought... I don't know what I thought. Like I said, she wasn't the most energetic person in the world to start with."

Weber knew about altitude sickness. Every year at least one or two flatlanders who came to the mountains to escape the desert heat exhibited symptoms of dizziness, shortness of breath, and sometimes chest pains. Usually, as soon as they descended to a lower elevation things cleared up for them. But every once in a while they lost someone when their condition became acute.

"According to the Medical Examiner, Jill had a heart disease. Something called hypertrophic cardiomyopathy. He said it's usually something that's passed down from parent to child. I remember you said that her father died a long time ago. Did she ever tell you what he died of?"

"No, not that I recall." Cotter raised his head and said, "Wait a minute. This doesn't make any sense. If she died of a heart attack, why was she in the lake? And why was she naked?"

"We don't know that yet, Tom," Chad said. "We're still working on figuring those things out. That's why we need your help."

"Tom, did Jill ever drink very much?"

He shrugged his shoulders. "I don't know, not a lot. She'd have a few drinks now and then, but it wasn't like she was a lush or anything like that."

"What about drugs?"

"Drugs? Why are you asking me about drugs?"

Weber tried to keep it as gentle as possible when he said, "According to the ME, Jill was intoxicated and had cocaine in her system when she died."

Cotter shot out of his recliner like it was an ejection seat and shouted, "Don't start that bullshit again, Jimmy! You're trying to paint my wife like she's some kind of drugged out whore or something, aren't you?"

"I'm just giving you the facts as they were told to me by the Medical Examiner, Tom."

"You can take your facts and your medical examiner and stick them up your ass. Jill wasn't like that!"

"Calm down, Tom. We're not trying to smear your wife's reputation. But the facts are the facts, whether you like them or not."

He grabbed Weber by the front of his shirt and jerked him upright, knocking things over on the coffee table that sat in front of the sofa. "You keep talking about my wife like that and I'm gonna kick your ass!"

Chad was on his feet and grabbed the man by the shoulders and pulled him backward. "Stop it, Tom!"

But Cotter wouldn't listen to him. He struggled and tried to pull away, leaving Chad no choice but to put his foot in front of the man and push forward, knocking him off balance and onto the sofa. Behind them the coffee table tipped over and crashed to the floor. Putting his weight on top of him, Chad pulled his arm backward and up, drawing a yelp of pain from Cotter.

"Stop resisting, Tom! Just stop. Right now. Nobody wants to hurt you, but you can't be doing this."

"Just kill me, you bastards. Just shoot me and get it over with! I don't have anything to live for anymore anyway."

"Nobody's going to kill anybody," Chad said, as the man beneath him stopped fighting and began sobbing. "We're your friends, Tom. Whether you believe that or not. Nobody's trying to make Jill look bad. Nobody's trying to cause you any more grief than you've already got, okay? But we can't just pretend that the things we know didn't happen. Don't you want us to find out what happened to her?"

"It just doesn't matter anymore. I just want her back. I just want my Jill back."

He was wailing now, giving into his grief. Chad got off of him and looked down at him with pity, then at Weber, who shook his head.

They let him cry for a moment, then Chad sat down beside him and pulled him upright.

"It's okay, buddy. Just let it out. We're here for you."

Like a child that has been hurt too much, Tom buried his face in the deputy's shoulder and cried. Chad had been a Little League baseball coach for many years, as well as a long time deputy, and he knew that sometimes a person just needed to let go.

"I love her so much! I don't want to go on without her. I can't do this."

"It's okay," Chad said gently. "It's okay, Tom. You're going to get through this. I know it doesn't seem like it right now, and it's not going to be easy, but you will get through this."

Weber sat on the edge of the couch and said, "Tom, I know this hurts. I know it sucks, and you wish you could just wake up and it was all a bad dream. I wish you could, too. But it isn't a dream. You need to know that a lot of people love you. I talked to your sister today. She's hurting, too. Kathy, and Greg, and Don all want you to know that they're there for you. Whatever was done in the past, whatever was said, it doesn't matter at this point. They're your family, and they love you. You're a good man and you've got a lot of friends in this community. A lot of people who respect you and would do anything for you. You need to hold onto that, okay?"

Cotter nodded, and after another moment or two he managed to compose himself enough to pull away from Chad. He seemed embarrassed by his emotional breakdown, but at the same time unwilling to believe that the things his family members had told him about his wife could be true.

"I don't want to see Kathy or any of them. Not after what they said about Jill."

"That's your right," Weber told him. "Just know that they care."

"Tom, we still need to find out how Jill died and how she ended up in the lake like she did. Do you know where her car is?"

"Her car? No, I just assumed you guys had it."

"No, it wasn't at the lake when we found her."

"I don't know," he said, shaking his head.

"Could it be in the lake, too? Maybe she drove it in?"

"I don't think so," Weber said. "We had an airplane fly over the lake several times looking for any holes in the ice. They didn't see anything."

"Did Jill have any friends around here that she hung out with when you were gone, Tom?"

"No. That's one of the things she always complained about. Me being gone and her being alone all the time. I tried to get her to make friends with people but she just didn't seem to be able to do it. To be honest with you, Jill didn't like it here at all. She didn't like the town and she didn't like the people. I know that makes her sound like a snob, but she never did fit in. Maybe I should have listened to her and moved to Barstow like she wanted to. Or Vegas, or wherever she wanted to go. But this was always my home, the place I could come back to after I was on the road and feel like I was part of something. Jill never got the fact that it's lonely for me when I'm out there, too. And I just can't handle those big cities, where you don't know anybody and you're just one more face in the crowd."

"Do you know what Jill did with her time when you were gone? Did she ever say anything about what she did to keep busy?"

He shrugged his shoulders and shook his head again. "Not really. At first she tried stuff like crocheting and scrapbooking and things like that, but she always got bored with them. That's why she wanted to move to someplace bigger. Someplace with movie theaters and things happening all the time. I wish I'd have done it. She was so unhappy here."

"Do you know if Jill had any enemies?"

"Enemies? She hardly knew anybody here. How could she have enemies?"

"I don't know," Weber said. "Maybe one of the neighbors she got into an argument with, something like that?"

"Mrs. Zimmerman next door is a pain in the ass, just like she was when she was teaching. A few times she bitched about my truck being parked out there and she kept saying she was going to call the Sheriff's office and have you guys give me a ticket. But I knew I wasn't breaking any zoning laws, so I just ignored her."

"Anybody else?"

"No. The house on the other side of us has been empty ever since the Donahues moved back to Kansas. That's been two or three years. As fast as places are selling around here, I thought someone would grab it up by now, but I think they're asking way too much."

"How about the people across the street?"

"Old Herb Dawson's in the two-story place. He's about 90 and never even comes outside anymore. He's got a caregiver that comes over every day, and she waves once in a while but that's about it. And the people in the place next to him have only been there a year or so. They've got a couple of kids but I haven't even met them. And Jill never mentioned talking to them, either."

"Could there be anybody from back in Barstow that had some kind of grudge against her from when she lived there? From before you guys met? Did she ever mention anybody like that?"

"No. At least nobody that I can recall. She had a roommate when I first met her, and they seemed like they were pretty close. After Jill moved here they'd call each other once in a while, but then it kind of died away."

"No old boyfriends that were jealous when you two got together?"

He thought for a minute, then said, "There was a guy who worked at the hotel where she did that she said kind of had a crush on her. Ernie? Arnie? Something like that. He was a real nerdy guy, typical geek with the thick glasses and always talking about computer games and stuff like that. She said he asked her to go to some kind of comic-con thing or something like that and she just laughed and told him she was a grown-up. She said he didn't talk much to her after that."

"And how long ago was that?"

"Six years. Almost seven."

That was a long time to hold a grudge, but Weber asked if he could remember anything else about Ernie or Arnie.

"Not really. I mean, I saw him around there when I'd stay at the place, he was the desk clerk or something. He was never real friendly but it wasn't like he was rude or anything. Just off in his own world."

"Okay, I have to ask you this again, and please don't go flying off the handle like you did before," Weber said. "Did Jill use any kind of drugs that you know of? Pot, coke, anything at all?"

"No, Jimmy. She wasn't like that! We'd have a few drinks once in a while but that was it. That medical examiner said Jill was drunk? Yeah, I guess it's possible. But drugs? No way. I just don't believe it."

Looking at him, Weber thought Tom Cotter was telling him the truth. Maybe his wife did use drugs, but if she did, he had no idea that she did. He truly believed his wife was all that she

100

appeared to be, or least all that his heart and his mind saw her as being.

Chapter 18

"What do you think?"

They were in Weber's Explorer, driving back to the Sheriff's office.

"I think that guy is one hurting puppy," Weber said.

"Yeah, he's taking it hard. And the thing that sucks, Jimmy, is that it's only going to get worse for him once we learn more about what happened to his wife."

"I know. I appreciate you pulling him off of me, Chad."

"I didn't really want to go hands-on with him, but he didn't leave me any choice."

"Sometimes there's no other way."

"So what's our next step?"

"I think we need to go see a man about a cowboy hat," Weber said.

~***~

Welch's Western Wear was a family-owned business that had relocated from its original building on Main Street to a block of stores with false fronts that replicated an Old West town, though they had been erected within the past year by one of the many real estate developers who had come to the once quiet little mountain town to cash in on the building boom. His neighbors included a shop selling Minnetonka moccasins and Birkenstock shoes, the popular Big Lake Brewpub, a shop that sold taffy and a dozen varieties of fudge, and one of the many stores in town offering Native American jewelry, pottery, and rugs. Weber sometimes thought there were almost as many places selling Native American souvenirs to the tourists as there were Native Americans on the nearby White Mountain Apache Reservation.

Scott Welch was a slender, good-looking man with collar length brown hair and a short, well-groomed beard. He was wearing hand tooled cowboy boots, jeans, a belt with a big silver buckle, and a western shirt with pearl snaps instead of buttons. Weber didn't know him well. Scott had taken over the day-to-day operation of the business when his parents semi-retired, moving it to its new location and bringing in a lot of inventory that appealed to the tourists and replacing the heavy duty Carhart jackets and vests and outdoor clothing that had always been steady sellers to local people.

"Howdy, gentlemen. How you doin' today?"

Weber wasn't sure if the greeting was all part of the act or not, but he just nodded and said, "Good to see you, Scott. I was wondering if we could have a few minutes of your time?"

"Sure. What do you need? I've got some nice Stetsons in, and if you're looking for boots we've got the biggest selection on the mountain."

"Actually, this is a little more personal," Weber said, looking around. Two young women were looking at shirts on the other side of the store, a middle-aged woman who Weber assumed was a clerk hovering nearby. "Is there someplace we can talk in private?"

"Sure, come back to the office. Bonnie," he called to the clerk, "can you hold down the fort for a few minutes while I talked to these gentlemen?"

She nodded, and he led them past displays of jeans and shirts and hats to a short hallway in the back of the store. There were men's and women's restrooms on one side and a door that opened into his office on the other. Scott motioned them to chairs in front of his desk and sat down behind it.

The office carried the same Western theme as the rest of the store. The wall behind the desk held several large color photos of rodeo cowboys on bucking broncos and bulls, another wall had a large buffalo head hanging from it, and branding irons and a display of barbed wire covered a third wall. The whole office was a tribute to the Great American West. Or at least the modern version of it.

"So, what can I do for you?"

"We need to talk about Jill Cotter," Weber said.

If Welch was a poker player, the sheriff suspected he was a good one, because no hint of recognition crossed his face when he heard the dead woman's name.

"I'm sorry, I'm not familiar with that name. Who is she?"

"She's the dead woman we pulled out of the lake on Sunday at Snowdaze."

"I heard about that. Do you know what happened to her? Somebody said she was naked?"

"We don't know what happened to her, yet," Weber replied. "That's what we're trying to find out."

"Like I said, I don't know the name, so I'm not sure how I can help you."

"If you don't know the name, maybe you'll recognize the face," Weber said, handing him a picture of Jill that Tom had given them.

Welch studied the picture intently, like he was trying hard to remember if he had ever met the woman. Then he shook his head and said, "I'm sorry, but I don't recognize her. Is she a local or a visitor? We get so many people coming and going through here that I can't remember everybody I see. It's not like the old days when this was such a small town. Not that I'm saying progress is bad, mind you, because it's certainly been good for our business."

"That's good to hear," Weber told him. "I always like to see our business community doing well. But back to this woman. Take another look, Scott. Are you sure you don't recognize her?"

He shook his head. "No, I don't. That's not to say she hasn't been in here, but if she has I don't remember her. Let me check with Bonnie, maybe she does."

"That's not necessary," Weber said. "I wasn't actually talking about you knowing her from the store."

Welch looked at the photograph again and shook his head once more. "You know how it is, guys. There are so many new people around here that I can't keep track of everybody. I'm involved with the Chamber of Commerce and a couple of other things. Would I have known her from something like that?"

Weber felt himself growing irritated with the man's denials, but he considered himself a pretty good poker player too, and didn't let it show.

"Where do you live, Scott?"

"Where do I live? Up on Juniper Ridge. We just had a new home built there last year."

"How about before that? Where did you live before you had the new house built?"

"What's this all about, Sheriff?"

"Just some routine questions."

"Hey, just because I run a store in a small mountain town doesn't mean I'm some kind of hillbilly or ignorant redneck. What is it you guys are fishing for? What does where I live have to do with anything? I told you I don't know that woman. What more do you want from me?"

"Well, right now I want to know where you lived before you moved to Juniper Ridge."

"What's that got to do with this dead woman?"

"Is there a reason you don't want to answer the question, Scott?"

"No, no reason. But I don't appreciate you guys coming in here asking me a lot of questions and not telling me what's going on."

"I did tell you. We're investigating the death of Jill Cotter."

"And I told you I don't know her," Welch said his voice rising.

"We've heard otherwise."

"Well, you heard wrong. End of discussion."

"Before you moved to Juniper Ridge, did you live on Echo Lane?"

"No. I don't even know where Echo Lane is. We lived in Cottonwood, and then when we moved here to take the store over from my mom and dad, we rented a place a block from the post office."

"Look, Scott, we're not trying to cause you any problems," Chad said, trying to calm the waters a little bit so the interview didn't go sour. "If you knew this woman and there's some reason you don't want to tell us, I understand. We're all guys here, we know how it works."

"What is this, good cop, bad cop? I watch TV, too. And if you're implying that I had some kind of relationship with this woman, you're wrong. I'll say it one last time. I don't know her. I don't recall ever meeting her. Not here in the store, not around town, not on Echo Lane, nowhere. Is that plain enough for you?"

"Scott, what's going on?"

They turned to see a pretty young woman with black hair hanging loose to her waist and a developing baby bump standing in the office doorway.

"Darcy, do you know who this woman is?" Her husband held up Jill's picture.

She looked at it and shook her head. "No, I don't think so. Should I?"

"She's the woman that they found dead in the lake."

She studied the picture again. "You know what? I think I do know her. Not her name or anything, but I'm pretty sure she's come through my checkout lane at the grocery store. I think she's a local."

"Her name is Jill Cotter," Weber said.

"And apparently these two clowns think I knew her," Scott told his wife.

"Has she been here in the store before?"

"If she has, I don't remember her. But these two are implying we had some kind of thing going on. And they keep asking me if we ever lived on Echo Lane."

"Sheriff Weber, I don't know what you're thinking, but you're wrong. Scott isn't like that. He's pretty much a workaholic, and when he's not at the store he's home with me. If he says he didn't know this woman, he didn't."

"I'll take a polygraph test or whatever you want," Welch said. "But you've got the wrong guy if you think I was messing around with her. I don't care who told you what they saw, they were wrong. Now, if you're done with your questions, I've got a business to run."

He stood up, dismissing them. Weber looked at Chad and shrugged his shoulders, and they stood up.

"Thank you for your time. Darcy, it was good to see you again."

~***~

Back in the Explorer, Chad said, "Either that guy's telling the truth, or he's got the biggest pair of balls I've ever seen. What guy who's cheating on his wife comes right out and tells her he's being accused of it?"

"She seemed pretty adamant that he was telling us the truth," Weber said. "For what that's worth."

"Obviously she believes him, even if we don't."

"Well, at this point, I don't," Weber said. "We need to figure out what the connection is to that place on Echo Lane."

"Could Greg Sterling be wrong, Jimmy? He said he knew it was Jill he saw out there, but could he be mistaken about it being Welch?"

"I don't know," Weber said. "Let's go talk to him."

Chapter 19

The showroom was empty when they entered the furniture store, but a chime sounded somewhere in the rear to announce their presence. Greg poked his head out of the back room and asked, "Back again, Sheriff?"

Weber and Chad walked to the rear of the store and followed him into the back room. There was a noticeable but not unpleasant smell of some kind of chemical.

"I'd shake hands, but I'm kind of grimy right now," Greg said.

He was holding a cotton cloth in one hand and wiping the surface of a large wooden table. As he did so the grain in the wood seemed to spring to life.

"That's a pretty piece of furniture," Chad said.

"Thank you. It's called a library table and they're pretty popular these days. Lots of people have started appreciating the older stuff again. Decorating tastes seem to run in cycles. For a year or two it's all chrome and glass, then they go back to heavy old wood, then it's on to something else."

"That must be hard to keep up with."

"It is, but I have a big warehouse out back and when they change to something new I just buy all the stuff they're replacing and hang on to it until it comes back in style, then I sell it back to them again at twice the price."

Chad laughed and said, "Sounds like you've got it all figured out."

Greg finished rubbing the polish into the wood, stepped back to inspect his work, and then, satisfied, he set the can of polish and rag on a workbench.

"Kathy told me you talked to her and said Tommy's back in town. How's he doing?"

"He's having a pretty rough time of it," Weber said.

"Man, I wish there was some way we could help him. Kathy wants to go over there but she said you told her it's not a good idea right now."

Oftentimes part of a policeman's job is to be a family counselor, and this was one of those times. "I know you guys want to be there for him, and the truth is, he needs family around him right now," Weber said. "But I really don't think he's going to be receptive at this point."

Greg shook his head sadly. "I should have never gone to their house that day to drop that desk off in the first place. And I wish I'd never said a word about what happened when I did."

"You can't change the past, Greg. You did what you thought was right at the time."

"Yeah, but if I had kept my mouth shut maybe..."

"My old man used to always say that if a frog had wings it wouldn't bump its ass. Playing the "if" game and second-guessing yourself isn't going to change anything. If I'd have been in your position, I probably would have done the same thing."

"Do you know anything else about what happened to Jill?"

"We're still trying to figure things out," Weber said, reluctant to reveal any details until the investigation was complete. "That's why we're here now. You said that you saw Jill kissing Scott Welch, the guy from the western wear store, right?"

"Yeah."

"And that was up on Echo Lane?"

"Yeah. Like I said, it was a few months ago, but it was him and it was her."

"Are you absolutely sure it was him, Greg?"

"What are you getting at, Sheriff?"

"We just talked to Scott, and he swears up and down he never met Jill. He said he has no idea who she is and that he never had anything to do with any place on Echo Lane."

"Then he's lying to you. I know what I saw."

"I'm not questioning that," Weber said. "Can you give us the address where you made that delivery the day you saw them together? And the date, too?"

110

"Yeah, I can find it for you if you've got a couple minutes. I need to clean my hands first."

"Take all the time you need."

Just then the door chimed again. Greg looked out into the showroom. "Hi there, Mrs. Barnes. Back for that China cabinet?"

"I'd like to take another look at it, if you've still got it."

"Yes, ma'am. Right over there in the next aisle. I've got furniture polish all over my hands. Let me clean up and I'll be right with you."

He looked at Weber and Chad apologetically, and the sheriff said, "We're in no hurry, Greg. Take care of business."

They browsed through the store as Greg pointed out the features in the cherry wood curved glass China cabinet to his customer.

"He's got some nice stuff in here," Chad said, opening the drawers on an old oak roll top desk. "I was picturing some kind of junk shop, but this is classy merchandise."

"That's the same thing I thought, at first," Weber replied.

"I need to bring the wife here. She's been wanting a roll top desk forever."

It took close to half an hour for the woman to make up her mind about the China cabinet, but she did, and after ringing up the sale and making arrangements to deliver it to her home the next day, Greg thanked her for her business. As soon as she was out the door he was back to them, shaking his head.

"I'm sorry about that."

"No need to be sorry," Weber told him. "We get paid the same amount of money whether we're standing outside in the snow writing traffic tickets, or hanging around here looking at everything you've got. And it's a lot warmer in here!"

"Let's go over here to my office and I'll see if I can find that information you need."

His office was a tiny cubicle with barely enough room for a desk and chair, and two large metal filing cabinets.

"Sorry I can't offer you any place to sit," Greg said, sitting down at his desk and opening a file on his computer. "Let's see, I know it was back late summer, August I think."

He did a search and said, "Here it is. I was wrong, it was September 2nd."

"That's pretty close to August," Weber said.

"Yep, September 2nd. I delivered a bedroom set to JoAnn and Richard Wycliffe, 627 Echo Lane."

Weber wrote down the date and address in his notebook. "And you said it was right across the street, where you saw Jill and Scott together?"

"That's right. Broad daylight in the middle of the afternoon and there they were, like they didn't have any shame at all."

"Can you describe the house, Greg?"

"Typical of so many of the places they're putting up around here. Wood, with a garage and a front porch. You can't miss it because there aren't that many houses up there yet, and it's the only one directly across the street from 627, where I made the delivery."

"You said after she saw you, Jill got in her car. Her Toyota?"

"Yeah, her red Toyota."

"Was there another vehicle in the driveway?"

Greg's forehead wrinkled as he tried to remember.

"I think so, but I really can't remember."

"So, Jill got in the Toyota and left alone, right?"

"Yeah. The guy went back inside and closed the door when she left."

"Okay, Greg. I'm not questioning your judgment at all, so please don't take me wrong. But are you absolutely, beyond a doubt, sure it was Scott Welch she was with?"

"Would I bet my life on it? No, he could have one of those, what do they call them? Doppelgängers? But aside from that, or him having a twin brother, it sure looked like him to me."

"Between zero and 100%, how sure are you that it was Scott?"

"Jeez, Sheriff, now you've got me questioning myself."

"I'm not trying to confuse you," Weber said, "and it's not that we don't believe you. We just need to be as sure as we can be that it was Scott Welch before we go much further with him."

"Do you guys think he had anything to do with what happened to Jill?"

"We really can't say," Chad told him. "We're still early in the investigation."

"I hate to make accusations that could mess up someone's life and be wrong," Greg said.

It wasn't the first time Weber had seen witnesses second guess themselves, and though it could be frustrating, it was all part of the process. If Scott Welch was the man that Greg had seen with Jill that day on Echo Lane, it was an important lead they had to follow up on. But if Greg was wrong, pressing too hard could damage the man's reputation in a small town, something Weber didn't want to do.

"No," Greg said shaking his head, "it was him."

"Scott Welch?"

"Yeah, if I had to pin it down, I'd say I'm 95% sure it was him."

Maybe it wasn't 100%, but it was close enough for Weber. They needed to have another talk with Welch. But first he wanted to check out the man's background, and see what his connection was to the house on Echo Lane where Greg had seen him and Jill Cotter together.

~***~

The house at 628 Echo Lane was pretty much as Greg had described it. Built to give it a rustic look, with naturally stained wood and a green metal roof. A covered porch stretched across the front, and an attached two-car garage was on the right side. It could have been any one of the two hundred or more houses that had appeared during the town's building boom. Most were only occupied in the summertime, some of them only on weekends.

"Sometimes I can't believe how fast this place is growing, Jimmy," Chad said. "Two or three years ago, I hunted deer in this area. This road wasn't even here. Now there's what? Seven, eight houses here?"

"It doesn't look like anybody's been home for a while," Weber said, noting the fact that there were no car tracks in the snow-covered driveway.

"Doesn't surprise me," Chad said. "People with more money than common sense come up here and buy these places, and what do they do? Spend a few weeks in them in the summertime? If that much?"

"I can't decide if you're one of those traditionalists who hates to see change, or if you're just jealous of people who have so much money they can blow it this way," Weber said.

Chad chuckled and said, "Probably a little bit of both, Jimmy."

"I know what you mean. Any of these places on this road are bigger than my house. I don't think anybody lives up here year round. We made the only tracks coming down the road."

"Should we make some more?"

"Why not?"

Weber pulled into the driveway and they got out and walked around the house. Not because they really expected to find anything connected to Jill Cotter's mysterious death, but also because the summer places were prime targets for vandalism and burglary when they sat vacant during the winter.

Curtains covered all of the windows and they couldn't see inside, and there were no windows in the garage.

"What do you think?"

"I think we need to find out who owns this place and what kind of connection it might have to Scott Welch."

"Did you notice that?"

"What?"

"The lockbox on the front door." Chad waded through the snow in the front yard and brushed snow off something with a rectangular shape that was sticking up from the ground. A real estate sign.

"Hargis Real Estate. Which one is that?"

"Hell if I know," Weber said. "Every time I turn around there's some new real estate place opening up around here. Everybody's trying to cash in and make a buck."

114

He wrote down the telephone number on the sign and the broker's name, Debra Hargis.

"Let's go see if we can find her."

Nick Russell

Chapter 20

Debra Hargis reminded Weber of so many of the real estate agents he had met since Big Lake had been discovered by the outside world and started its transformation from a sleepy little mountain town, known only to the locals and the occasional fisherman who came to try their luck against the lake's trophy trout, to a summer playground for desert dwellers looking for an escape from the heat.

She was wearing some type of cable knit sweater over designer jeans, and suede boots with a rolled fur top. Somewhere in her late-40s to early 50s, she was an attractive woman in spite of carrying a few extra pounds, who realized that time was her enemy and was fighting hard to hold it off. Her blonde hair contrasted with her dark eyebrows, and her full lips hinted at collagen injections.

"Gentlemen. Welcome to Hargis Real Estate. I'm Debra Hargis. How can I help you today?"

"I'm Sheriff Weber, and this is Deputy Chad Summers."

"It's nice to meet both of you," she said, shaking their hands. "Which one of you is in the market for a new home? I've got some wonderful listings right now."

"Sorry, ma'am," Weber said. "We're not looking to buy anything, but we do need to get some information from you about one of the houses you have listed."

"Information? What kind of information?"

"628 Echo Lane," Weber said. "What can you tell us about it?"

"628 Echo..." she thought for a moment, then said, "yes, that's the Mitchell home. It's a lovely house whether you're looking for something as a year round residence or a summer retreat."

"Like I said, we're not in the market to buy something. We just need some background on the house, if you could give us any."

"Well, it's a three-bedroom, open floor plan with two baths and an island kitchen. All new stainless steel appliances, including a beautiful restaurant quality Jenn-Air range. The master bedroom has a walk-in cedar closet and a garden tub in the master bath. It's got a propane furnace and a fireplace, and beautiful wood flooring. It was built in the last three years and has had very little use. The owners are very motivated to sell."

Weber didn't really need to hear all of the house's features, he just wanted to know who owned it and when it was last occupied.

"You said the owners are motivated to sell. Why is that?"

"Oh, you know how it is, Sheriff. Some people come up here and they fall in love with the natural beauty of the area and the quaintness of the town, and they buy on impulse. Then they find out that their lives are just too busy to make full use of it and they decide to sell."

Weber couldn't picture being in such a financial position that one could buy a house simply on impulse, but he didn't say it. Instead, he asked, "You said they didn't use it very much? Do you know when the last time they were there was?"

A look of concern crossed the real estate broker's face and she asked, "Has something happened to the house?"

"No, ma'am, not that we know of," Weber said. "We were just up there and it looked like we were the only vehicle to go down the road since the storm hit last week. We walked around the house, just sort of a security check, and didn't see anything to worry about."

"You walked around the house for a security check? Why?"

"I'm sure you know that places get vandalized sometimes when they sit empty like that," Chad told her. "It's usually kids getting into mischief. We like to do occasional checks on places. Sort of a preemptive type thing."

"I'm glad that nothing's wrong, but why do you want to know about when the last time someone was there?"

118

"We just like to check on things like that," Weber said. "If we know a place isn't getting used much and we do happen to go by and see tracks in the snow or a car there, or some indication someone's been around, we know to check it out."

She looked relieved and said, "Okay, that makes sense. I appreciate that."

"You said the owners haven't been there recently?"

"No, I don't think they've been back up here since early spring," she lowered her voice even though no one else was in the office to hear her, and said, "The truth is, they're getting divorced. That's why the house is for sale. Of course, we don't want to say that to prospective buyers. I'm sure you understand."

"Yeah, that makes sense to me," Weber said.

"Anyway, they've split up and the divorce is pretty contentious, from what I can gather. I think the house is about the last thing holding proceedings up. They both wanted it when they bought it, but now neither one has any interest in it. But they each want their half of the money they invested in it back out, plus a profit, obviously."

"Obviously."

"I know you said neither one of you are interested in purchasing a home right now," she said, ever the professional hoping for a sale, "but let me just say that you could pick it up for way below market value."

"That's good to know," Weber told her.

"When was the last time you showed the house?" Chad asked.

"I'm not sure, it's been a while. Let me check." She went to her desk and opened the file on the Mitchell home on her computer. "It's been at least six weeks. I had a gay couple from Sedona looking at it. Rynald and James. Lovely young men. I need to follow up with them, they seemed very interested at the time. I think if they made any kind of reasonable offer at all, the Mitchells would be quick to take it."

"Well, we've taken enough of your time," Weber said. "Thank you very much, Ms. Hargis."

"Just call me Debra. And seriously, if either one of you is looking for an excellent deal on a house, let me know. Or if you know somebody who's looking. And I've got other listings besides that one."

"We'll keep that in mind," Weber told her.

~***~

"I managed to get some background information on Jill Cotter," Robyn said when they returned to the Sheriff's office.

"Let's have it," Weber said, sitting down at his desk.

"Her maiden name was Jill Hubbard, born March 11, 1983, in Fresno, California. Father's name was Roland Hubbard, mother's name is Claire. The most recent last name I have for the mother is Lucas, with an address in Temecula, California."

"That ties in with what Jill's husband told us," Weber said. "He said his wife and her mother didn't get along very well, but that the last he heard she was living in Temecula and working in a bar. He said she'd gone through a long line of husbands and boyfriends."

"It looks like it," Robyn agreed. "Besides Lucas, I've got four other last names for her. She's got a history."

"Such as?"

"Nothing major. Three DUIs, driving on a suspended license, drunk and disorderly, disturbing the peace, and I found five domestic violence reports in which she or whoever she was living with at the time was the aggressor, depending on which story you want to believe."

"It sounds like Jill had one heck of a role model," Chad said.

"Yeah, but the mother is still better than the father."

"What do you mean?"

Robyn referred to her notes and said, "Roland Frank Hubbard spent about half his life in jail, beginning when he was a teenager. He started out with joy riding and petty thefts and worked his way up to strong-arm robberies. At some point between incarcerations he started hitting convenience stores.

Then he graduated to the big time and decided to become a bank robber."

"Really?"

Robyn looked at her notes again, then looked up and said, "According to what I've been able to find out, he robbed three banks in the space of about eight months. The FBI tracked him down after the last one and he was sentenced to 28 years in federal prison. He died there of a heart attack in 1990."

"The Medical Examiner said Jill's heart condition was genetic and was passed down from one of her parents."

"What about Jill herself? Did she have a record?"

Robyn shook her head. "Not really, Chad. One ticket in California ten years ago, for driving on an expired license plate, and another here last year for running a stop sign in a school zone. That's it as far as anything to do with the police. She did have two cars repossessed when she was living in California, before her and Tom got together. But compared to her parents, it looks like she was pretty straight."

"Nothing about drug use?"

"Nothing at all, Jimmy."

"Anything else?"

"Yeah. I talked to her boss at the hotel in Barstow where she was working when she met Tom. He still owns the place and he still remembers her. He said she was a pretty girl, and good with the customers, but that she didn't have the best work habits in the world. He said she'd show up late at least once a week, and always had some kind of drama going on."

"Drama?"

"Yeah, either her cat got out of the house and she couldn't find it so she was late for work, or her roommate borrowed her car and forgot to fill the tank so she ran out of gas, or she got in a fight with her boyfriend and was up all night dealing with that."

"I'm surprised he didn't fire her if she was that bad of an employee."

"I asked him about that," Robyn said. "He said she was really sweet and pretty, and the customers all loved her. Especially the truckers that stop there quite a bit. So he said he let her get away with a lot of stuff that he probably shouldn't have. I got the feeling he probably had a crush on her. He seemed really sad when I told him about her being dead."

"Tom mentioned something else, about some geeky guy who worked with her and asked her out. Were you able to find out anything about that?"

Robyn shook her head. "The manager said people come and go and he couldn't remember who that might be. I think the only reason he remembered Jill was because she was so cute, and he maybe had a little thing for her."

"When you say he maybe had a little thing for her, is that something we need to look into more?"

"I really don't think so," Robyn said. "He sounds like he's much older. I think just one of those infatuation things men get for pretty young women who work for them."

"I can relate to that," Weber told her with a smile, then added, "She was supposed to have a half-brother somewhere in the Pacific Northwest. Were you able to find out anything about him?"

"Not a thing. Sorry."

"Don't be sorry," Weber told her. "We know more than we did when we started out."

He looked at his watch and added, "I've got time to get something to eat before I have to be at the Town Council meeting for my weekly reaming session. Let's go to the Roundup and get a steak. With Chet on the warpath about Snowdaze, I'm going to need a healthy dose of red meat before I go in there."

Chapter 21

The mayor was indeed on the warpath, opening the weekly Town Council meeting with a litany of sins the sheriff and his deputies had committed, all leading to the ruination of Snowdaze.

"Not only did they make us all look like a bunch of buffoons with that stunt with the Santa Claus, but then they blocked off half the park when they found that dead woman! How much more are we going to put up with before we take action?"

"Now hold on there, Chet," Councilman Frank Gauger said. "That whole malarkey with the Santa Claus was your idea. I told you it was stupid right from the get-go."

"It wasn't stupid," the mayor snapped. "It would have worked out fine if it wasn't for Sheriff Weber."

"I've seen a lot of your twisted reasoning over the years, Chet, but I fail to see how you can connect Sheriff Weber to this. It was your idea to do the Santa Claus drop, right?"

"Yes, it was. And it would have been perfect if they hadn't ruined it."

"Who is they, Chet?"

"Sheriff Weber and his people, that's who! They made me the laughing stock of the whole state. Not just the state, but the whole country. Do you know people took videos with their cell phones and put it on Facebook? And it was even on the national news!"

"I saw that," Councilman Mel Walker said with a smile.

"Can I have your autograph, Chet?" someone shouted from the audience.

The mayor rapped his gavel. "Silence!"

"Forget the autograph, can I be your groupie?" Harley Willits called out in a high-pitched falsetto voice."

"I said silence," Chet said again, pounding his gavel on the top of the dais.

It took a moment for the laughter to die down, but when it did, Councilman Gauger continued his line of questioning. "So it was your idea to do the Santa Claus drop, right?"

"That's what I said."

"Was Sheriff Weber flying the airplane?"

"No, it was Larry Parks."

"Larry Parks, the FBI agent?"

"That's right."

"Well, I must admit that I'm a little confused, Chet. If it was your idea, and Mr. Parks was flying the airplane, how is any of that Sheriff Weber's fault?"

"It was one of his deputies in the airplane with Special Agent Parks. Deputy Northcutt."

"Okay. So there's you, and there's Mr. Parks, and there's Deputy Northcutt. You are the three people involved in this thing, and those two were following your directions. Is that correct?"

"Yes, but..."

"So, either this was a dumb idea of yours that went bad, just like I told you it was going to do when you first brought it up, or else this was some kind of conspiracy, and you are the ringleader. Which was it, Chet?"

People in the audience laughed, and a couple of the Town Council members couldn't hide their smiles either.

"You're not paying attention to what I'm saying," the mayor said. "It should have worked out just fine."

"Well, it didn't. How about the next time you decide to bomb the town, you think again, Chet?"

"Okay, forget the Santa Claus thing. Do you know how many disappointed children we had because they couldn't make snow angels where we had planned? And why? Because Sheriff Weber had the whole area sealed off, that's why!"

"He had it cordoned off because there was a dead body there, Chet," Councilman Kirby Templeton said.

"They could have moved her quicker than they did."

"Chet, how many crime scene investigations have you conducted yourself?"

"None, but that's not the point. And according to the sheriff, he doesn't even know that a crime has been committed yet."

"It doesn't matter how that poor woman got in the lake," Kirby said. "The fact is they found her and they needed to deal with it."

"Yes, they found her right in the middle of our Snowdaze celebration. It ruined the whole weekend for everybody!"

"I hardly think Sheriff Weber and his people found a dead body just so they could ruin Snowdaze. Come to think of it, if you want to split hairs, it was one of the fire department volunteers that found the body, wasn't it?"

"It doesn't matter who found the body, Kirby," the mayor argued. "The whole thing was handled wrong."

"Can we move on to something more productive than this nonsense? Every week we come here and we sit at this dais and we listen to the same old story. Sheriff Weber did this, Sheriff Weber did that, if anything goes wrong in the whole wide world, it's Sheriff Weber's fault. Why don't you get yourself one of those voodoo dolls that looks like him and just stick pins in it and be quiet so the rest of us can get some work done, Chet?"

"I don't have to sit here and take that from you!"

"No, you don't," Kirby agreed. "And Sheriff Weber does not have to sit here and take anything from you, either. I want to put it on the record right now that I've lost total faith in you as a mayor, Chet Wingate. I don't know what your problem is, but it's gone past the point of ridiculousness. You need to grow up, or get some counseling or something."

There were murmurs from the crowd and Weber noticed a couple of the council members subtly nodding their heads.

"Let's move on to other business, shall we?"

"I think that's a good idea, Councilman Walker. Ms. Murdock, Snowdaze was originally your idea and was put together by the Chamber of Commerce. In spite of the unfortunate incidents we've already talked about, I think you did an excellent job with it and are to be commended."

There was applause from the crowd and the Chamber director beamed.

"Can you give us a report?"

"Certainly, Councilman Templeton." She stepped up to the small lectern in front of the dais and said, "First of all, I want to thank the Council for cosponsoring the event with the Chamber, and everybody that helped out and supported the event, from the folks at Cat Mountain Ski Resort, to our business owners, the Sheriff's Department, the Volunteer Fire Department, and all of the citizens who volunteered their time to make the event a success, and everybody who came to take part in it. Even with the little problems we've already talked about..."

"Little problems? Santa Claus exploded!" Harley Willits' comment got another round of laughs from the crowd.

Juliette Murdoch smiled good-naturedly and waited for it to die down. "Yes, there was that. Someone suggested maybe next year we should have a Santa Claus drop contest and see who could come the closest to hitting a target. But I think we need to work on that idea little bit."

There was more laughter, and then she gave a quick rundown of the estimated number of attendees at Snowdaze and the overall cost of the event. "Talking to the business community, a lot of our stores and restaurants saw a noticeable increase in business over the weekend."

"Not me," said Todd Norton. "I told you when you came up with the idea that it wasn't going to do me any good."

"Todd, if I come by and buy a spark plug, would you shut up?"

Harley was in rare form that night and had the crowd laughing again, though the auto parts store owner glared at him.

"I'll tell you what, Harley, *I'll* buy the spark plug if you'll stick it in your ass," said Harley's brother-in-law, Arnold Foster.

"Okay, enough! Let's move on," the mayor said, slamming his gavel down again.

"Be that as it may, Todd," Juliet said, "as a whole, Snowdaze did benefit the business community. And we're looking forward to having the event again next year."

"Thank you," Kirby said as she sat down to another round of applause.

"I want to know what's going on with the investigation into the dead woman," said Councilman Adam Hirsch, a short nerdy man who had even less love for the sheriff than the mayor did.

"It's an open investigation," Weber said, "and I'm not at liberty to discuss it."

"Why not?"

"What part of *it's an open investigation* didn't you get?"

"Do you have any leads? Anything at all?"

"No comment."

"What are you holding back, Sheriff? Why are you being so secretive?"

"And here we go again," Kirby Templeton said, his frustration obvious. "Sheriff Weber, you know I've got a lot of respect for you as a man, and as the sheriff. But I've got to tell you, sometimes I think you're not all that smart. You've got years of experience and an excellent record, but you sit there and put up with this nonsense every week. I wouldn't blame you for one minute if you told the mayor and Councilman Hirsch here to stick it where the sun don't shine and go get a job someplace else where they would appreciate you."

The audience burst into applause, and the mayor rapped his gavel so hard that the head broke off and bounced to the floor, leaving him holding just the handle.

"This isn't going anywhere," Councilman Walker said. "I move we close the session for this week."

His motion was quickly seconded and approved, and Weber walked out of the Council chambers shaking his head.

"What was that all about?"

"I don't know, Paul," Weber told the newspaper publisher. "I know Kirby gets fed up with Chet's games sometimes, but he tore him a new one tonight. Him and Adam both."

"At least I've got something juicy to write about in this week's paper. Between this tonight, and the Santa Claus episode, and the dead woman, I'm going to have to add some more pages to this week's edition."

"Jimmy, got a minute?"

Weber turned to see Councilman Templeton standing on the sidewalk.

"Go ahead," Paul said, "I need to get back to the office and start writing."

"Okay, catch you later," Weber told him, then turned to Kirby. "What's up?"

"How's Tom Cotter doing?"

"He's having a hell of a time."

"He's a good man. I hate to see him going through this."

"Me, too."

"Listen, about tonight's meeting. I don't know why Chet's got a bug up his butt. For a while there it almost seemed like he was going to start to mellow out. I don't know if it's because Gretchen's over in Prescott or what, but I've had it with him."

"I got that impression," Weber said. "Maybe when she gets back Chet will start to calm down."

"Last time I talked to her, she said it was going to be at least another six weeks."

Councilwoman Gretchen Smith-Walker had always been the mayor's right hand, supporting him and everything he did. The previous summer their relationship had morphed into open romance, something Weber suspected had been going on all along, or at least in her mind it had. But a month earlier she had taken a leave of absence from the Council to go to Prescott and help care for her sister, who had suffered a debilitating stroke. While the mayor had been somewhat tolerable before she left, he had reverted to his old, cranky ways within a week or so after she was gone. Weber suspected Chet just needed to get laid, but that was something he hesitated to say to Kirby, a no-nonsense, churchgoing man.

"The way you were talking in there tonight, I half expected you to announce that you were going to run against Chet in the next election."

"I really don't want the job," Kirby said. "Running the pharmacy and being a Councilman takes enough of my time. But somebody's got to get control of things in there. Every week it's the same old crap. And I've got to tell you something, Jimmy. I meant what I said. I'd hate to lose you, but I don't think anybody could blame you if you found a better job someplace else."

Weber had been born and raised in Big Lake, and except for a few years in the Army, it had always been his home. True, there had been a time when he didn't want to return to the little town in the mountains of northern Arizona, but circumstances beyond his control had brought him back, and now he could not see himself ever leaving again.

"I appreciate that, but don't worry about me, Kirby. I'm not going anywhere. And as for *you*, I think you'd make an excellent mayor. You'd certainly have my support all the way."

"Well, I'm not making any announcements anytime soon. But like I said, something's got to change."

Chapter 22

"I'm confused. What are we looking at, Jimmy?" Coop asked when the deputies assembled Wednesday morning for a quick rundown on the case. "The ME is listing Jill Cotter's death as a heart attack, but under suspicious circumstances. There's obviously more to it than that. Are we in the middle of a homicide investigation or what?"

"I don't know," Weber admitted. "Like you said, this is more than a simple heart attack. Just how complicated and convoluted it is, we don't know yet."

"Have you been able to verify the husband's alibi, or whatever you want to call it, since we don't know if we have actually a crime?"

"He wasn't anywhere around here," Dan Wright said. "Even though he doesn't have an electronic locator in his truck, he left a very plain trail between his logbooks, delivery slips, and fuel purchases. He was everywhere he said he was, when he said he was."

"He said something about his wife always accusing him of cheating on her," Coop said. "Do you think there's any truth to that?"

"I wouldn't believe that for a minute," Weber said.

"Are you basing that just on what you know about the man, Jimmy?"

"Do you think my judgment is clouded by friendship, Coop?"

"Hey, no offense, boss. I'm just throwing stuff out there. Spit balling ideas."

"There's no way to know what a guy's doing when he's out on the road like that," Weber said. "So yes, I guess I am basing that on what I know about Tom. But I just don't see it as being something he would do."

"Fair enough."

"Robyn, what have you been able to find out about Scott Welch?"

"Quite a bit, Jimmy, but nothing that raises any red flags. He was born and raised here in Big Lake. Left here to go to college and got a business degree from Arizona State University. After he graduated he took a job with one of the big box stores and worked there for six years, working his way up to assistant manager. Then he was hired by a competitor to run one of their stores in Phoenix. He married Darcy Blackburn two years ago, and they moved up here six months later so he could start taking over the family business."

"Nothing in his background we need to know about?"

She shook her head. "Nothing at all, Jimmy. Not even a traffic ticket."

"He's young enough that I don't remember him when I was growing up," Weber said. "Do any of you know anything about him?"

"He played Little League for part of one season, then just stopped showing up," Chad said.

"You coached him?"

"No, he was on one of the other teams. I don't remember who his coach was. He was just a kid that was there and then wasn't anymore."

"From what I remember of him, he was always a good kid," Dolan said. "Always polite, I don't remember him ever getting into any kind of trouble."

"Me, neither," Buz added.

"From what I hear, him taking over from his parents wasn't a smooth transition," Mary Caitlin said.

"What do you mean?"

"Welch's was always a working man's store," Mary said. "That's where all the farmers and ranchers got their clothes. But Scott wanted to focus on the whole Western theme, the fancy boots and the shirts and all that. His dad, Bernard, didn't want to change things around but Scott kept insisting that it was needed. Evelyn, his mom, says that him and his dad argued about that quite a bit at first. Scott said Big Lake is growing past the days of the ranchers and farmers and has a whole new customer base. He said that the store needed to keep up with the times or go under. Evelyn said he told them he didn't give up his career to come back here and run a business that was going to fail."

"Sounds like so many of the new breed we see up here these days," Dolan said.

"I know his wife," Robyn said. "I mean, not like we're good friends or anything like that, but we always say hi and chat for a minute or two when I go through her checkout line at the grocery store. And a few times I've seen her around town and would stop to visit on the sidewalk for a couple of minutes."

"Did she ever give you any indication that there were problems at home or that she suspected her husband might be cheating on her? Anything like that?"

"No, she always seemed really happy. On top of the world. In fact, the last time I saw her she was all excited because they're going to have a baby."

"Sounds like the perfect couple," Coop said. "Pretty wife, handsome husband, a bright future, and a baby on the way."

"I've got to be honest with you, Jimmy. I hope that guy at the furniture store was wrong and it was somebody else he saw with Jill Cotter," Robyn said. "It's bad enough to think that he would be cheating on his wife, let alone be involved in her death."

"He seemed pretty adamant it was Scott," Weber replied. "But we all need to keep in mind here that even if it was Scott and he was messing around behind his wife's back, that doesn't mean he had anything to do with her dying, or her ending up in the lake. It's no secret that she played the field whenever Tom was on the road."

"Maybe we need to be looking into that angle, too," Chad said. "Even if she was playing footsie with Scott Welch, I don't think it was an exclusive thing."

"You've got a point there. Why don't you and Coop start looking into who else Jill may have been involved with. The rest of you, keep your ears open. The way people gossip in this town, we might hear something. But guys, out of respect for Tom

Cotter, we need to keep this as low-key as possible, just because of all that gossip."

When the meeting ended, Mary corralled Weber before he could slip away and sent him to his office with a stack of requisition forms and payroll sheets he had to sign off on. He started to argue, because paperwork was the thing he hated most about his job, but one look at Mary's stern face told him resistance was futile. At least he could take some comfort in the fact that the pile of forms was only half as thick as normal.

He was just finishing that task when there was a knock on his door and Larry Parks stuck his head in.

"You busy, Bubba?"

"I'm always busy," Weber replied. "I'm not some federal government employee who can sleep half the day and goof off the rest of it."

"Too busy to buy me lunch?"

"No, I'm too *poor* to buy you lunch. Christmas is coming and I'd really like to get Robyn something nice. But every time I pick up the bill in a restaurant with you it maxes out my credit card."

"There you are thinking about money again, Jimmy. I keep telling you, it's just pieces of paper with numbers printed on them."

"Yeah? So are the bills that fill my mailbox."

"How about I buy lunch this time around?"

"Let me mark this day on the calendar," Weber said. "I want to remember it forever. And I'm gonna need two signed and notarized affidavits swearing that you're going to pick up the tab before we leave here."

"Really, Jimmy? Do you think I'd stiff you with the bill?"

"Oh, I have no doubt about that," Weber replied. "I just want something in writing that I can show people to prove I'm telling the truth when I say you even offered."

They walked down the street to the ButterCup Café, nodding and saying hello to people on the sidewalk. As so often happened in the mountains, last week's snowstorm was long gone and it had warmed up into the low 40s. The snow that had accumulated was melting off and turning into slush, and they had to step back

134

quickly as they started across the street to avoid getting splashed by a car whose driver didn't really believe pedestrians had the right-of-way, even in a marked crosswalk. Weber turned to see if he could recognize the vehicle, but he didn't and it was gone before he could see the license number.

It was warm inside the restaurant and they shucked off their jackets and hung them on the back of their chairs at the table they took in the rear.

"Coffee?"

"Please," Weber said and watched the waitress fill their mugs. She was new in town and he remembered her name was Gwen. A tall, rail thin woman in her mid-30s who wore her auburn hair in a French braid and had half a dozen earrings in each ear. What had caught his attention the first time she had waited on him was her unusual eyes. One was brown and the other was hazel colored.

At first he thought she might have been wearing some sort of tinted contact lens in one eye, but when he had mentioned it to Parks, the FBI agent had told him that it was caused by heterochromia, a condition in which the iris of each eye was a different color. "Kind of like some of those Alaskan huskies they use to pull dogsleds," Parks had said. "The ones with one blue eye and one brown one."

Weber wished Parks had never said that, because now every time Gwen took his order at the cafe, he thought of sled dogs and wanted to yell "mush!"

"The specials today are goulash or meatloaf sandwiches. What can I get you boys?"

"I think I'll go for that pork tenderloin sandwich on the regular menu," Weber said.

"Fries or mixed vegetables?"

"What the hell, let's go with fries. If I'm going to clog my arteries up, I might as well do a good job of it."

"I'll have the same," Parks said, "but double fries, please."

"And he gets the check," Weber said, making sure his friend didn't renege on his offer to buy lunch.

"Hey, Jimmy, how you doing?"

"No complaints," the sheriff said to the old rancher sitting at a nearby table. "How about you, Gus?"

"Oh better than some, and not good as others, I guess."

"Well that's good to hear. How's the wife?"

"She's down with the gout, but otherwise she's good."

"I hope she gets to feeling better soon."

"Talk around town is that you haven't figured out what caused that woman to end up there in the lake like she did."

"Not yet, but we're working on it."

"You'll get to the bottom of it. You always do."

"We try, Gus. We try."

The man stood up and left some money on the table with his bill, and patted Weber on the shoulder as he left.

"You take care of yourself, Jimmy."

"You too, Gus. And say hi to Miss Elizabeth for me."

"Will do."

Weber watched as the man walked away, pausing to say hello to people at booths and tables on his way to the door. "That there is Gus Haskell. Him and my dad were best friends from the time they were kids. Gus and his wife are both salt of the earth people. They had a boy my age named Danny. Heck of a nice kid. Got killed by a drunk driver getting off the school bus when we were in about the fourth grade, as I recall. Guy ignored the flashing lights and went right around the bus, hit Danny when he was crossing the road."

"Man, that sucks."

"It took them a long time to get over it," Weber said. "A very long time."

"I can't imagine what that must be like."

"You know, Parks, I'm glad Robyn can't have any kids."

"Really? I think you'd make a pretty good father."

"Thanks, but with all that's going on in the world these days, I'd hate to have to raise kids in it. Does that make me cynical?"

"Face it, Jimmy, you've seen a lot of loss in your life, what with your parents dying so young, and losing your sister. Not to mention all the stuff you see every day in our line of work. So yeah, maybe you are cynical. Or maybe you just know more than the average person who goes through life fat, dumb, and happy, without a clue."

The waitress brought their orders, refilled their coffee cups, and moved away to check on other customers.

"Are you guys getting anywhere with this dead woman?"

"Not yet. At least, not very far. We've got a person of interest, but it's too early to tell if that's going to pan out or not."

"Well, keep at it. Like your friend there said, you'll get to the bottom of it. You always do."

"Thanks, Parks" Weber said as he poured a puddle of ketchup onto the edge of his plate, though he wasn't very confident, given the small amount of progress they had made so far.

Nick Russell

Chapter 23

"I'm tellin' ya, that man's got me frustrated as a firebug in a petrified forest," Kallie Jo Wingate was saying when Weber returned to the Sheriff's office. "Mr. Chet ain't never been easy to get along with, but this is somethin' else altogether."

"What's going on?" Weber asked.

"Kallie Jo here was just telling us that Chet's been getting underfoot at the hardware store lately," Mary told him.

"Now don't get me wrong, I love him because he's my husband's daddy, and it *is* his business. I'm just runnin' it for him. But I just don't understand why in tarnation he wants to come in and change everything around that I've done. If you was to look at the books, you'd see that sales is up over 12% since this time last year. That's because I got rid of a lot of stock that was sittin' there forever and I filled those spaces on the shelves with stuff that's movin.' Fer instance, flashlights. He had boxes of flashlights, and they was all the old-style with a bulb. Now I'm askin' ya, who do you know that uses those anymore? Nobody, right? 'Cause everybody's usin' those there LED lights these days. That's what Archer carries in his flashlight for work, just like the rest of the deputies. So I done closed those things out at giveaway prices just to get them gone, and I brought in a selection of new LED flashlights. And you know what? They's sellin'! Used to be we might sell half a dozen flashlights in a busy month. In November we sold fourteen. Yes, sir, we did! But does Mr. Chet appreciate that? No sir, he don't. He just wants to complain because I got rid of the old stock that weren't movin', at cost. He said we don't make no profit sellin' at cost, and I told him we don't make no profit bein' a museum either. But that's what that stuff was, just somethin' to look at."

Kallie Jo was a tiny woman from Georgia who had met the mayor's son online and showed up in town unexpectedly to claim her man. The fact that Archer was an overweight bumbling young man with few social skills and not the brave, handsome deputy solving crimes on a daily basis that he had portrayed himself to be hadn't phased Kallie Jo for a minute. As she told Weber and Mary, the heart wants what the heart wants. And from the moment she set eyes on him, she wanted Archer Wingate.

Several months earlier, when he was going through what everyone referred to as the mayor's invalid stage, riding around on a motorized cart and sucking on an oxygen bottle, Chet had turned the day-to-day operations of his hardware business over to Kallie Jo. It had proven to be a wise decision, and the little ball of energy had gone through the place from top to bottom, rearranging things, eliminating dead stock, bringing in new merchandise, and revitalizing the business. Until now it had seemed to be a good arrangement. But for Kallie Jo, who always seemed to be in top spirits, to become so frustrated as to openly complain showed that there were big problems afoot.

"Have you tried talking to Chet?" Weber asked, knowing that attempting to reason with the mayor about anything was unrealistic.

"Oh, Sheriff Jimmy, I've done talked to that man 'til I'm blue in the face, and it don't do no good."

"I'd offer to shoot him for you, but if I did, Mary here would make me fill out a truckload of paperwork."

"He don't need shootin', he needs bootin'," Kallie Jo said.

Weber thought she was referring to the slang word used to describe a woman's posterior, and he was reminded of his thought the night before that the mayor needed to get together with his girlfriend and work off some of his frustrations, but Kallie Jo put that idea to rest.

"Yes, sir, someone needs to put a boot in that man's rear end! Now, I know that ain't ladylike, and it ain't respectable to say that about my father-in-law, but it's kind of like my daddy always said, "you got to call 'em like you see 'em." Do ya know what I mean?"

"I do, and I don't disagree with you, or your daddy," the sheriff told her. More than once he had been tempted to do exactly that to the mayor.

"Anyways, I didn't come in here just to complain about Mr. Chet. No sir, I have a problem I need to talk to you about, Sheriff Jimmy."

"A problem besides Chet? What did Archer do now?"

"No, it ain't about Archer either. Can we talk in your office, please? No offense to you or Robyn, Miss Mary, but this is kind of personal."

Weber didn't really want to get cornered in his office alone with Kallie Jo. He liked the woman, even admired her. There was no doubt that she had been a good influence on Archer. He was never going to be a shining example of what a deputy should be, but since marrying Kallie Jo, at least he showed up for work on time, his boots were shined, and he didn't have food stains on his uniform. Well, he didn't until the first time a jelly donut crossed his path. But if she had a problem she thought she could only confide in him about, Weber couldn't turn her away.

"Sure, let's go in my office."

He held the door for her and motioned her to a seat next to his desk, then sat down.

"What's up, Kallie Jo?"

Normally the woman was like a rapid fire machinegun, talking so fast that it sometimes gave Weber a headache trying to keep up with her. So he knew something must be amiss when she hesitated before replying. Her face colored, and she said, "Like I said out there in the main office, this is kind'a personal. And I'd just die if it got out to anybody else."

"Whatever you tell me stays in this room," Weber assured her.

Kallie Jo looked up at the ceiling as if asking for direction from above, then took a deep breath and looked down toward the floor before she said, "Well, there's this guy."

"A guy?"

Of all the things Weber could have possibly thought might be troubling Kallie Jo, another man would never have entered his mind. She seemed completely devoted to Archer, though the sheriff never really understood why.

"Yes, sir. His name is Tony Hurley and he works for this big wholesale company over in Albuquerque where we get a lot of our merchandise for the store. He comes up here every week to call on us and take our order. And he's due back here tomorrow."

"Okay."

"Well, here's the thing, Sheriff Jimmy. He keeps wantin' to talk about things that ain't got nothin' to do with the business."

"What kind of things, Kallie Jo?"

Her head was still downcast and she shrugged her shoulders. "You know, personal things."

"Can you be a little more specific?"

"This is embarrassin'."

"I understand that. But this is just between you and me."

She sighed and said. "Man and woman stuff, if ya know what I mean."

"Like sexual stuff?"

She nodded her head, then looked up at him and she had tears in her eyes. That was something Weber had never seen before. Kallie Jo was the happiest person he had ever known in his life.

"I swear, Sheriff Jimmy, I ain't never encouraged him one bit. But he keeps askin' me about things between me and Archer. Things that happen behind closed doors."

"Have you told him that's not something appropriate to talk about?"

"'Course I did! But he don't pay that no never mind. He keeps tellin' me what a cute little thing I am and how he knows ways to make a woman really happy. Sayin' he can do things to me that Archer never thought of. Sayin' that me and him should get together sometime when he's up here. I'm a good girl, Sheriff Jimmy! The only man I've ever been with is Archer, and there ain't no way I'd ever think about cheatin' on him. But Tony just keeps pushin' me and pushin' me, and last time he was up here put his hands on me."

"He touched you? How did he touch you?"

"He squeezed me right on the butt, that's what he did! Then he squeezed me up here," Kallie Jo, said, pointing at her chest.

"Ain't no man ever touched me like that but my husband. Ain't no man got a right to touch me like that 'cept Archer."

"What did you do, Kallie Jo?"

"I'll tell you what I did. I slapped him right across his face. That's what I did!"

"And did he get the message?"

"No, sir. He just laughed and said he liked his women with a little bit of fire in them. Then he said he'd see me in two weeks, and those two weeks is up tomorrow. I got to be honest with you, Sheriff Jimmy, it makes me sick to my stomach just thinkin' about havin' to see him again."

"Did you tell Archer about this, Kallie Jo?"

"No, Sheriff Jimmy. I can't."

"He's your husband. Don't you think he has a right to know?"

"I can't. What with his hands being lethal weapons registered with the U.S. government and all that, I'm just worried sick about what might happen if Archer ever found out about what Tony did!"

"Lethal weapons? Archer's hands are lethal weapons?"

"Well sure they are. What with all that special commando trainin' and stuff he's had, who knows what could happen if he ever got wind of the way Tony's been actin'?"

Weber knew that Archer had told Kallie Jo some tall tales during their online courtship, but this was a new one on him. He wondered how she could still believe such a thing, knowing how clumsy and ungainly Archer was. But then again, maybe she was just as blinded by love as Tom Cotter was to Jill's shortcomings.

Whatever, it was obvious she was miserable, and Weber could feel his anger building toward anyone who would try to take advantage of someone as sweet as Kallie Jo.

"I tried handlin' this myself. I really did. I even tried callin' the main office there where he works, but it turns out his daddy owns the place. When I got him on the phone and told him 'bout the way Tony's been actin' he just laughed at me and told me I was bein' uptight. He said if I was goin' to be runnin' a store, I needed to grow up a little bit and understand how the real world works. Said if there was a problem, maybe we needed to find some other company to do business with. And I'd do that, Sheriff Jimmy. But there ain't no other place that carries all the stuff they have that we need."

"He said that, did he? I've got a feeling that Tony and his father are both going to get a lesson in how the real world works before much longer. What time is Tony supposed to be here tomorrow?"

"11 o'clock in the morning. That's the time he always comes, every Thursday. He made a point of tellin' me he always comes right on time, then he gave me one of those looks and said a woman 'preciates that in a man, if I got his drift. Well I got his drift all right. And I didn't 'preciate it one little bit."

"Don't you worry about it, Kallie Jo. You're not going to have any more problems with this jerk. I promise you that."

She looked visibly relieved at his promise and got out of her chair to throw her arms around his neck. "Thank you, Sheriff Jimmy. I knew I could count on you."

"You can," he assured her. "You just leave everything to me."

"And you won't tell Archer nothin' about all this?"

"No, he'll never hear about it," Weber told her. "I wouldn't want him and those lethal hands of his going off on some unsuspecting civilian."

Chapter 24

"Were you guys able to pick up any information at all that could help us?"

"Only that Jill Cotter always seemed to be on the prowl when Tom was on the road," Coop said. "She's been seen around town with several different guys."

"Any names?"

"Mike Sanders."

"The guy that runs a muffler shop?"

"That's him. The two of them were seen drinking and dancing at the Redeye Saloon a couple of times. And I've heard tell that Jill was kind of cozy with Reggie Sosin, too."

Sosin was the owner of the recently opened Redeye, a western-themed saloon that featured waitresses in skimpy outfits that consisted of midriff shirts and short calico skirts. Weber had only interacted with him a time or two, but it was enough to know he didn't like the man.

"Anybody else?"

"Lonnie Henderson."

That didn't surprise the sheriff. Lonnie drove a bread delivery truck, making the rounds in the early morning hours to stores and restaurants throughout the region. He was a known player even though he had a wife and two kids at home. Twice Weber had stopped to check out suspicious vehicles parked on some dark back road at night and found Lonnie and whatever woman he was currently messing around with doing the nasty. He knew Lonnie's wife, a chubby woman who was very dedicated to her children and enjoyed being a mother. He wasn't sure if she knew about her husband's infidelity. And if she did, why she tolerated it.

"She's been seen with other guys, too, but, we couldn't get any names on them." Chad said.

"Yeah, I saw her with a couple of guys at the Antler Inn a while back."

"She was stooping pretty low if she was hanging out at the Antler."

Housed in a square cinder block building two miles outside of town on the road to Round Valley, the Antler Inn had always been a trouble spot. Weber and his deputies were called there on a regular basis to deal with drunken fights between the establishment's rough clientele. Margo Prestwick, the bar's owner, was an overweight, bleached blonde with a perpetual bad attitude and a strong dislike for Weber and any other member of law enforcement who might darken her door.

"Have you guys talked to Sosin or Mike Sanders? Or Lonnie?"

"Not yet," Chad said. "We didn't know how you wanted us to handle it."

"You're not handling anything this afternoon," Mary Caitlin told Chad. "Did you forget you've got a doctor's appointment in Show Low for your annual physical?"

"Is that today?"

"At 3:30. Sometimes I'm not sure if my job title is administrative assistant or den mother around here. I spend as much time keeping track of you guys and where you're supposed to be as I do anything else."

"And you're darned good at it," Chad added.

"You'd better get a move on so you're not late."

"Yeah, right, I'll get there on time and he'll still keep me waiting for a couple of hours."

"I don't doubt it," Mary agreed. "Be careful driving back in the dark. With all this snow melting off and then freezing to black ice, you may wind up needing a doctor on your way home from the doctor."

"Yes, den mother," Chad said, heading for the door.

"Well, I guess that leaves you and me, Coop. Let's go see if we can talk to these guys."

~***~

They found Mike Sanders standing in a shower of sparks underneath a red Ford Escape. He was so tall he stood hunched over, even though the car was raised on the lift. Weber and Coop stood back a distance to avoid getting any burn holes in their uniforms. With a welding mask over his face, Sanders wasn't aware of their presence until Weber called out his name the second time. He stopped what he was doing and pushed the mask up.

"Sorry Sheriff, didn't know you were there."

He turned off the welder and laid the torch on the concrete floor of his garage, then pulled the mask off and set it aside.

"What can I do for you guys?"

"Mike, this is Deputy Ted Cooper."

"Yeah, I've seen you around town," he said shaking Coop's hand.

"We need to talk to you about a woman named Jill Cotter," Weber said.

The man sighed and said, "I knew this was coming. I heard about what happened to her. Damn shame."

"So you knew Jill?"

"Come on, Sheriff, you wouldn't be here if you didn't already know that."

"What can you tell me about your relationship with her?"

"That it was a mistake."

"Why do you say that, Mike?"

"I knew she was married. Hell, I've worked on Tom's truck. So I know it was a pretty chicken shit thing to do. I'm not proud of it. But she told me he had left her."

"Left her? Like they were separated?"

"That's what she led me to believe at first. I met her at the Brewpub one night, bought her a drink, and we got to talking. I asked why she was there all by herself and she said that Tom had left her and she was tired of sitting home alone staring at the walls."

"When was this?"

"I don't know, sometime last summer. It was just before Pioneer Days, when that fellow who worked at the Indian reservation got shot. I know, because I asked her if she wanted to go to the park with me to see the fireworks, and she said no. I guess that should have been my first clue, that she didn't want to be seen in public with me."

"But I heard that you two were at the Redeye Saloon at least once."

"A couple of times. I guess Jill didn't consider bars to be public places. I don't know."

"When did you find out that her and Tom were still together, Mike?"

"When I went to her house. She'd been acting so down that I bought her some flowers. I thought I'd surprise her and maybe they would cheer her up. But when I got there, Tom's Kenworth was parked beside the house. I thought maybe he had just come back to pick up some stuff so I just kept driving since I didn't want to cause any problems. I called her cell phone the next day and Tom answered."

"How did that go over?"

"Man, I didn't know what to say. I knew it was his voice as soon as I heard him on the line, so I just told him I had dialed the wrong number and apologized. Then I didn't know what was going on. I thought maybe they were getting back together so I bowed out. But a few days later Jill called me and asked if I wanted to get together. I asked her what the deal was with Tom and she said he was back out on the road. I asked if they were patching things up between them and she kind of laughed and said I must have misunderstood her. They weren't separated, he had just left to go on a run in his truck and would be gone a couple weeks."

Mike shook his head and said, "That ended it for me right there. I swear to God, Sheriff, if I would have known they were still together it wouldn't have never started in the first place. I ain't no saint, not by a long shot, but messing around with a married woman? No way!. That's not something I would do. Tell you the truth, I'm ashamed of myself."

"When you guys were together, you never went to her house?"

"No, never did. She said she had this nosy neighbor and she didn't want the whole town talking about her, knowing her business. So we always went to my place."

"Mike, did she ever show any signs of any kind of illness?"

"What do you mean?"

"Just that. Did she ever act like she was sick?"

He thought for a moment, then shrugged his shoulders. "If she did, I never noticed and she never said anything about it."

"How long did this thing between the two of you go on?"

"I honestly don't know, Sheriff. A few weeks at most. It wasn't like we were seeing each other every day or anything like that, either. I think we hooked up five or six times before I found out about her and Tom still being a couple."

"How did she handle it when you broke things off with her?"

"Not too good. First she started saying it didn't matter about Tom, what he didn't know wouldn't hurt him. Then when I told her I didn't ever want to see her again, she got really pissed. She started cussing me out and said she was the best I ever had, best I'd ever hope to have, and that I was an idiot for ruining a good thing like we had going."

"And that was it? You never saw her again?"

"I saw her once after that. I had to meet Howie McDermott at the Antler Inn to get a check from him for putting a new exhaust on his Jeep. Jill was in there with some cowboy, hanging all over him. She saw me and kind of gave me this look like what was I going to do about it?"

"Do you know who the guy she was with was?"

"Not really. I've seen him around town a couple of times but I don't know his name or anything like that."

"Did you and Jill talk at all, there at the Antler?"

Mike shook his head. "There was nothing I wanted to say to her, and I figured the further I stayed away from her the better. I had a beer with Howie, he paid me for my work, and I left. That was the last time I ever saw her."

"From the time that you guys stopped seeing each other until you saw her with that cowboy, about how long was that?"

"If I had to guess, I'd say a month or so. Sorry, I don't really keep track of everything I do on a schedule."

"That's okay," Weber told him. "We appreciate your time, Mike. And as for the whole deal with Jill being married and all that, things like that happen sometimes."

"Honest, Sheriff, like I said, if I had known she was married..."

"I believe you," Weber told him. "Thanks for your time."

They turned away and started to leave and Mike said, "You know, you hear about guys being dogs and running around and cheating. Stuff like that. I guess there are some women that do it, too, huh?"

"Unfortunately, that's true," Weber acknowledged.

"I'm really sorry she's dead. For all her faults, cheating on her husband like that, Jill was a nice girl and I liked her a lot. Hell, I was beginning to see a future for the two of us. When I found out it was all a big lie, it really took the wind out of my sails."

"I'm sorry," Weber told him.

"Me, too. Jill was right about one thing, though."

"What's that?"

"She was the best I ever had. Best I'll ever hope to have."

He shook his head sadly, bent down to pick up his torch, and went back to work on the SUV.

Chapter 25

Mike Sanders may have been remorseful about his involvement with a married woman, but Reggie Sosin obviously didn't see why that would be a problem.

"Jill? Yeah, she was one hot little piece of ass."

"Really? That's the way you talk about a dead woman?"

"Come on, Sheriff, it's not like she was Mother Teresa or something."

Weber hadn't liked Sosin the first time he met him, and the man wasn't doing anything to gain points with the sheriff with the casual way he referred to Jill Cotter.

"We understand you two had a thing going on for a while."

"A thing? Naah. I mean, we hooked up together a few times, sure, but it wasn't a thing."

"Then what would you call it?"

"I don't know," Sosin said, shaking his head as he took chairs off of tabletops and put them in place for the evening's drinkers. "Like I said, we hooked up. Sex, okay? She was a freak. She liked it and she liked a lot of it. I'm telling you guys, nothing was off-limits with that bitch. She would do things I'd only seen in porn videos before."

Weber was having a hard time not smashing the man's face into one of the tabletops. He knew Jill had cheated on her husband more than once, but he still didn't appreciate the bar owner's locker room talk.

"How about you show a little respect?"

"Respect? What's to respect? You act like she was your sister or something."

The snicker was halfway out of Sosin's mouth when Weber grabbed him by the collar of his shirt and jerked him upright, the chair the bar owner was holding toppling onto the floor.

"Hey man, you can't treat me that way!"

"Oh yeah? Then call a cop. You listen to me, asshole, and you listen real careful. Jill Cotter may not have been perfect, not by any means, but she was still a person. And she was the wife of a friend of mine."

"Yeah? Well maybe if your friend knew how to take care of business, his woman wouldn't be out screwing around behind his back, would she?"

Coop caught Weber's fist before he could smash it into the other man's smug face.

"Easy, Jimmy. This punk isn't worth it."

The deputy pushed his sheriff and the bar owner apart.

"Man, I'm gonna have your job," Sosin declared.

Cooper turned to him and put a finger in the man's face and said, "Shut up. Close your pie hole and keep it closed. Because I can think of a hundred reasons to shut this place down every time I walk in here. So unless you want to spend the rest of your life explaining to the liquor board why your bar got closed down as a public nuisance, you need to cut the crap right now."

"Nobody grabs me like..."

Coop jabbed his finger into the bottom of the man's throat. Not enough to do any damage, but enough to get his attention.

"And besides dealing with all the violations I'm sure we can start finding in here, some night when you close up, you may just find you have yourself some company."

"Are you threatening me, Deputy?"

"No, sir," Coop said. "You need to stop thinking of me as a deputy and start thinking of me like one of those psychics that can predict the future. And I can tell you right now, your future is looking pretty grim. That's not a threat, that's a prediction. But it's a prediction I'd bet money on."

"Okay, sorry. Look. I don't need any trouble. I'm just trying to get by here, you know?"

"The best way for you to get by right now is by answering our questions without all the bullshit and disrespect. Are we on the same page?"

"Yeah, I get it. Same page."

"Good," Coop said, taking a step back. "Now, tell us everything you know about Jill Cotter and about your involvement with her."

"She started showing up in here right after I opened the place up. We'd talk and bullshit, and one thing led to another."

"As in bed?"

"In bed, on the desk in my office, right there on the bar one night after I closed up." Sosin looked at Weber and hurriedly added, "I'm not trying to be disrespectful, that's just the way it was. I was telling you the truth when I said she was a freak."

"How long did this go on between the two of you?"

"Shit man, I don't know. Almost a year, I guess."

"Did she say anything about her and her husband having any problems?"

"No, he wasn't really a topic of conversation, if you get my drift. But I got the impression everything was okay with them. She never had anything bad to say about him, just that when he was gone she needed someone to keep her company. I'm not gonna lie to you, I enjoyed doing it."

"When was the last time you saw her?"

"A couple weeks ago, maybe three weeks. There was never any schedule or anything like that. It's not like we were dating. I never called her. She'd just show up here and we'd get it on."

"Did she ever mention any health issues to you?"

"No."

"How much did she drink?"

"A bit."

"How much is a bit?"

"She'd get loaded once in a while, but she was always able to navigate out the door and find her way back home."

"Did you ever see her use drugs?"

"Okay, stop right there," Sosin said, raising his hands, "I don't allow drugs in my place. None. Nada. Zero. I may not be an altar boy, but I worked long and hard to get this place open and I'm not gonna get shut down because of shit like that. You can bring one of those drug sniffing dogs in here and go over the place anytime you want, day or night. You're not going to find anything."

"I didn't ask if you use drugs, I asked if you'd ever seen Jill use drugs," Weber said.

"No. And if I would have, that would've been the end of it right there. I've got a sister back east who was a good person. Had a husband and three great kids. She started doing the blow and within a year she was fried. It ruined her marriage, she lost her husband and her kids and her job and everything. Last I heard, she wasn't any more than a streetwalker. Like I said, I don't want nothing to do with that shit. And I don't want nothing to do with anybody who uses it, either."

Weber was surprised that even a man like Sosin drew the line someplace. Apparently everybody has their own set of morals, even if they don't conform to society's.

"Do you know anybody else that Jill was messing around with?"

"It's not like we had an exclusive thing going. Yeah, I saw her in here with different guys a time or two."

"Do you know any of their names?"

He shook his head. "I make it a point not to become friendly with my customers. That's what the waitresses are for. As long as they have cash to pay for their drinks or their debit cards are good, and they don't get drunk and start tearing the place up, I don't need to know their names."

"All right, is there anything else you can tell us about Jill?"

"Not really. I don't think I even knew her name until the second or third time we screwed. She was just a woman in the bar."

~***~

When they got back in the sheriff's Explorer, Coop said, "That is one despicable man. I probably should have let you pound his face in."

"No, you did the right thing," Weber replied. "Mary would have had a field day with all the paperwork that would cause."

"Now what?"

"What the hell, I already feel the need for a long hot shower. Let's go to the Antler Inn and add another coat of sleaze before we call it a day."

~***~

Margo Prestwick frowned when she saw Weber and Coop coming through the door of her bar.

"What the hell do you guys want?"

"Is that any way to be, Margo?"

"Every time you pricks come in here I've got trouble."

"That's because every time we come here, there's trouble going on. How about the next time a bunch of the derelicts that hang out here start beating on each other we just ignore you when you call and let them tear the place up? Would that make you happy?"

"Just tell me what you came for and get the hell out of here. I've got better things to do than stand here talking to you two."

Weber looked around the large open barroom, noting the tables with empty bottles and glasses that had not been cleared and the general shabbiness of the place and said, "Whatever you've got to do, I bet it's not cleaning, is it?"

"The slobs that come in here don't care what the place looks like. They just care that the drinks are cheap."

If the three half drunk men sitting on stools at the bar took any exception to her words, they didn't show it.

"Okay, enough of the pleasantries," Weber said, "I think we've fulfilled our social obligations. What can you tell me about this woman?"

He laid the picture of Jill Cotter on the bar, making sure that the surface wasn't wet before he set it down.

Margo looked at it briefly, then shrugged her shoulders. "Nice enough looking, I guess. That your new girlfriend?"

"We know that she came in here sometimes."

"As long as she's 21 years old, that's none of your business."

"Actually, it sort of is our business. She's dead."

"That the one they found in the lake?"

"That's her," Weber said. "Her name was Jill Cotter. What do you know about her?"

"I know that she was pretty, from that picture, and I know she's dead, because you just told me. That's about it."

"You don't recall ever seeing her in here?"

"No, I don't pay any attention to who they are or what they look like. I'm just here to supply the booze."

"Given the kind of people that are normally in this place, I'd think a good looking woman like that would stand out like a daisy in a cesspool," Coop said.

"I never noticed. I don't swing that way, if you get my drift."

"You're telling me she's never been in here?"

"No, I'm not saying that. I'm saying if she was, I never noticed her."

"Can we get a refill over here?"

Margo looked toward the men at the bar and said, "Keep your shorts on. I'll be right there."

She started to turn away, then turned back to Weber and Coop and said, "Whoever that bitch was, if she was in here, I never paid any attention to her."

"Why do I think you're being less than forthright with me?" Weber asked.

"I don't know. Maybe because you're the suspicious type."

"Look again, Margo. We need to find out who she might have been hanging out with in here."

The woman used the tip of her finger to flick the photo back across the bar. Weber caught it before it fell to the floor.

"I told you, I don't know anything about her and I don't know anybody she was with. Now, unless you're planning to order something to drink, I've got customers to take care of. Believe it or not, some people come in here to spend money, not to waste my time."

She turned away, dismissing them, and pulled three more bottles of beer from a cooler under the bar, popped their caps off, and set them up for her customers.

"You know, boss," Coop said when they got back in the Explorer, "if we did just ignore Margo the next time she calls for help and just let the rowdies tear this place apart, we might be doing a public service in the long run."

"The way I   see it," Weber said, buckling his seatbelt and turning the key to start the engine, "this is kind of a maggot sanctuary. As long as the scumbags stay here, at least they're not wandering into the other places in town, bringing down the property values."

The sheriff looked at the Antler Inn one last time, then shook his head and drove away.

Chapter 26

Weber was up and out of bed early, leaving Robyn sleeping as he carried his clothes into the bathroom and got dressed. He leaned over to kiss her cheek and she mumbled something and rolled onto her side.

It had snowed again, leaving an inch or so of fresh powder on the Explorer's windshield overnight. He started it, and while the engine was warming up, called Dispatch on his radio.

"Big Lake One."

"Go ahead, One."

"Anything going on this morning?"

"Got a fender bender on Autumn Drive, no injuries, officer on scene. Nothing else."

"10-4. I'll be on the radio if you need me."

"10-4, One."

There was only one car in the parking lot of the Stop and Go, its snow covered windows telling him it had been there overnight. The bored clerk standing behind the convenience store's counter looked up from the aquarium magazine he was reading and said, "Morning, Sheriff."

"Morning, Cleve. What's going on?"

"I was reading an article here about the Green Spotted Puffer fish. Have you ever heard of them?"

"Can't say that I have," Weber replied, pouring coffee into a Styrofoam cup and stirring in powdered creamer and sugar.

"They're fascinating creatures. They're native to Southeast Asia and they exhibit some interesting behavior and personality traits. I'm thinking about adding another aquarium and getting one."

"Why don't you just get one and put it in one of your regular aquariums?"

"They have to be by themselves, they are very aggressive and will attack and kill other fish in their tank."

Weber was tempted to ask how the fish ever managed to reproduce if they had to be kept alone, but he didn't because he knew that if he did, Cleve would launch into some long lecture about the fish, which he really didn't have either the time nor the interest in listening to.

Cleve had many interests, from stamp collecting (he preferred American commemoratives) to ham radio, to tropical fish (he limited himself to freshwater species and was partial to African cichlids and the various types of tetras). All nerd hobbies, but perfect for a loner like himself.

An intelligent young man, graduating in the top five percent of his class at Big Lake High School, Cleve did not interact well with others. It wasn't that he didn't like people, he just could never find the right thing to say at the right time. So usually he just nodded or mumbled some unintelligible response on the rare occasions when somebody took the time to notice him. Unless he liked you, in which case he could go on and on about obscure topics that nobody but he was interested in.

And for some reason, Cleve liked the sheriff. Weber had learned all sorts of things from him, not only about tropical fish, but also the Inverted Jenny, a 1918 postage stamp printing error in which the image of the Curtiss biplane was printed upside-down, and the benefits of different models of ham radio microphones that included mention of something called amplitude, and measuring it on an oscilloscope.

Glancing at the bread rack, Weber asked, "Has Lonnie been in with the delivery this morning?"

Cleve shook his head. "Should be here anytime." Cleve didn't like Lonnie. The bread truck driver was a handsome man who carried the confidence of so many attractive people, knowing that he would be accepted based just upon his looks anywhere he went. Short, fat, and socially awkward, Cleve had never experienced that, and he resented men who took their looks and their popularity for granted.

He started telling Weber about how the Green Spotted Puffer was successfully bred in captivity at the University of Florida for the first time in February, 2009, and about the challenges of raising them in aquariums, explaining that they could not be fed manufactured fish food exclusively because their teeth continued to grow throughout their life, and how in nature they ate hard invertebrates, which helped to grind their teeth down. Apparently, from what Weber could understand, the store-bought fish food was too soft, so they had to be fed snails and ghost shrimp on occasion to provide some wear for their teeth.

Weber was glad the coffee was strong, because he needed to stay awake as Cleve droned on, pausing only long enough to ring up sales of gas, cigarettes, and coffee from the customers that stopped on their way to work. He was rescued when the big FreshlyMaid bread truck pulled into the parking lot and backed up to the store.

Weber stood aside while Lonnie Henderson carried in a large plastic tray holding loaves of bread, along with hot dog and hamburger buns. He stacked them on the shelf, took away three loaves of outdated bread from his last delivery, and had Cleve sign a receipt for the delivery.

As he started out the door, Weber asked, "Got a minute, Lonnie?"

"Sure, Sheriff, what do you need?"

Weber handed Cleve a dollar for his coffee and said, "Fascinating stuff about those puffer fish. Thanks for educating me."

Cleve rang up the sale, but didn't reply, resentful that once again he was being pushed aside in favor of a more popular man like Lonnie.

Weber followed Lonnie outside and watched while he threw the day-old bread into a large plastic bin in the back of his truck.

"Does that just get thrown away?"

"Oh, no," Lonnie replied. "The boss don't throw nothing away. The dated stuff gets donated to the safe house and the senior citizens center."

"That's good of him, I'd hate to see it go to waste."

"He don't do it because he cares about helping people," Lonnie said. "He keeps track of everything we donate and writes it off on his taxes."

"Sounds like a smart businessman to me."

"I guess so. After all, he's the one sitting behind the desk in a nice warm office all day long, and I'm out here in the cold, in the dark before the chickens wake up, making deliveries."

"Lonnie, I wanted to ask you about Jill Cotter."

The delivery driver pulled the rollup door in the back of the truck closed and latched it.

"That was a terrible thing. I was really sorry to hear what happened to her."

"So you knew Jill?"

"Yeah, I knew her."

"Can I ask how well you knew her?"

"Let's just say that we were more than casual acquaintances, okay, Sheriff?"

"No, I'm afraid I need more than that."

"Okay, you caught me again. I banged her a few times."

"How many is a few?"

"I don't know," Lonnie said, shrugging his shoulders. "I never kept track."

"How did it start between the two of you?"

"How does anything like that start? I'd seen her around town different places and always thought she was hot. One night I saw her in some bar, don't remember which one it was now, and I bought her a drink and one thing led to another. You know how it goes."

"Where did you guys usually hook up?"

"She'd call me when her husband was out of town and we'd meet someplace."

"Did you ever go to her house?"

"A couple of times, but then Jill saw this old woman that lives next door to her looking out the window as I was leaving and was afraid she would say something to her husband. After that, she never wanted me to come around the house anymore. So we'd just find ourselves someplace to park and... you know."

"When was the last time you saw Jill?"

Lonnie thought for a minute, then said, "It was at Halloween. The wife took the kids to trick or treat and Jill called. I met her on the road that goes up to the fire lookout tower."

"And you never got together after that?"

"No, that was the last time."

"How come? Did you guys have an argument or something?"

"No. It just kind of died out, I guess. It wasn't like we were in love or anything, It was just casual sex."

A green Jeep Cherokee pulled into the parking lot and a woman got out, saying hello to Weber as she hurried inside to get her morning caffeine rush.

"Did Jill ever drink much?"

"She'd have a drink or two, but that was about it."

"How about drugs?"

"No, never saw her using drugs. I remember we talked about when that medical marijuana dispensary opened up in Show Low and her saying that she had a brother that lived in Oregon someplace and pot was legal up there, but that it wasn't her thing."

"Okay, another question, Lonnie. Did she ever seem to have any health problems?"

"What do you mean? Like an STD or something?"

For the first time, Weber saw a look of concern in the man's eyes.

"Anything, any health issues at all?"

"Not that I know of. Is there something I should know, Sheriff?"

"I'm tempted to tell you that you should know you're a married man and you should keep it in your pants when you're not at home. But I think I'd be wasting my breath."

Lonnie gave him a rueful grin and replied, "What can I say? If it's out there and it's offered, I take it."

"I just don't understand that," Weber told him. "I've met your wife. She seems like a nice lady to me."

"She is, no question about that. Couldn't ask for a better mother for my kids."

"So then why do you do it, Lonnie? Why are you always running around, cheating on her?"

He shrugged his shoulders, then said, "I don't know. I never really gave it much thought, to be honest with you. I guess maybe it's because you got it right. She's a lady. Sometimes a guy wants a woman who forgets she's a lady now and then."

Weber gave the man a sour look, but did not comment except to ask, "Is there anything else you can tell me about Jill? Did she ever talk about having any problems at home, anything like that?"

"Not really. She was always bitching about her husband being gone all the time. She said if he would stay home and take care of business she wouldn't be out running around on him. I guess she blamed her cheating on him."

Weber was struck by the irony of all that. Jill Cotter blamed her husband for her infidelity. If he had not been working so hard to provide a good home for her, she might have been faithful to him. Lonnie blamed his wife for being a good woman and a good mother to his children for his cheating ways.

He was done talking to Lonnie, but Weber made a mental note to himself to drop a hint to his deputies that if they saw Lonnie Henderson so much as failing to use his turn signal when changing lanes, or not coming to a complete stop at an intersection, they should exercise a zero-tolerance policy toward him.

"You have yourself a good day, Lonnie. Thanks for your time."

Chapter 27

"We've talked to all four of the guys we know that Jill was fooling around with and what do we know so far?"

"We know she didn't take her marriage vows very seriously," Robyn said, distastefully.

"Neither does Lonnie Henderson or Scott Welch," Chad said. "That's assuming that Greg Sterling was right and it was Scott he saw Jill with up there on Echo Lane."

"I don't think Greg is lying to us, and I think he really believes he did see Scott and Jill together. I just can't figure out what the tie-in is between the two of them and that house."

"Something else comes to mind," Robyn said.

"What's that?"

"You just said you talked to all four of those guys, right?"

"Yeah."

"And what do they all have in common?"

Weber thought about it for a moment, then shrugged his shoulders. "I don't know. The only thing I can think of is that they all live here in town and they were all messing around with Jill Cotter."

"Okay, so what *don't* they have in common?"

"What are you getting at, Robyn?" Coop asked.

"Think about it guys," Robyn prodded, "what don't they have in common?"

"Two of them, Lonnie Henderson and Scott Welch, are married, and Reggie Sosin and Mike Sanders aren't?"

"Okay, that's one thing. What else?"

"Sosin, Welch, and Sanders all run their own businesses, and Henderson works for the bread company in Show Low?"

"Something else."

"Can't you just tell us without making us play Twenty Questions?"

"Hey, Jimmy's kept me here in the office doing background checks while you guys get to go out and play. Give a girl a break."

"I give up," Chad said. "What else don't they have in common?"

"Three of them, Sanders, Sosin, and Henderson, all freely admitted they had been doing the deed with Jill. Only one of them has completely denied it."

"Scott Welch."

"Bingo," Robyn said. "Why is that?"

"Either Greg Sterling was wrong and Scott really wasn't messing around with Jill," Weber said, "or else maybe he's got something to hide besides the obvious, that he was cheating on his wife."

"Either way, I think we need to talk to him again," Chad said.

"Before you do that, can I try something?" Robyn asked.

"What do you have in mind?"

"I know that Darcy takes her lunch break about 12:30 every day. I've seen her about that time in the ButterCup Café, and I thought maybe I would just sort of bump into her and ask if she wants some company."

"I don't know if that will do any good or not," Weber said. "When we saw her at the western wear store, she was pretty adamant that her husband would never think of cheating on her."

"I'm not planning to question her about him or the case," Robyn said. "I'll make it like it's just girl talk, talking about our wedding coming up, and her and Scott having a baby. Just kind of get a feel for how things are between the two of them. You never know."

"It's worth a shot," Weber said. "See what you can find out. Meanwhile, I need to get over to the hardware store. There's a man coming that I want to talk to."

The intercom on Kallie Jo's desk beeped and Norma Foster announced that Tony Hurley from Hurley Wholesale Hardware Supply was there.

Kallie Jo looked up nervously at Weber standing in the corner across from her, who nodded.

"Send him in, Norma."

At one time Chet Wingate's office had been a showcase to the man's ego. The walls had been covered with framed photos of the mayor with every major or minor celebrity or politician who ever passed through Big Lake or came within fifty miles of the little mountain town. What space wasn't adorned with photographs held certificates of achievement or membership in everything from the Arizona Hardware Retailers Association to the Kiwanis Club. An upright glass-fronted case held small trophies and awards from Chet's civic and business activities. Now that his daughter-in-law was running things, most of that had been boxed up, and the only decorations were a picture taken on her wedding day with Archer and photographs of the local wildlife and mountain scenery.

There was a knock on the door and it opened. A casually dressed man in his mid-30s wearing jeans and a heavy suede coat over a knitted sweater came into the office.

"How you doing, sweetheart? Did you miss me?"

"Have a seat, Mr. Hurley," Kallie Jo said, motioning to a chair in front of her desk.

"Don't call me Mr. Hurley, sweet cheeks, that's my old man."

"Yeah, I talked to your father after your last visit."

The salesman laughed and said, "Yeah, he told me about that. Said I'm supposed to be nice to you. But I keep telling you, darling, you give me half a chance and I'll be *real* nice. Nice in ways you never imagined. Have you thought about what we talked about?"

"I didn't have to think about it," Kallie Jo said angrily. "I told you I ain't interested. The only thing I want to do with you or your company is to order things we need for the store. Why can't you get it through your head I'm a married woman?"

"Awww, come on baby. You can't really expect me to believe that you'd rather have that than me," he said, nodding at the picture of Archer and Kallie Jo on their wedding day. "You don't know what you're missing."

He reached across the desk and put his hand on top of Kallie Jo's. She tried to pull away but he held on.

"Let go of me!"

"Oh, you still want to play that game? Come on, girl, you know you want it. How about we lock the door and get to know each other a little better?" He let go of her hand and reached out and touched her on the breast.

Tony had never noticed Weber standing behind the door when he came in, and the first time he became aware of the sheriff was when the hand slapped him across the back of his head. The blow was hard enough to rock him forward, and he turned around, saying, "What the hell?"

"I believe the lady told you to let go of her. Are you hard of hearing?"

"I don't know who you are, asshole, but you can't go around hitting people like that!"

"What, like this?" Weber slapped him on the side of his head, the sound of flesh hitting flesh loud in the small office.

"Hey man, stop it," Tony said throwing up his left arm to protect his face.

Weber ignored him and slapped the other side of his head, almost knocking him off the chair. "I hear you like it rough, Tony. Is this rough enough for you?" This time he slapped the top of the man's head, hard enough that he heard his teeth slamming together.

"You're a cop," Tony said, seeming to realize Weber was in uniform for the first time. "This is police brutality."

"No, this is just me getting your attention," Weber said, slapping him again. Weber had hit a lot of people in his time, and he knew how to make it hurt without leaving any evidence.

"Don't worry, when I get brutal, you won't be conscious long enough to know it."

Tony had curled into a ball crouching in the chair, both arms over his head and face to ward off the next blow. "Stop it," he whined. "Stop, please! I'm sorry."

"You're sorry?" Weber grabbed the front of his jacket and pulled him to his feet. The chair fell over and Weber asked again, "Sorry? What are you sorry for, Tony?"

"I'm just sorry. I was just kidding, okay? Just having a little fun, that's all."

"Sure, I understand that. And that's all I'm doing, just having a little bit of fun."

Weber slammed his fist into the man's stomach, then stepped back as a whoosh of air was forced out of Tony's mouth as he fell to the floor. The salesman rolled into a fetal position and began sobbing. "Don't hurt me anymore. Please don't hurt me."

"Oh, trust me, I haven't even begun to hurt you yet."

"No more," Tony pleaded, "don't hit me again. Please don't hit me again!"

"What? You come in here and put your hands all over a helpless woman, but suddenly you're not such a big stud after all? I don't get that. What's that all about, Tony?"

"I'm sorry! It won't happen again. I promise."

"You're right. It won't happen again," Weber said jerking him to his feet and slamming him against the wall so hard that a picture of a squirrel perched on the limb of a Ponderosa pine tree fell off. Snot and tears were running down Tony's face and he flinched when Weber raised a finger and pointed it at him. "Here's the way it's gonna work from now on, Tony. Your daddy is going to send someone else to call on this business. I don't care who it is, but it's not going to be you. And you're not going to try to cut Kallie Jo off from things she needs to order. Got it?"

"But I'm the one that covers this entire area."

Weber backhanded him across the face. "I'm sorry, did I give you any reason to believe this was some kind of a negotiation?"

"No."

"Okay then. Your company needs to find somebody else to cover this territory. Because I'm going to tell you something right now. If I ever see you in Big Lake again, I'm going to pull you over and we're going to have us another talk. And the next time, I'm not going to be so gentle about it. Understood?"

He nodded his head.

"I asked if you understood me?"

"Yes, I understand."

"And I believe you need to say something to Kallie Jo here, don't you?"

Tony hung his head and said, "I'm sorry."

"You look her in the eye like a man, and you apologize," Weber ordered.

He looked at Kallie Jo and said, "I'm sorry. I'm really sorry."

"That's better. Now call your old man."

"What?"

Weber raised his hand again and Tony yelped in pain even though the blow was never delivered. "Don't make me repeat myself. Call him, now."

Pulling his cell phone from his pocket, Tony pushed a button with a trembling finger and Weber took the phone away from him. It rang four times and a gravelly voice answered, "What's up, kid?"

"Is this Mr. Hurley?"

"Yeah, who's this?"

"My name is Jim Weber, Mr. Hurley. I'm the sheriff in Big Lake, Arizona, and I'm afraid I've got some bad news for you about your son."

"Tony? What happened to Tony?"

Weber could hear the concern in the man's voice.

"Your son had to learn a lesson today about being a gentleman around women. Now that he's learned that lesson, I'm trying to decide if I need to arrest him for attempted sexual assault or not."

"You're kidding me. Tony would never do anything like that."

170

"Yeah, he did. And according to the information I have, the victim, Kallie Jo Wingate, called and told you that she was being harassed by him. Apparently you thought that was just boys being boys. Now, the penalty for sexual assault in Arizona can range from a minimum of five years for first offenders to life imprisonment. I'm sure that Tony here would only get the minimum sentence, but trust me, Mr. Hurley, five years is plenty of time for him to learn all about boys being boys and what sexual assault feels like."

"Do I need to call a lawyer?"

"That's entirely up to you," Weber said. "Like I said, I'm trying to decide about that. You know how it is when something like this happens. Word gets out and people start coming out of the woodwork claiming that they were victims, too. And given what I've seen of Tony here, I'm pretty sure that they would be telling the truth. The next thing you know it's all over the news, and then the social media goes crazy with it. All of a sudden there are lawsuits coming in from every direction. That could be really rough on a business."

"How do we make this go away, Sheriff?"

"As I was telling Tony, starting immediately, your company is going to send somebody else to call on your customers in this part of the country. Because if I ever see him in my town again, things are going to get real ugly. Do you understand me?"

"Yeah, loud and clear."

"That's good. And I don't believe that Kallie Jo's going to have any problems with shortages of inventory or anything like that, is she?"

"No, nothing like that. I promise you."

"Your promises don't mean a lot to me," Weber told him. "So here's what I'm going to do. I am going to arrest Tony and I'm going to fill out a booking slip on him. But I will hold off on formally filing the charges for a while, just to make sure that you remember this little conversation of ours. What happens with Tony from here on out is entirely up to you and him."

"Thank you, Sheriff."

"You need to keep him in the office and put a leash on this punk, Mr. Hurley, since he seems to want to run around acting like a dog all the time. Because around here, there are people that tend to shoot dogs that are out of control. You think about that."

Chapter 28

"If Scott Welch was messing around with anybody behind his wife's back, Darcy doesn't have a clue about it," Robyn said that afternoon when she returned to the Sheriff's office.

"You asked her about it?"

"No. Like I said I was going to do, I just happened to bump into her as she was going into the restaurant and asked if she wanted some company. We talked about our wedding coming up and about her and the baby, and married life, and then she brought it up. She said that you and Chad had been at the store asking Scott about Jill Cotter, and how wrong you guys were to even think that he would be doing something like that. She said it really hurt Scott's feelings for anybody to think that he would be unfaithful to her."

"You said she doesn't have a clue if something is going on," Weber said. "Do you think that's all it is, that she's clueless?"

"I don't know, Jimmy. She's a pretty sharp woman. I'm not saying she's right about him, but if her husband has been stepping out on her, he's doing a darn good job of hiding it. She's completely convinced that he's a loyal, dedicated husband. She said that the only time they're not together is when they're working, or when he's at a Chamber of Commerce meeting or something like that. She said lately all they've been doing is talking about how excited they are about the baby coming and getting a room ready for it."

"Either Greg Sterling was wrong and it wasn't Scott he saw with Jill that day," Chad said, "or this guy should forget about running the family business and head for Hollywood, because he's a hell of an actor."

"I keep coming back to what you said earlier, about Scott being the only one who denied having been with Jill. Could we be barking up the wrong tree? Could Greg possibly be wrong?"

"Anything's possible, Chad," Weber said, "but you heard him when we were in the store. He seemed pretty darned sure of it."

"What did he say, 95% sure? That still leaves some room for error."

"That's true. Do you want to go talk to Scott again?"

"What have we got to lose?"

~***~

"Boy, you guys just won't take no for an answer, will you? I've told you before I had nothing to do with that woman, I don't remember ever meeting her, and I know I wasn't involved with her, or anybody else. I'm happily married and I've got a baby on the way. There's no way I'm going to screw that up."

"Look, Scott, we're not trying to set you up or frame you, or anything like that. But we've got a witness who swears he saw you and Jill together at that house on Echo Lane. How can you explain that?"

"I can't explain it, because it never happened," Scott said heatedly. "Your witness is wrong, or he's lying to you, or something. I don't know. But you need to stop coming in here and accusing me of stuff I didn't do!" His face was red and his mouth was a tight angry slash. "I told you when you were here before, I'll take a lie detector test if that will satisfy you. Anytime, anyplace you want. You just tell me when and where."

Weber looked at Chad, then back at the man behind the desk. Did Greg Sterling get it wrong, he wondered, or was Scott Welch indeed an accomplished actor able to cover up his misdeeds? He wasn't sure, since both men were convincing in what they had told him about any involvement Scott might have had with Jill Cotter or the house on Echo Lane. The sheriff decided to call his bluff.

"I'll tell you what, Scott, let's do that. I can have a polygraph examiner come up tomorrow and we can put an end to this once and for all. What time works for you?"

"I already told you, you name it and I'll be there."

"Fine, I'll call you first thing in the morning to let you know when to come by the Sheriff's office."

"Okay. Now are we done here? Because I've got a business to run."

"We'll see you tomorrow," Weber said, and he left the office with Chad following him.

"What do you think?" Chad asked when they were out on the sidewalk.

"I don't know what to think at this point," Weber admitted. "But he sure doesn't seem hesitant to take a polygraph."

Chad pulled his cell phone out and said, "I'll call Mary and have her set it up."

~***~

"It was short notice, but DPS can have someone here by 2 p.m. tomorrow," Mary said when they got back to the office. A small organization like the Big Lake Sheriff's Department did not have a trained polygraph examiner, so when there was a need for one they reached out to the Arizona Department of Public Safety, who would send someone from Flagstaff or Phoenix.

"Good," Weber said, "because I want to put this thing with Scott behind us, one way or the other."

He had barely gotten the words out of his mouth when the door opened and an indignant Darcy Welch stormed in with fire in her eyes.

"How dare you, Robyn? I can't believe you did that!"

"What are you talking about, Darcy?"

"You just happen to meet me for lunch and act like you're my friend, and all the while you're pumping me for information about Scott so you guys can try to pin that woman's death on him? I can't believe you. I can't believe any of you people. My husband is a good man! I keep telling you that. He would never cheat on me."

"Calm down, Darcy. Nobody's trying to..."

"Don't tell me to calm down," she shouted. "You guys are trying to blame my husband for something he didn't do and

175

destroy our lives, and you tell me to calm down? I don't think so!"

"Darcy, nobody's trying to hurt you, or Scott," the sheriff told her. "But the fact is, there is a dead woman, and accusations have been made that she and Scott were seen together."

"Who made those accusations? I want them to tell me that right to my face."

"I'm sorry, I can't reveal that information," Weber said.

"You can't reveal it? Why not?"

"Because it's an open investigation and we can't compromise a witness. I'm sorry."

"But yet you're going to believe this witness of yours over my husband. What do we have to do to get you off our backs?"

"Scott has volunteered to take a polygraph test tomorrow," Weber said. "If he passes it..."

"*If* he passes? You sound like you already expect him to fail it."

"No, ma'am, that's not what I mean. What I'm trying to say is that the polygraph test will help us clear your husband so we can move on to the next person."

"And what do you think all of this is going to do to Scott's reputation in this town, Sheriff? When word gets out that he was a suspect in that woman's death, people are going to believe whatever they want, right or wrong."

Weber knew that was true, and he couldn't deny it. Sometimes small town gossip could ruin a person's good name. It was a sad fact of life, but there was no way around it.

The phone rang at the dispatch desk and Judy Troutman answered, then waved Mary over. She spoke to the person on the phone, then turned to Weber and said, "I'm sorry to interrupt, Jimmy, but you need to take this call."

"Look, Darcy, I'm sorry for all this, and we're going to do everything we can to clear Scott's name. That's what the polygraph is all about. But right now, I've got something I've got to deal with."

He went to the dispatch desk and took the phone from Mary. "Sheriff Weber here."

"Sheriff, it's Debra Hargis. You were here in my office the other day to talk about the house at 628 Echo Lane."

"Yes, ma'am, what can I do for you?"

"I'm at the house now, Sheriff, and I think you'd better get up here right away. There's something you need to see."

~***~

There was a white Lincoln Navigator parked in the driveway, and Weber pulled in beside it. Debra Hargis was sitting in the SUV with the engine running. She got out when Weber and Coop arrived.

"What's going on, Ms. Hargis?"

"Someone's been in the house."

"You mean like somebody broke in or what?"

Weber wouldn't be surprised. They had already had reports of three or four summer places being burglarized that winter.

"No, nobody broke in," the real estate broker told them. "But somebody's been in there. I'll show you."

They went onto the porch with her and she unlocked the door and opened it. Weber and Coop didn't see anything out of place.

"Okay, what's going on?" The sheriff asked. "I don't see any evidence of somebody's being here."

"Well, they have," Debra said, leading them through the kitchen and a utility room with a new GE washer and dryer set that looked like they had never been used. She pointed to a door on the other side of the room and said, "Look in the garage."

Cautiously, Weber put his hand on his holstered Kimber .45 semiautomatic pistol and pushed the garage door open.

"Well, I'll be damned. No wonder we couldn't find it," he said, looking at Jill Cotter's red Toyota Corolla.

Chapter 29

"There weren't any tire tracks on the road or in the driveway when we were up here the other day," Chad said, "which means this car has been here since before the snowstorm last week."

"Which ties into the estimated time Jill went into the lake," Dolan said. He opened the car's door and there was a chiming sound. Leaning inside, he said, "Keys are in the ignition."

"So let's try to establish a timeline," Weber said. "Tom Cotter said the last time he talked to his wife was last Tuesday, sometime in the morning. The snow storm hit the next day, Wednesday afternoon. We found Jill's body on Sunday morning. So that has to mean that sometime between Tuesday morning and Wednesday afternoon she drove the car into the garage. And the ME down in Tucson said she was in the water no more than four days. Which means she died sometime Tuesday or Wednesday, right?"

"Sounds about right to me," Chad said.

"You've got one thing wrong, Jimmy."

"I do? What's that, Dolan?"

"I don't think Jill Cotter drove this car into the garage."

"What are you getting at?"

With the driver's door open, Dolan said, "Look at the position of the seat, pushed back that far. I'm six feet tall, and with the seat in that position it would fit me pretty good. Jill Cotter wasn't more than about 5'2" or maybe 5'3". I don't think she could have reached the brake and gas pedal comfortably with the seat this far back."

"Maybe not for driving very far," Jordan Northcutt said, "but I imagine she could drive it a short distance into the garage."

"Yeah, but it's her car," Dolan explained. "I doubt very much that she drove around town all the time with the seat in this position. Why would she?"

"You're right. That doesn't make any sense," Jordan said. "I'm about four inches taller than my wife, and Meghan always has to move the seat forward before she drives if I've been the last person to use our Durango."

"Something else," Dolan said. "With the seat back there, the mirrors are adjusted wrong."

"So somebody besides Jill got in the car and drove it into the garage."

"That's what it looks like to me, Jimmy."

"But if the place was locked up, how did whoever it was get it in here?"

"I don't know, but I intend to find out," Weber said. "Meantime, I want this place searched from top to bottom. See if you can find anything out of place, any indication of who was in here."

Debra Hargis was standing in the living room with Robyn and Dan Wright.

"Who would have keys to this house besides the owners and you, Debra?"

"Nobody that I know of."

"You didn't give the key to anybody to let them get in here?"

"Absolutely not," she said with a note of aggravation in her voice. "Do you think I would just let someone go wandering through a client's house alone?"

"That's not what I meant," Weber said, holding up his hands in apology. "I meant like maybe a service guy. A plumber, an electrician, or somebody like that, that had to get in to fix something."

She thought for a moment, then shook her head, "No, nobody at all."

"Well, there's no sign of forced entry. Could the owners have given a friend a key for some reason?"

"I guess it's possible," Debra acknowledged.

"Do you have a number were we can call them and find out?"

"Is that really necessary, Sheriff?"

"Yes, it is. Is there a reason you don't want to do that?"

"You have to understand where I'm coming from. When a house is listed with a real estate agent, the owners are placing a lot of trust in that agent. Not just in terms of selling the property, but also in making sure that it is protected. It's not going to look very good if my clients get a call from the police telling them that somebody's been parking a car in their garage without my knowledge."

"Debra, as of now this place is a crime scene. I'm not sure you can keep your clients from knowing that. Meanwhile, I need to call them and find out if anybody else has a key, so I need their contact information."

"Can I call them for you? Maybe I can soften the news and do a little bit of damage control."

Now that same note of aggravation she had exhibited a moment before had slipped into Weber's voice when he said, "Look, I understand you don't want to look bad in front of your customers, but right now that's not my concern. As far as I know, a woman died in this house, and if she did, we need to find out what happened to her."

"Died? What are you talking about?"

"That car belonged to Jill Cotter. She's the woman we found in the lake Sunday during Snowdaze."

"Oh, my God. This can't be happening!"

Debra sank onto the couch, a look of horror on her face.

"I'm afraid so."

"No, this has to be some kind of bad dream."

Robyn looked at Weber, then back at Debra.

"Did you know Jill Cotter?"

"Who?"

"The dead woman Sheriff Weber just told you about. Jill Cotter."

Debra thought for a moment, then shook her head. "No, I don't think so. Why?"

"Well, because you look like you just got some terrible news or something."

"Of course I just got terrible news. When my clients find out about this, when the word gets out around town, it's going to ruin my reputation! How would you feel if you trusted your house to a real estate agent and then something like this happened in it? How could this happen to me?"

"This didn't happen to you," Robyn said. "You're not the person who is dead."

"I might as well be," Debra lamented. "When the competition finds out about this and starts telling potential clients they can't trust me to keep their homes safe, I'm finished in this town!"

~***~

Robyn was still seething an hour later when Randy Laird backed his tow truck into the driveway and loaded the Toyota onto the back of it. Since the Sheriff's Department didn't have any place big enough to securely store the car while it was processed for evidence, he agreed to take it to Weber's cabin and put it in the garage there.

"I can't believe that woman," Robyn said, looking at Debra's Lincoln SUV as it drove away. "Somebody is dead, and all she's worried about is what it's going to do to her business reputation? How shallow do you have to be to act like that?"

"I don't know," Weber said. "But we both know there are some people that only think about themselves, and to hell with the rest of the world. Why don't you go back to the office and call the folks that own this place, see if you can get anything out of them."

"Okay. I'll let you know what I find out."

After she left, Weber walked back inside. Dolan and Buz were standing at the kitchen counter comparing notes.

"Did you guys find anything?"

"Nothing real obvious, but come with us, Jimmy."

He followed them down a hallway and Dolan paused in the doorway of two bedrooms. "These are the guest bedrooms. Notice how neatly the beds are made?"

"Yeah."

"And here in the bathroom across the hall, everything looks nice, doesn't it? If you are looking for a house to buy, it's pretty impressive, right?"

"Maybe not impressive, but it looks nice," Weber said. "What am I missing so far?"

"This," Dolan told him, leading him into the master bedroom. "What do you see?"

"A bedroom?"

"Yeah, Jimmy. It's a bedroom. But look at how the bed's made. Robyn noticed it right away, but you still being a bachelor, I guess you don't."

"You're right, I don't," Weber admitted.

"Go back and look at the beds in the guest bedrooms and you'll see how tight they are. Bedspreads adjusted just perfect so they're the same distance from the floor on both sides, not a wrinkle in the surface of them. Then look at this one. This bedspread is a good three inches higher on one side than the other. And it's not pulled tight and smoothed out like in the guest bedrooms. Those beds were made up to give the best impression when a potential buyer sees the house. But if you're buying a house, the master bedroom is where you're going to be sleeping and what you'll notice the most, right?"

"Yeah, I see where you're coming from now, Dolan."

"Somebody made this bed in a hurry, Jimmy. And more than likely, it was a guy."

"And if that doesn't seal the deal, look in the master bathroom there."

It didn't take any explanation for Weber to see what was amiss there. "The toilet seat's up."

"Yep. I don't know how many houses you might have looked at that are for sale, Jimmy, but I doubt you will ever see one with the toilet seat up."

"Which reinforces the whole thing about a guy being here. And maybe a guy who needed to get out of here in a hurry."

"That's right," Dolan said. "And I'd venture to say that guy is probably somewhere around six feet tall."

Nick Russell

Chapter 30

Buz and Dolan, with Coop's help, spent hours processing the house, looking for any evidence of Jill Cotter and the man who had been with her there. Late in the afternoon Weber returned to the Sheriff's office.

"Have you been able to find out anything at all from the owners of the house, Robyn?"

"I found out divorces can be really ugly," she said. "Depending which one of them you choose to believe, either Mason, the husband, is a deadbeat skirt chaser who would hump anything that moves, or else the wife, Samantha, is a frigid bitch who cares more about her career than she does her marriage."

"See, that's just one more perk of this job. You get to meet all kinds of interesting people and find out the most intimate details of their lives."

"Yeah, I feel so blessed," Robyn said, rolling her eyes.

"Aside from finding out about all their character flaws, did you learn anything that might help us in our investigation?"

"They're not living together, and according to them, neither one has been up here in quite a while. Samantha said she was here in May, over Mother's Day weekend. She's a nurse practitioner at a hospital in Phoenix and said she knows it was then, because it's the only holiday weekend of any kind she's had off all year. Mason said he was up in early June to pick up some stuff he still had in the garage, and he hasn't been back since."

"Anything else?"

"Both of them said that they are really frustrated that the house hasn't sold quicker, and they both blame the other one for buying the house in the first place. Samantha said Mason wanted some kind of macho man cave in the mountains where he could, and I'm quoting her here, Jimmy, walk around in his underwear, thump his chest and fart like some kind of Neanderthal."

"He sounds like my kind of guy," Weber told her.

"Don't get any ideas. Keep your pants on and your sphincter shut," Mary Caitlin advised him.

"Why do you seem so obsessed with my ass lately?"

"Maybe I'm becoming one of those cougars I keep reading about in *Cosmopolitan*. I hear the mature woman/younger man thing is pretty hot right now."

"Cougar? At your age you are damn near a saber tooth tiger," Weber told her. "And why does it concern me that you read *Cosmopolitan*?"

"Anyway," Robyn continued, ignoring their banter. "According to Mason, they could have gotten a lot of use out of the place, but Samantha is more married to her job than anything else, and anytime he wanted to come up here she couldn't get any time off. He said he finally stopped waiting for her to clear her schedule, and was coming up by himself for a while. But he said when he did that, she was always accusing him of bringing some woman with him, so he finally just said to hell with it and they put it on the market."

Robyn was quiet for a minute, then asked, "How do people end up like that, Jimmy?"

"What do you mean?"

"Like those two. I mean, they must have been in love when they started out, right? And now they're at each other's throats. Look at Tom and Jill Cotter. He's busy working and she's sleeping with guys behind his back. What happened in their marriage to make her do that? Heck, look at my parents. They are always bickering back and forth at each other. How did they get from standing together and saying "I do" to where they are today?" She looked up with tears in her eyes and asked, "Are we going to end up the same way, Jimmy?"

"No, Baby," Weber assured her. "That's them. We're different."

"Are we, Jimmy? How do we know we're different? Do you think any of them started out ever dreaming they would wind up like they are today?"

Robyn had grown up in a home where her parents always seemed to be at war with each other, and he knew that had caused her to be wary of marriage since the time he had first proposed to her. It was something that Weber could not completely relate to, because his own parents had been completely devoted to each other. He could never remember hearing them argue, although he was adult enough to understand that they certainly must have had their problems from time to time. But whatever those problems may have been, they handled them behind closed doors, not in front of their children.

"Lots of people are different. Look at Mary and Pete. They tease each other to death, but you can't deny they are in love and have been, forever."

"That's true," Mary said. "He's a cantankerous old fart, but he's the only man I ever wanted."

"And look at Greg Sterling and Kathy. All the medical problems she's had, and he's right there with her, every step of the way. That's what it's all about, Robyn, being there for each other all the time. That's us. I don't know what your parents' problem is, or why a couple of overachievers like those two you talked to today get off track, or why all those people we have to go break up domestic disputes between get like they do. But I also know there are millions of couples who live happy lives together. And something else I know, Robyn, is that you and me, we're going to make it."

She looked at him and nodded, rubbing the tears away. "Yeah, you're right. We aren't those other people." She put her arms around his neck and held him close. "Just remind me of that when I get scared, okay?"

"I promise," he said, holding her tight. "You can count on that."

Chapter 31

Weber was shocked when Tom Cotter opened the door to his house. It didn't look like he had changed clothes or shaved or bathed since he got back to town. His face was gaunt and his eyes deeply sunken. His wife may have been the one whose funeral he was supposed to be arranging, but Tom looked more dead than alive himself.

"Are you okay, Tom?"

The man stared at him wordlessly, like he didn't know who Weber was or could not understand what he was saying to him.

"Tom? Are you in there?"

Finally, he nodded his head, but still didn't reply.

"Can we come in, Tom?"

He stepped back to make room for them. Weber and Robyn went into the living room, noting that it looked even messier than it had before. There was a blanket and pillow on the couch and a staleness to the air. They sat down on the couch and Tom plopped down in his chair. Weber had seen a lot of grieving people in his time, but few that had seemed to suffer as much as Tom was doing.

"Have you eaten anything?" Robyn asked.

He looked at her dully, as if he couldn't understand the question.

"Tom, you need to eat," Weber said.

Finally he spoke, just two words. "Not hungry."

"I know you're not hungry," Robyn said. "But you need to eat. Your body needs fuel. You can't go on this way or you're going to collapse.

"Don't care."

"I know you don't care right now," Weber said. "But you need to care, Tom. As terrible as all this is, you need to take care of yourself. Jill wouldn't want you sitting here staring at the walls and wasting away to nothing."

"I should have moved her back to Barstow. Never should have taken her away in the first place. She was happy there."

"Maybe so, Tom, I don't know. But I do know you need to take care of yourself."

"Why, Jimmy? What's the point?"

"The point is, you owe it to Jill, and you owe it to yourself, and you owe it to the rest of the people who love you, to get through this."

"And then what? If she's not here, I don't care anymore."

"I know you feel that way now, Tom. This is all part of the grieving process. I've been through it and I understand. But things do get better, eventually."

Robyn had left the couch and gone into the kitchen. Weber heard cupboard doors opening and closing and then the sound of a pan being put on the stove. A few moments later there was the aroma of something cooking. But if Tom Cotter noticed it, he gave no indication.

"Tom, we found Jill's car."

"Okay."

He didn't ask where it was or anything about the Toyota.

"Have you been able to talk to Jill's mother?"

"No. I guess I should try to find a phone number for her, but..." the words trailed off and he didn't finish.

Robyn came back into the living room with a plate of corned beef hash and a glass of water and sat them on the coffee table in front of Tom.

"Why don't you have a little bit to eat, okay?"

"I'm sorry. I'm just not hungry."

"I know you're not," Robyn said. "But just a couple bites."

He looked at her and nodded, then picked up a fork and with a shaking hand managed to put a bit of the hash in his mouth.

"You need to eat it," Robyn said, as if coaxing a reluctant child.

Tom nodded, chewed a few times, and swallowed.

"Good. How about some more?"

He managed to get down half a dozen forkfuls, and then pushed the plate away. "Sorry, ma'am, I'm just not hungry "

"That's all right. At least we got a little bit of food in you," Robyn told him. "I'm going to put this in the refrigerator, okay? Maybe you will want more later."

Tom nodded his head. "Thank you."

"Are you up to answering a few questions for us, Tom?"

"I guess," he said listlessly.

"You said the last time you talked to Jill was on Tuesday of last week, right?"

"I think so."

"Can I look at your phone, Tom?"

"Yeah, go ahead. It's here someplace."

The phone was lying on the floor next to his recliner. Weber picked it up, found the call log, and scrolled through it. "It looks like you talked to her at 11:27 AM on Tuesday of last week. Does that sound right, Tom?"

"Yeah. She got mad at me because I wasn't making it back in time for the winter festival thing. Maybe if I would have..."

"Tom, you couldn't have changed anything. You were in Oklahoma when you called her the last time. From what we have been able to figure out, Jill died sometime that day or the next. If you hadn't taken that last load to go to Tulsa, you still couldn't have driven home in that time. And even if you were here, Tom, it was a heart attack. Who's to say that even if you were home, you could have gotten help for her in time?"

"Still should have been here."

"Tom, does Echo Lane mean anything to you?"

He shook his head in answer.

"Did Jill ever mention knowing anybody who lived on Echo Lane, anything like that?"

Another head shake.

Weber hated to ask the next questions, but he had to.

"Have you ever heard of a man named Scott Welch?"

"Sounds familiar. Are they the folks that run the western wear store?"

"Yes. How about Lonnie Henderson?"

"There's some Hendersons around here, I think, but I don't know any of them."

"How about Reggie Sosin? Does that name sound familiar?"

"I don't think so."

"Okay, one more. Mike Sanders."

Tom nodded his head. "I know Mike. He put a new exhaust on my truck a while back."

"Did Jill ever mention knowing any of those people?"

"Not that I can recall." He looked at Weber, then asked, "Are those the men?"

"What men, Tom?"

"Are those the men Jill was messing around with when I was gone?"

Weber knew they were on a slippery slope and he had to tread carefully. He never wanted to reveal too much information during the course of an investigation. And then there was the fact that while Tom Cotter was usually a pretty levelheaded man, he was in the middle of a crisis. The last thing Weber needed was for a distraught, vengeful husband trying to track down his dead wife's lovers.

"They're just names that have come up in the course of the investigation," Weber told him.

Tom seemed to accept that and didn't ask any more about the men Weber had mentioned.

"When you were out on the road and you called home, did Jill ever say that she was with a friend, anything like that?"

"What kind of friend?"

"Anybody, Tom. Did she ever mention any friends that we might be able to talk to, to get a better picture of what was going on with her?"

"No. All she ever did was complain that she was sitting by herself staring at the walls while I was gone. She said it was driving her crazy, and I guess it's true. I was just too dumb to believe her. If I would have listened to her, maybe things would have been different."

"What do you mean by that, Tom?"

"It took me a long time to accept it, but you were right about her, Jimmy. I didn't believe it until I found her birth control pills last night, in the bottom of one of her dresser drawers. From the

192

time we met, Jill let me know right up front she did not want any kids. She insisted I get a vasectomy, and I did, right before we got married. We used to say that was my wedding present to her, sex with no babies."

"I'm sorry, Tom."

"You were right about her, and Don was right, and Kathy was right. Everybody knew it but me. I heard what they were saying, but I just couldn't believe it could be true. There was no way that I thought Jill would ever cheat on me."

"I'm sorry, Tom. I really am."

"Why would she do that? I loved her so much, and she said she loved me, too. Why did she do that, Jimmy?"

"I don't know. I wish I had an answer for you."

Robyn caught Weber's eye and nodded her head toward the gun cabinet, then tilted her head toward the kitchen. Weber followed her there and she asked, "He's really down, Jimmy. Do you think it's safe to leave those guns here?"

"I don't know," he said.

Going back into the living room he said, "Tom, can we call anybody for you?"

"No. Thanks anyway."

"You know, your sister and brother and Greg really do care about you."

"I know. And I've treated them like crap for a long time when all they were trying to do was protect me."

"Do you think it's time to have a talk with them?"

"Not yet, Jimmy. I will, in my own time. I'm just not ready yet."

"Okay. Listen, Tom, we need to get out of here. But before we go, there's something I'm concerned about."

"What's that, Jimmy?"

"Your guns."

"My guns? Do you think I'm going to go off and shoot somebody?"

"It's crossed my mind," Weber said.

"Well, don't worry about that. I have no intention of hurting anybody."

193

"What about yourself, Tom?"

The man looked at him and didn't reply.

"You've been through a lot in the last few days," Weber said. "I'd be lying to you if I said I wasn't worried about you hurting yourself, too."

Tom shook his head. "That's not going to happen, Jimmy."

"You're sure about that?"

"If it makes you feel better, take them. But I absolutely promise you, I will not shoot myself, or anybody else. I give you my word on that, Jimmy."

Weber thought for a moment, then said, "Your word has always been good enough for me, Tom." He extended his hand and they shook hands.

Chapter 32

Parks, Marsha, and Christine Ridgeway were already at Mario's Pizzeria when Weber and Robyn arrived a half hour later.

"About time you got here," Christine said, "smelling all this good food has me starving!"

"Did you two stop for a quickie on the way?"

"No, Marsha, we did not stop for a quickie," Robyn said as she sat down at the table. "Don't you ever think about anything but sex?"

"Hmmm.... let me think about that," Marsha said putting her hand under her chin and seeming to be in introspection for a moment. Then she shook her head and grinned. "Nope, to be honest with you, while I was thinking about whether or not all I ever think about is sex, I was thinking about sex."

Christine laughed and asked, "What would you rather have us think about, Robyn? Famine and wars and global warming?"

"I should know I wouldn't get any help from you," Robyn said, laughing.

"Ahhh, there you are. Sheriff Jimmy, Miss Robyn, so wonderful to see you," said a large man as he came out of the kitchen to deliver a steaming basket of garlic knots slathered in butter to their table. "Look at this," he said, holding his hands out, "Wonderful people come to my restaurant, and it is an honor to serve you."

"Sal, you are one silver-tongued devil," Christine said.

"And you, my beautiful Miss Christine, every time I see you I hear angels sing." He bent and gallantly kissed her hand. Robyn and Marsha exchanged grins.

Salvatore Gattuccio, the owner of the restaurant, was a huge man with an even bigger heart, who had never met a stranger. Sal made everyone he met feel special, but none more so than Christine.

A large woman herself, Christine and Weber had been friends since childhood. Blessed with a great sense of humor and a tremendous amount of compassion for others, Christine had moved away to Southern California and a career as a social worker. There she had been faced with and had overcome personal tragedies before returning to Big Lake, where she opened and was the director of SafeHaven, a shelter for battered and abused women and their children. Surprising everybody, including themselves, in the last few months the friendship between the pizza shop owner and Christine had blossomed into something more, much to the delight of everybody who knew them.

"I don't take your order, because I know what everyone wants," Sal said. "So please, enjoy the garlic knots while I cook your pies."

"Can't you join us?"

"For the people I love, Sal has to cook the pizza. The young people in the back, they are hard workers and they do a good job. Sal has tried to train them right, and for other people yes, it is okay to let them make the pizza. But for you people, no. No, only Sal can make the pizza for you!"

"Well, will you at least sit with us and eat some when it's done?" Christine asked. "It's not fair that these two girls get to have their special guys with them, and I'm sitting here all by myself while you're in that hot kitchen." She put an exaggerated pout on her face and looked at him with lowered eyes.

"How can I resist such a beautiful woman? It's not possible. Sal won't even try. Yes, my darling Christine, once I make the pizzas I sit here and we visit."

"Yay," Marsha and Robyn said in unison, clapping.

Sal bowed and returned to the kitchen.

"Now that is how you train a man," Robyn said.

"Girlfriend, you just need to understand that men are like carpet," Marsha told her. "If you lay them right the first time, you can walk on them for life."

"Hey, now. That's not nice," Parks said.

Marsha looked at him with arched eyebrows and asked reproachfully, "Do you have any complaints, mister?"

Parks looked at her and hung his head, shaking it and muttering, "No, ma'am. Please don't hit me again."

"Now *that's* how you train a man!"

It had taken Robyn quite a while to become accustomed to Marsha's often outlandish ways, and hadn't taken her long after Christine came back to town to realize that the two of them were kindred souls, one seeming to try to outdo the other at times, while Robyn sat back quietly observing, and sometimes secretly admiring their openness. She had told Weber once that she was sure her uptight, straight laced mother would have been shocked to hear some of the conversations that took place when they were all together.

"So, I hear you found the missing car," Parks said.

"Yep. It was sitting in the garage at that place on Echo Lane all along."

"That's amazing. Hidden in plain sight."

"If the garage would have had a window in it, Chad and I would have probably seen it the first time we were up there."

"How is Tom doing?" Marsha asked.

"Not too good," Weber told her. "We were just out at his house before we came here. Apparently he's coming to terms with the fact that his wife was cheating on him, which only makes things worse."

"Can you know somebody did you wrong and deceived you like that, and still grieve for them?"

"Yeah, it's possible," Christine said. "As bad as my ex-husband was to me, I have to admit that I shed some tears when I found out he was dead. Don't ask me why, but I did."

Even back in high school, all the girls had loved Mark Wagner. At least until they got to know him better. He was handsome and a charmer, but there were rumors that two or three girls who went out with him said Mark didn't believe in the word "no" and tried to push things way past their comfort points. After he and Christine had married and moved to San Diego, he had been an abusive husband, both physically and mentally. He had also chased every skirt that crossed his path, until one day he found a younger, slimmer woman and abandoned his wife and their young son. Some said it was karma that after a couple of years his new wife grew tired of his abuse and shot him dead.

That seemed to put a damper on the conversation, but not for long, because before they were fully into their bread knots, Sal returned with two large pizzas and put them on the table.

"And now," he said, taking off his white chef's apron and draping it over the back of a chair and sitting down next to Christine, "I stop being Sal, the pizza man, and I become Sal, the man enjoying dinner with three lovely ladies and two brave men who I respect and admire."

"Hey, us ladies are brave, too! Don't forget, Sal, Robyn's a cop just like Jimmy and Parks are. And your lady Christine here, she protects a lot of women and children from bad men, and she's not afraid of anyone. And me? I'm the bravest of all. I have to look at Parks, naked!"

"What's with all the abuse tonight? Do I have a sign on my back that says kick me?"

"Come on, Parks, you know you love it," Robyn told him.

The front door of the restaurant opened and a couple came in, then stopped abruptly. Something was said between the two of them, then they quickly reversed course and went back out the door. Looking at them, Sal asked, "I wonder why they left so quick."

"Hard to say," Christine replied. "Maybe they got the wrong place?"

"They eat here all the time," Sal said.

Watching the couple get in their truck and drive away, Weber knew the reason they had had a sudden change of plans. He just wasn't sure if it was Scott Welch or his wife Darcy who had not wanted to be in the same restaurant with the sheriff and Robyn.

Chapter 33

"Except for her car being in the garage, on visual examination we weren't able to find anything that puts Jill Cotter or Scott Welch in that house," Dolan Reed told Weber Friday morning as he and Buz examined the Toyota in Weber's garage. "However, we did find a strand of blonde hair on one of the pillows on the bed in the master bedroom. We can send it off for DNA analysis and see if it matches Jill's. And there was a fingerprint on the underside of the toilet seat in the master bathroom that might tell us something."

"I imagine there were a lot of other fingerprints "

"Oh, yeah. Too many to even try to guess at. People don't wipe their house down before they list it with a real estate agent, so there's no telling how many sets we would find. We did take the one off the toilet seat because we know that was recent. Ms. Hargis, the real estate lady, insists the seat was down, along with the toilet lid, the last time she was there."

"We can assume that's going to be a man's print," Weber said, once again hearing Mrs. Zimmerman tell him that making assumptions was lazy thinking. He needed to get his encounter with that woman out of his head.

"And we know Jill didn't park the car in the garage herself," Buz said. "Hopefully we can find a print on it that matches the one from the toilet seat."

"Assuming that it was the same person that raised the toilet seat and moved the car," Dolan said.

There was that word again. So far a lot of their case was based on assumption. If he would have taken heed of the rest of Mrs. Zimmerman's lessons as much, he might have graduated from high school with a higher grade point average. But as with most of her students, Weber had allowed most of what she told him to go in one ear and out the other. In his memory, the majority of her time spent in the classroom was not in teaching, but in telling the students how many ways they didn't measure up. Mrs. Zimmerman seemed to have the eyes of an eagle and the ears of a bat, and nothing slipped past her. The slightest whisper between classmates in the back of the room, a gaze out the window, and she was on you like white on rice. She never missed anything.

Never missed anything. Damn! She never missed anything!

"You guys go ahead and do your thing," Weber said. "Something just occurred to me and I need to check it out."

~***~

"Tell me again, why are we going back to talk to this woman? It was bad enough the first time."

"Because she never misses anything," Weber said. "Right away she assumed Tom Cotter had killed his wife. Of course she would never admit assuming anything, because that's lazy thinking, according to her. But when I asked why she thought that, she said something about, how did she put it? Something about Jill fornicating with every Tom Dick and Harry that came her way or something like that."

"How did she know that? I don't picture her sitting around with the girls, having a cup of tea and gossiping," Robyn said.

"Exactly. Lonnie Henderson told me that Jill didn't want him coming to the house anymore because the neighbor woman had seen him leaving. I'm wondering who else Mrs. Zimmerman might have seen."

The reception they received from the retired schoolteacher seemed to be even colder than it had been on their previous visit.

"I do not appreciate people stopping by, unannounced," Mrs. Zimmerman said when she opened the door to find them on her front porch. "I am very busy."

"Yes, ma'am, we understand that." Weber said apologetically, "But we need to ask you a few more questions about your neighbors."

"I told you all I know about them already. Now, good day."

She started to close the door but Weber put his hand on it to stop her. Mrs. Zimmerman glared at him for his rudeness.

"Please, we just need a few moments of your time."

"Very well," she said, not trying to hide the frustration in her voice. "Let's get on with it. I really have better things to do with my time than talking about people like them."

She led them into the living room, which was just as dimly lit as it was before, and they sat in the same places. Mrs. Zimmerman did not offer them coffee or tea, or do anything to make them think they were guests in her home, merely an intrusion into her day.

"Mrs. Zimmerman, you said something the other day about Jill Cotter being involved with different men. Where did you hear that?"

"Hear it? James Weber, do you believe I have time to waste in idle gossip?"

"No, ma'am, I don't. I'm just wondering where you came up with that. How do you know Jill was cheating on her husband?"

"Because I saw it with my own eyes, that's how!"

"You saw it?"

"There were two different men, at least, that I saw coming and going from that house when Tom was away in that truck of his. Speaking of which, I really wish you would do something about making him move it. I hate looking out my window and seeing that ugly thing sitting there."

"I'm sorry about that, Mrs. Zimmerman. But as we told you before, it's a zoning issue. The way this area is presently zoned, he is within his rights to park it there. You would have to go to the Town Council and see if you can get them to change the rules before we can do anything about it."

"You always had an excuse for not doing what you were supposed to, even when you were a student."

"Getting back to these men you saw next door, do you know who they were?"

"One was somebody I had never seen before. The other was a former student of mine. Another person who is wasting his life and not living up to his potential."

Weber wondered if anybody ever truly lived up to their potential in his former teacher's eyes. "And who was that, Mrs. Zimmerman?"

"Lonnie Henderson. He was always such a handsome boy, and talented, too. But he would rather spend his classroom time staring at the girls than studying. And where did he end up? Driving a bread truck!"

"How many times did you see Lonnie coming and going from the Cotter house? Or the other man, the one you didn't know?"

"I have no idea," Mrs. Zimmerman said peevishly. "As I've told you before, I have better things to do with my time than to waste it spying on the neighbors."

Weber laid drivers license photos of Reggie Sosin, Scott Welch, Mike Sanders, and Lonnie Henderson on her coffee table. "Do you recognize any of these men, Mrs. Zimmerman?"

"That is Lonnie Henderson there," she said stabbing a finger into the appropriate photo, "and that is Michael Sanders."

"Was Mike one of the ones you saw coming and going next door?"

"No. I told you there was a man I didn't know and there was Lonnie Henderson."

"But you recognized Mike's picture, too."

"Are you questioning my judgment?" she asked sharply.

"No, ma'am, not at all. I just wondered how you recognized Mike's picture."

"He put a muffler on my car last year, that's how. Michael was another student who grew up to become a ne'er-do-well."

"Don't you think that's a little bit harsh? Mike is a successful businessman with an excellent reputation," Robyn said.

"I did not say he wasn't competent at his trade." She made the word trade sound distasteful, akin to being a pickpocket or a panhandler. "But there is so much more one could do with their life than working with their hands. Are we done here?"

"Almost," Weber said, as eager to get away from the dark room and its judgmental occupant as she was to see him gone.

"You said you saw a man you didn't know coming out of the house. What can you tell me about him?"

"I can't tell you anything about him because, as I said, I don't know who he was."

"How about his height, weight, hair color? Anything?"

"I have better things to do with my time than to spy on my neighbors and write down the details of their visitors."

"Of course you do," Weber said. "When these men visited, did any of them stay overnight, to the best of your knowledge?"

"Again, I don't know. As I've told you before, I saw those two sneaking in or out on different occasions. I did not keep track of them because I did not care to have that much involvement in whatever disgusting things were going on next door. Those are just observations I made upon seeing those men."

"You also said you heard a lot of fighting from next door. I know you weren't spying on them, but could you hear anything that was being said?"

"No, just a lot of shouting."

"Could you tell who was doing the shouting? Was it Jill, or Tom, or both of them?"

"Mostly her. As time went on, it seemed like she was shouting at him every time he was home. Occasionally I would hear him, too, but for the most part it was her."

"Can you think of anything else that might help us, Mrs. Zimmerman?"

"I'm sorry. What gave you the impression that I care to help you? I tried to help you when you were a student. You didn't want my help then and ignored anything I ever said to you. Why would I consider helping you now?"

"You're right, ma'am. It would be a waste of time. Thank you for talking to us, Mrs. Zimmerman. We'll see ourselves out."

~***~

"Since you call her Mrs. Zimmerman, I assume she was married at one time," Robyn said as they drove away. "Whatever happened to her husband?"

"I have no idea," Weber replied. "She was always just Mrs. Zimmerman."

"Can you imagine being married to somebody like that?"

"No, I can't," Weber said, taking one hand off the steering wheel to hold hers. "It had to be a pretty miserable experience. It was all I could do to get through a 60 minute class with her."

Chapter 34

"Either Mr. Welch is an excellent actor, or else he is telling the truth," said Gordon Schmidt, the Department of Public Safety polygraph examiner. "I did not see any noticeable deception on his part to any of the questions I asked him."

"You say noticeable deception. What does that mean?"

"As you know, Sheriff Weber, a polygraph measures and records a person's physiological responses when they answer a question put forth by the examiner. Their pulse rate, breathing, blood pressure, and galvanic skin response. Nothing is 100% positive, but when a person is lying there is usually a noticeable indication on the graphs. There will always be some variance between individuals, and even a little bit of variance with one individual, depending on the question being asked. But in most cases when a person is outright lying, there's a strong indication on the graphs. I didn't see any of that with Mr. Welch when I asked him if he had any involvement in Jill Cotter's death or with her body ending up in the lake. Now, I did see a little jump when I asked if he had ever met Mrs. Cotter. First he said no, then he said he didn't think so. When I asked him to answer yes or no, he said no."

"Did that mean he was lying?"

"Not necessarily. If he didn't know for sure if he had met the woman or not, that could cause the variance I saw."

"Scott never said for sure he didn't know her," Chad said. "He said right up front that if he had met her, he didn't remember doing so."

"So except for that one little variance about whether or not he knew Jill, you feel like he's telling the truth?"

"Based upon my knowledge and experience, and my interpretation of the responses he gave, yes, I feel like he's telling the truth," Schmidt said.

"Which means that Greg Sterling either wasn't telling the truth, or was mistaken in who he saw."

"It looks that way, Chad."

"Greg seemed really sure he knew what he was talking about to me. And I really don't know why he would be lying about what he saw."

"Given that we found Jill's car in the garage there, it's obvious he was telling us the truth about that part. But as to who the man she was with was, it looks like he was wrong. What did he say, he was 95% sure it was Welch? I guess that other 5% kicked in."

"You said nothing is 100% positive," Robyn said. "How often are the polygraph tests wrong?"

"It's not so much that they are wrong as that they can be misinterpreted," Schmidt said. "An inexperienced examiner might miss something that someone with more time in would pick up on."

"But you've been at this a long time," Robyn said.

"Over eighteen years."

"So, again, what's the failure rate with these tests?"

"The commonly accepted numbers are 10-15% of the time."

"Which is why they're not admissible in court."

"Yes, ma'am."

"Could this guy be able to beat the polygraph? I've heard it can be done," Weber said.

"It can, Sheriff, no question about that. But it's not as easy as one might think."

"Then how do they do it?"

"As I'm sure you know, we begin the process by asking both relevant and irrelevant questions. For example I might ask an examinee what his name is, or if he has blue eyes, knowing that he does. Those are control questions and I measure the response when he tells me the truthful answer. Then I will ask him if he has ever stolen anything in his life, or if he has ever taken anything that didn't belong to him. Or maybe, I will ask them if they have ever told a lie to keep from getting into trouble. We all have at one point or another. Maybe we shoplifted a candy bar when we were a kid, or snatched a cookie out of the cookie jar when our mother told us not to, and fibbed when she asked us about it. But you'd be surprised how many people say no, they never have. The theory is that when they lie to those questions, even though it's a tiny white lie, it helps us establish a baseline for deception."

"Okay, then how do they tell a lie and get away with it to fool the machine?"

"There are several ways it can be done. One way is to think of something terrible when you answer a truthful question. I ask you if you have blue eyes, and you say yes, but at the same time you force yourself to think of your dog being run over when you were a child, or of your mother dying. That's going to give your body a different reaction than normal, and that's going to skew the results to the control questions. At the same time, if you're guilty of, let's say, embezzling funds from the office and I ask if you took the money, you may think of something entirely pleasant, like sitting in a boat out in the middle of the lake in the summertime fishing. Again, the theory is that that's going to skew your body's responses downward. I've also heard of people putting a thumbtack in their shoe and pressing down on it when they answer a truthful question, or maybe biting their tongue just before they answer."

"And that works?"

"Not every time. Not even most of the time. Very few people have that much self-control that they can manipulate their body's responses. But it can be done."

"Are there other factors that can come into play to change the examiner's interpretation of the final result?"

"Some. I have heard of people with heart murmurs or other physical conditions which will throw off a polygraph. And, while some of my peers would strongly disagree with this, there are also people who are simply excellent liars who can beat a polygraph. If you lie all the time about every little thing, just for the sake of lying, there's a darned good chance you could deceive a polygraph."

~***~

"One of two things is happening. Either Welch has been telling us the truth all along about not knowing Jill Cotter and not being up there on Echo Lane, which means that Greg Sterling was wrong, or else Scott is one of that small percentage of people who can fool a polygraph," Weber said. "I guess we just have to figure out which one it is."

"How do we do that?"

"Beats me," the sheriff admitted.

"And what does that place on Echo Lane have to do with it anyhow? Why was Jill and whoever she was with there? How did they have access to the place?"

"Maybe we have been focusing on Scott too much," Chad said.

"What do you mean?"

"Well, Greg Sterling told us he was 95% sure it was Scott he saw up there. Which means we've still got that margin for error. But back to your question, Jimmy. Why that place on Echo Lane? There was no sign of forced entry, so how did they get in?"

"I'm not following you, Chad."

"Robyn, what was it that guy's wife said? The couple that are selling the house. Didn't she say something about her husband bringing women up to their place here?"

"No, she didn't say it. When I was talking to the husband, Mason, he said he would come up once in a while by himself because his wife was always too busy working. But he said he stopped doing it because she was always accusing him of bringing some woman with him."

"Could this be a case of where there's smoke, there's fire?" Chad asked. "Was she accusing him because he's got a reputation for messing around behind her back?"

"And you think there's a possibility Jill Cotter could be one of those women?"

"It's worth checking into," Robyn said.

"Yeah, it could be true," Weber said. "But then again, Jill was always accusing Tom of being unfaithful, and all the while she was the one doing the cheating. Like you said, it's worth looking into. Why don't you make some phone calls, Robyn? See what you can find out."

~***~

Dolan and Buz had spent most of the day processing Jill Cotter's car, and had not come up with much. Several different sets of fingerprints, which was to be expected of just about any automobile that had been on the road for a few years. They had taken some prints from the steering wheel and the gearshift, and Dolan had submitted them to AFIS, the Automated Fingerprint Identification System. The hope was that a database search would turn up a list of potential matches, but they were all aware that that wouldn't happen unless the fingerprints of any of their suspects were already in the system somewhere. There was no telling if any of them had ever been fingerprinted after an arrest, to join the military, or for a job.

When Weber told them about the results of Scott Welch's polygraph test, Buz whistled. "That muddies the water, doesn't it?"

"It sure would have made things easier if he was lying and we could prove it," Weber said.

"Does he know he passed the polygraph test?"

"What do you mean, Chad?"

"I mean, does he know? Did anybody tell him he passed?"

"I don't know. I didn't."

"How about the polygraph examiner?"

"What are you getting at?"

"Let's just say for a minute that Welch was lying and he somehow beat the test. He pulled some of that stuff about thinking about other things or pushing a tack into his foot, or whatever. Or maybe he's a pathological liar or something. However he did it, what if he was lying and he beat the test, and he doesn't know that he did?"

"I get where you're coming from," Coop said. "Jimmy, is there any way to get a hold of that guy from the DPS and ask if he gave Scott his results?"

"We can try," Weber said. He called the number on Gordon Schmidt's business card, and got someone at the Department of Public Safety switchboard. When he told her who he was, she said she would get in contact with Schmidt and have him call back as soon as possible. Ten minutes later the telephone rang, and Mary told him it was for him.

"Sheriff Weber."

"Sheriff, Gordon Schmidt. Did I forget and leave something there?"

The cell phone signal was scratchy, as it often was in different areas in the mountains. Weber hoped he wouldn't lose the call before he could get an answer to his question.

"No, sir. Just a quick question for you. When you finished up with Scott Welch today, did you tell him the results of the test?"

"No, sir, I never do that. I just told him that I would give you the results and thanked him for coming in."

"All right, I appreciate that. You drive careful going home."

"Will do, Sheriff."

"So, do we want to go visit Scott again?"

"It's worth a shot, I guess. But we have to be careful here, guys. The man is a business owner in the community and all we have is one person's word that he was there with Jill Cotter. And, he's passed a polygraph. So we can't go in like gangbusters expecting to force some kind of confession out of him by making him think he failed the polygraph. There is a very good chance that Greg Sterling is wrong and it was somebody else he saw with Jill."

Chapter 35

Scott Welch was not happy to see them when Weber and Chad entered his store just before closing time. He was arranging a selection of Justin boots on a display table and looked up and shook his head.

"Unless you're here to arrest me, I'm done talking to you guys. And if you are here to arrest me, I want an attorney."

"What makes you think we're here to arrest you?"

"Are you here to buy boots?"

"No, sir," Weber told him. "We just wanted to talk to you about the results of your polygraph test today."

"Did it say I was lying about something?"

"Why do you think it would be saying that, Scott?"

"I'm not playing these games with you, Sheriff Weber," the man said heatedly, slamming a boot down onto the table. "I've had it! I'm done. Like I said before, either arrest me or get the hell out of my store."

"Why don't we go back to your office and talk about this?"

"No, we're not going back to my office, and we're not talking about this. Not here, not back there, not anywhere. Because there's nothing to talk about! I've said all I am going to say. Now get out of here."

Weber looked at Chad, who shrugged his shoulders and shook his head slightly. They both knew they were pushing things beyond what was right, given the circumstances. Either Scott Welch was an innocent man who had been wrongly identified and was being persecuted for something he didn't do, or else he was a guilty man who had called their bluff. Either way, they had done all they could do at that point.

"Sorry to bother you, Scott," Weber said, and they left.

~***~

"I found out something," Robyn said excitedly when they got back to the sheriff's office.

"What's that?"

"Mason Mitchell definitely cheats on his wife."

"He told you that?"

"No, I wasn't able to get a hold of him yet. But his wife said he had been fired from his last job for having an affair with a female coworker."

"Were you able to verify that?"

"I called the personnel department at his last employer, and the lady there started giving me a bunch of flack about privacy and all that. She said she couldn't officially confirm nor deny anything without a court order from us. She said that was company policy."

"Okay, then how do we know his wife is telling the truth?"

"We talked for a few minutes," Robyn said. "Her name is Denise and she's always wanted to be a cop. In fact, she's taking criminal justice classes at Maricopa Community College. She thought it was cool to talk to a working policewoman. She had a lot of questions about the job, and I told her to call me sometime and we could talk. About five minutes later I got a call from her on her cell phone, telling me that she was on break and there was nobody around. She told me that while she still couldn't violate the company policy about privacy, speaking as one woman to another off the record, she said if we were friends and I was considering dating Mason, she would tell me to turn around and run the other way because I could never trust him."

"Interesting," Weber said. "Did you get anything else out of her, or the wife?"

"Nothing from her, but Samantha, the wife, said she knows of at least half a dozen affairs he had while they were married. Some of them are mutual friends. Or at least women she thought of as friends. She was able to give me the names of four of the women he had been involved with, and I called and spoke to three of them. One said she didn't have anything to say and hung up on me, but the other two confirmed that he is a big time player."

"Okay, so we know that. That doesn't mean he was involved with Jill Cotter. After all, he lives down in the valley and she was up here."

"Want to bet?"

"What do you mean?"

"Just for giggles, I ran him through records. Remember how he said he had not been up here since sometime in June?"

"Yeah?"

"He apparently forgot all about the traffic ticket he got from DPS for speeding, six miles from town out on the highway on September 3rd of this year."

"You're kidding me? The day after Greg Sterling said he saw Jill with a man at his house?"

"That's right. But there's more."

"What?"

"He's currently awaiting a court date on a charge of possession of cocaine."

"No way!"

"Yep, Phoenix P.D. pulled him over two weeks ago on a traffic violation and he was acting hinkey. The officer got suspicious and ran him for wants and warrants. He was clean, but had a prior possession charge. So the officer got him out of the car and patted him down. Mitchell didn't have anything on him, but when the officer asked if he could search the car, he said no. So he called in a K-9 officer and the dog alerted on the car. They searched it and found two rocks in a baggie in the console."

"This guy is sounding better and better all the time," Chad said.

"Oh, it doesn't end there," Robyn said smugly. "Look at his driver's license picture," she set a photograph down on her desk, "and then look at this one." She placed a second photo next to it.

"Well I'll be go to hell," Chad said.

"They're not identical by any means, but they could be related, that's for sure," Weber said, as he looked at the photograph of Mason Mitchell, the owner of the house at 628

Echo Lane. A slender, good-looking man with collar length brown hair and a short, well-groomed beard. Maybe Scott Welch didn't have a doppelgänger, but looking at photos of the two men side by side, it was easy to see that from the distance between one house and the front porch of a house across the street, it wouldn't be that hard to see a man in the doorway and confuse the two of them.

"According to their drivers licenses, there's less than six months between their ages, there's a two inch difference in their height, and about fifteen pounds difference in weight," Robyn said. She tapped her finger on the picture of Mason Mitchell and said, "I think this is the guy that Greg Sterling saw with Jill that day.

~***~

"Yeah, that's him," Greg said.

"That's the man you saw kissing Jill at that house on Echo Lane? Are you sure of it, Greg?"

"Yeah, Scott Welch. I'm sure that's who I saw."

"Absolutely sure?"

"What's this all about, Sheriff?"

"I'll tell you in a minute," Weber said. "But again, look carefully and tell me if you're absolutely sure that's the man you saw."

Greg studied the photograph and then shook his head. "Yeah, that's him. No question about it."

"Greg, that's not Scott Welch."

"What? What do you mean it's not him."

"That man's name is Mason Mitchell and he's the owner of the house at 628 Echo Lane."

"You're kidding me?"

"No, sir. This is Scott Welch."

Weber handed him the photo of the western wear store owner. Greg looked at both, side-by-side, and his face paled. He seemed to rock on his feet and Weber looked at him with concern "Are you okay, Greg?"

Greg sank onto a couch in his showroom and put his face in his hands. "My God, I accused the wrong man! Oh my God. How could I have been so stupid?"

"It was an honest mistake," Weber said. "These things happen sometimes. None of us could believe the similarity between the two of them when we saw both of their pictures."

"Yeah, but because of me, Scott Welch has been going through hell. I just can't believe I did that, Sheriff. I'm so sorry."

"Like I said, these things happen."

"I have to make this right somehow," Greg said. "What can I do to straighten this out?"

"You don't have to do anything. We'll handle it."

"Can I call him and apologize or something? No, I should do it face to face."

"No, you shouldn't do anything at all," Weber told him. "Scott doesn't know that it was you that identified him and there's no reason for him to know it."

"That's just not right, Sheriff. *I'm* the one who made the mistake and I'm the one who has to make it right."

"No," Weber said firmly, "you don't. I appreciate where you're coming from, and it says a lot about your character that you want to do the right thing. But in this case, it could lead to problems. Problems that neither you or Scott Welch need."

"Hey, if he wants to punch me right in my big mouth, I've got it coming."

"That's enough of that kind of talk," Weber said. "Look, Greg you're a good guy. You were being a good citizen by reporting what you saw. You didn't purposely misidentify Scott out of malice or anything like that. You made a mistake, and seeing how much alike these two guys look, I think I probably would have made the same mistake myself. You've got a lot on your plate already, and I admire you for the kind of man you are. Don't add this burden, too, okay?"

Weber wasn't sure if the man accepted what he was saying to him or not, but he had to let it go at that. He still had a long drive ahead of him and somebody he needed to talk to.

Nick Russell

Chapter 36

Mason Mitchell obviously had no affection for the police, and when Weber knocked on his apartment door and identified himself, the first thing he said was, "Whatever you're trying to railroad me for, I didn't do it."

"I'm not sure what you're talking about, Mr. Mitchell. Why do you think I would be trying to railroad you for something?"

"Because you're a cop, and that's what you do."

"Have police officers railroaded you in the past?"

"You're damn right they have! That's a bullshit charge they've got me on now. That cop planted that coke in my car just so he could make a bust. Just like they did the last time."

"Why do you think a police officer would do that to you? Not one, but two different officers on two different occasions?"

"I'll tell you why. Because of Samantha."

"Your wife?"

"My ex-wife. Or at least she will be once we get all the divorce shit done."

"I'm missing something here," Weber said. "You're telling me that your wife set you up? Or convinced those cops to set you up?"

"You're damn right she did! She works in the ER over at Valley Mercy and there are cops in and out of there all the time. She got cozy with a couple of them and they set me up. So now I'm wearing this damn ankle monitor and I'm under house arrest except when I'm at work."

Mitchell wasn't the first man to claim the police had framed him, and Weber didn't intend to stand in the hallway and debate the issue.

"Do you mind if we come in?"

"Got a warrant?"

"No, sir, we don't."

"Then yes, I mind."

"Mr. Mitchell, I don't know what happened here in Phoenix, but that's not why we're here. We need your help on something that took place up in Big Lake."

"I don't know what you're talking about, but why should I help you?"

"Because we've got a situation and we're trying to get to the bottom of it."

"That's your problem, not mine."

"Well, it kind of is your problem," Weber told him. "See, we found a dead woman floating in the lake last weekend."

"Yeah, so what? What's that got to do with me?"

"Her name was Jill Cotter. Does that name ring a bell with you?"

"Never heard of her."

Robyn showed him a photograph of the dead woman. "Does that help jog your memory?"

"Nope."

"When Deputy Fuchette talked to you on the telephone the other day, you said you hadn't been back up to Big Lake since sometime in June. Is that correct?"

"Yeah."

"That's part of the problem we have," Weber said. He handed him a copy of the traffic citation that was issued in September.

"If you weren't there, how did you get this ticket?"

"Oh, yeah. I forgot about that."

"You forgot you were up there? How does someone drive 250 miles to a place where they own a house, get a traffic ticket, and forget all about it?"

Mitchell tried to backtrack and failed miserably. "Okay, I was up there. But I misunderstood the question when you asked me about it. You asked about the house, and I said I hadn't been there since June. That was true. When I came up there in September I didn't stop at the house. I was scouting for elk for hunting season."

"So you drove all the way up there to scout for elk. How long were you there?"

"A couple of days."

"You were there a couple of days, but you never went to the house? Where did you stay?"

"What's with all the questions?"

"I told you, we've got a situation up there.

"And I told you that's your problem. That's all I got to say."

He started to close the door, but Weber put his hand against it.

"Hey, man!"

"Look, we can do this one of two ways," the sheriff said. "You can answer our questions standing here, or I can have a talk with the local police department and ask them to bring you down to the station, and we can talk there. Either way, it doesn't matter to me."

A woman from the apartment across the hall opened her door and looked out curiously, then closed the door again.

"Perfect. That's just what I need, the neighbors telling everybody the cops were here."

"Don't blame us," Weber said. "I asked if we could come in and you said no."

"You're a real asshole, do you know that?"

"It's been suggested a time or two in the past," Weber replied. "Now, what's it going to be? Do we talk out here, inside your apartment, or at the police station?"

Mitchell looked at him and shook his head, then stepped back to allow them to enter the apartment. The place was furnished in typical separated bachelor style. Cheap furniture, a big screen TV against one wall, a delivery pizza box sitting on a coffee table with the lid open. It looked like it had been there for more than a day or two.

"Okay, yeah, I was up at Big Lake. So what?"

"Making a false statement to a police officer is a crime. Did you know that? What with the legal problems you've got already, between your upcoming divorce and your possession charge, do you really need any more trouble?"

"How did I know she was really a cop when she called? It was just a voice on the telephone. For all I knew, it was some private investigator my wife hired. Or just some snoopy friend of hers."

"Maybe so. But how about you make all of our lives easier and just answer our questions so we can get out of your way?"

"Whatever."

"Take a look at this picture again. And remember, lying to a cop is against the law. Now, do you know Jill Cotter?"

Mitchell nodded "I know her name's Jill. I never bothered to ask her what her last name is."

"Was," Weber said. "Past tense. She's the woman we found in the lake."

"No way!"

"Yeah, way. Tell me what you know about her."

"Look, man, I've got a lot of hassles with this divorce and everything. If this gets back to Samantha she's gonna use it to make me look even worse when we get to court."

Weber wasn't sure how it would be possible to make this guy look any worse, but he didn't say that. Instead he said, "At this point there's no reason for your wife to know this conversation ever took place."

"Okay, yeah, I know her. But like I said, I never knew her last name. What happened to her?"

"That's what we're trying to find out now," Weber told him. "Tell me how you met her and anything else you can."

"I ran into her a couple of years ago when we were up there. Actually, I think it was last year. She was working as a waitress at some little diner there in town. We went there for lunch and she took our order, and I kind of thought she was hot. I didn't say anything about her being hot, but right away Samantha saw me looking at her and started accusing me of flirting with her. That bitch thinks if you ever even look at another woman you're cheating. So, just to piss her off, I left the waitress a nice tip."

"And?"

"And, I made it a point of stopping in there again the next day, while Samantha was doing something at the house. Jill and I got to talking and we kind of hit it off, and she gave me her phone number. It went by a couple of weeks and Samantha was pulling one of her marathon shifts at the hospital, and I went back up to the house and called Jill. She said her husband was a truck driver and was out of town, so I asked her to come over. I guess you can figure out the rest."

"This was last year?"

"Yeah, I don't remember exactly when. But it was before Samantha kicked me out."

"And did you see Jill after that?"

"A couple of times I went up there and we got together."

"When was the last time?"

"When I got the traffic ticket."

"And she came to your house? The place on Echo Lane?"

"Yeah. She said she had a nosy neighbor and didn't want me coming around there. She said my place made the perfect little love nest."

"And you're sure that's the last time you saw her?"

"Yeah, I'm sure."

"Think about it before you say that," Weber warned.

"It's the truth. I swear it."

"And when was the last time you were at the house?"

"Then. That time with her in September. I swear, I haven't seen her since. We talked on the phone a couple of times, and she talked about coming down here when her husband was out of town. But it never happened."

"Did you and Jill use drugs together?"

"No, man. I told you, that was all a frame up."

"And I told you, lying to a cop's going to get your ass thrown right back behind bars. Answer the question."

"No, I swear. She'd have a few drinks, but that was it."

"Did she ever seem to have any health problems?"

"Health problems? Like what?"

"Did she ever complain of being sick or not feeling good?"

"No, not that I can remember. We didn't spend a lot of time telling each other all about our lives or anything like that. It was just casual sex."

"You said the last time you were up there was in September, right?"

"Yeah, that was the last time."

"If that's the truth, can you tell me why we found Jill Cotter's car in the garage of your house up there on Echo Lane?"

"No way! I don't know what's going on, but I haven't been up there and there's no way that her car was in the garage."

"I'm afraid so. How do you explain that?"

"I can't, man. You can check my work schedule, or ping my phone, or whatever it is you guys do to tell where a person's been. The last time I was up there was that time I saw Jill in September."

"Did you by any chance give her a key to the house?"

"How stupid do I look to you?"

When he was growing up, Weber's mother had always taught him that if you didn't have anything nice to say, don't say anything at all. So he didn't reply to Mason Mitchell's question.

~***~

"Do you believe him?"

"I think he's a slimy, cheating SOB," Robyn said, buckling her seatbelt on the passenger side of her Ford Mustang as Weber started the engine. "But yeah, I think he was telling the truth about that being the last time he saw Jill. He's smart enough to know that we can trace phone records and the GPS locater on his ankle monitor and we would find out otherwise if he was lying. But just to be sure, I'll double check on that."

"So where does that leave us?"

"Well, we don't know much else about the case at this point, except that it was Mason that Greg Sterling saw with Jill, not Scott Welch."

"And?"

"That's as far as that goes, Jimmy. But as for where it leaves us, it's way too late to drive all the way back to Big Lake tonight. So I've got just two words for you."

"Oh yeah? What are those two words?"

She grinned at him in the reflected parking lot lights and said, "Motel sex."

"Oh, I like those two words," Weber said with a smile as he shifted the Mustang into gear.

Chapter 37

Robyn knew there would be hell to pay if her mother found out they had been that close and had not stopped in to visit, so Saturday morning they drove to Glendale to see her parents.

"What a surprise! What are you doing in town?" Renée Fuchette asked when she answered the door.

"We had to come down to take care of some business, and wanted to stop in and say hello," Robyn said.

"Good to see you, honey," her father said, wrapping her up in a big hug, then shaking Weber's hand. "Jimmy. Good to see you, too. Come in, come in."

"Can I get you something to eat? You must be famished."

"No, we're fine, Mom," Robyn told her. "We just had breakfast."

"It's only a little after 9 o'clock. How early did you have to leave this morning to get here by now?"

"Actually, we came down last night."

"What? You were here all night and you're just now coming by?"

"Like I said, we had to come down on police business. We took care of that last night, and we have to head back up the mountain pretty soon. But I at least wanted to stop and say hello."

"Well, I don't understand, Robyn. Where did you stay?"

"At a hotel. Where else would we stay?"

"Why would you do that? Your bedroom is still here, and we have a guest bedroom for him." Renée didn't like Weber, and didn't approve of her daughter's relationship with the sheriff. She seldom missed an opportunity to let that be known, either subtly or outright.

"*He* has a name, Mother."

"Of course he does. I'm sorry, I meant Jim. But why did you stay in a hotel when you could have come here?"

"Because it was late when we got in and finished our business. And besides, Mom, we're all grownups here, so let's be honest. We sleep together, not in separate bedrooms."

"I can't control what you do when you're somewhere else, but in this house..."

"Oh, put a cork in it, Renée," her husband said. "*That's* why they didn't stay here. And I can't blame them."

"Of course you see no problem with your daughter sleeping with a man outside of marriage. You have no standards, Bill Fuchette. Well, I'm sorry, but I do!"

"And with that, we'll say goodbye," Robyn said, starting to rise from the table.

"Please, stay a few minutes at least," her father said.

"No, Daddy, that's all right."

"I'm sorry," her mother said. "I should have just kept my mouth shut. Please don't leave. Let me at least make you some coffee. And I made some croissants. I know you just ate, but croissants were always your favorite, Robyn."

"They may be my favorite, but they're not my waistline's."

"Oh, hush now. You look just fine."

Her mother busied herself making coffee and warming up the croissants. Robyn looked at Weber and rolled her eyes. He gave her a slight smile in return. This wasn't their first rodeo.

"So the news has had the story about that woman you found in the lake. Is that what you're down here for?"

"Yes, Daddy. We had to talk to somebody about the case."

"Do you know what happened to her yet?"

"We're working on it."

While her mother hated the fact that Robyn was a police officer, her father had always been proud of her, and had even gone on a few ride-alongs with Robyn when her parents came to town for a visit.

"I think it's just scandalous. How did she end up in the lake, naked like that, anyway?"

"We don't know that yet, Mom. But we'll figure it out."

"I'm sure you will," her father said. "And what's the thing with the Santa Claus? Was that some kind of a publicity stunt?"

"Well, it got a lot of publicity," Weber replied, "But I don't think it's the kind the mayor wanted."

Bill laughed and asked, "Is he still being a thorn in your side?"

"I don't know about in my side, but he's a pain in another part of my body, that's for sure."

They chatted while they had their coffee and croissants, keeping the conversation light, and then said their goodbyes and left.

"Why do I always feel like I just came out of a battle every time I see my mother?"

Weber stopped at the entrance to their subdivision to let an elderly couple cross in front of them.

"She does have a way of getting under your skin, doesn't she?"

"Just once, Jimmy. Just once I'd like her to show a little bit of pride in me and the things I've accomplished. Pride hell, if she would just accept me for who I am, that would be enough!"

It was a conversation they had had before, and Weber knew they were not going to solve anything having it this time around either. But he also knew that Robyn needed to vent, so he listened as he began the long drive back to Big Lake.

~***~

"You really don't have to be here for this," Weber said, turning off the car's engine.

"Yeah, I do," Robyn told him. " I need to make my amends to Darcy, too."

They got out of the Mustang and walked up to the door of the house and Weber rang the bell. Scott Welch answered and gave them a withering look.

"Now what?"

"Scott, can we come in?"

"Are you here to accuse me of something else I didn't do?"

"No, sir, I'm here to apologize," Weber told him.

The man looked at them both for a long moment, deciding whether or not to slam the door in their faces, then stepped back and waved them inside. Darcy was just coming into the room, asking, "Scott, who was at the door?" She saw them and stopped in her tracks. There was no mistaking the look of anger on her face. "What do you guys want?"

"Scott, Darcy. We came to apologize to you. We have found out who the man was who was with Jill Cotter at that house on Echo Lane and we know now that it wasn't you, Scott."

"Isn't that what he told you all along? Isn't that what I told you?"

"Yes, it is," Weber said. "We were wrong."

"You were wrong? That's it? You were wrong?"

"We had a very good reason to think it was, Scott," Weber told her. "Someone positively identified him."

"Well, they were wrong!"

"Yes, ma'am, they were. May I show you both something?"

It was obvious by Darcy's body language, arms folded tightly across her chest, that she wasn't in a forgiving mood. But she did look at the photograph Weber showed them of Mason Mitchell.

"Okay, so he looks a lot like Scott. That's still no reason to blame him."

"Again, Darcy, it was an honest mistake. The person who told us he saw Scott with Jill Cotter really believed it was him. And I think if you saw the two of them at a distance you would think the same thing, too."

"I would know my husband when I saw him."

"That may be true, Darcy," Robyn said, "but it wasn't you seeing your husband, it was somebody else seeing someone who looks very much like a man he knew from here in town."

"And that's supposed to make it all right?"

"No, it doesn't make it all right," Weber said. "But you have to put yourself in our position. We have to go with the..."

"No, I don't have to put myself in your position," Darcy said, her voice rising. "I'm in *my* position! You guys accused my husband of having an affair and made him take a lie detector test and everything else. What are people going to say in this town?"

"Just to clarify, Darcy, Scott volunteered to take a polygraph test. And he passed it. Now, as for what people are going to say in town, as far as I know, nobody else knows about this. I can't guarantee that, but I know that none of my people will ever reveal anything about a case. Yes, there are tongues that wag all over the place. There always have been, and there always will be. None of us can control that. But as far as I know, nobody has any reason to even know that we talked to Scott about the case."

"Any reason? You and that one deputy came right to the store and took him back in the office twice."

"That's true, Darcy," Robyn said. "But that doesn't mean they were talking to Scott about the Cotter case. For all anybody knows they could have been investigating a shoplifting, or, I don't know, talking about hunting or fishing, or whatever guys talk about."

"I have to admit, the guy does look a lot like me," Scott said, looking at the photograph of Mason Mitchell. "I can see where someone could get the two of us confused."

"And that's all it was," Weber told him. "Simple confusion on the part of a witness who was trying to do the right thing. Nobody was trying to single you out, Scott. Nobody was trying to make your life miserable, ruin your reputation, or anything like that. It was just a mistake, and we were following up and doing our job."

Scott Welch nodded, seeming to accept what the sheriff was telling him. But his wife remained steadfast, arms still folded over her chest, her eyes boring through them. "Just doing your job. Isn't that the same excuse the Nazis used when they put those millions of people in the concentration camps? They were just doing their jobs."

Nick Russell

Chapter 38

It had been mid-afternoon by the time they got back to town, and after their uncomfortable visit with Scott and Darcy Welch, Weber and Robyn checked in at the sheriff's office to see what had happened while they were out of town.

"Nothing much going on last night," Coop said. "A couple of routine calls for things like barking dogs and loud music. Tommy nailed a guy for doing 80 miles an hour in a 55 zone out on the highway, and him and Jordan broke up a fight at the Redeye. No injuries, they sent both guys home and told them that if they gave them any more trouble or were seen out on the street again all night, they were going to jail. See boss, you can actually leave town and the sky doesn't fall."

"Thank you, Coop, I keep telling him that," Robyn said. "If he had his way, we'd have our honeymoon right here in town."

"Come on guys, I'm not that bad."

"I beg your pardon? You micromanage everything, Jimmy. You think if you are gone for more than a couple of hours the whole damned office is going to collapse into chaos."

"Boy, talk about the pot calling the kettle black," Weber said. "What are *you* doing here on a Saturday, Mary?"

"I'm just passing through. Pete's at the barbershop getting his hair cut, and then we're driving over to Show Low to see my nephew Alan's new baby."

"Oh cool," Robyn said. "You're a great-aunt."

"Trust me, girl, I'm great at everything I do!"

"I never had a doubt in my mind," Robyn assured her.

"So it looks like this Mitchell guy wasn't the one that was with Jill Cotter when she died, even though everything points right at him?"

"I wish it was him, Coop," Robyn said. "Because he's a guy I would definitely like to put the cuffs on. But we checked with the P.D. down there and according to the tracking unit on his ankle bracelet, the only places he's been to are work and home. He's being a good boy. Or at least as good as a maggot like him can be."

"Maybe this last bust woke him up and he's learned a lesson."

"Oh, please," Robyn said. "He's trying to keep out of trouble until his court date, and hoping everything will blow over before the final divorce proceedings. Guys like that don't change. You know that as well as I do. You could beat them over the head until your hands fell off, and it wouldn't make any difference."

Something she said niggled at Weber's mind, but he couldn't get a handle on it at the moment. And before he could say anything, his cell phone rang.

"What's up, Parks?"

"I'm in need of a big, bloody steak, and Marsha threatened to feed me something called tofu. What the hell is that?"

"Trust me, it's not something you're going to like."

"Do you guys want to meet us at the Roundup in about an hour?"

"Fine with me. Let me ask Robyn." He took the phone away from his ear and asked, "Roundup in about an hour?"

"Sounds good. That breakfast and my mom's croissant wore off a couple of hours ago."

"Do you and Roberta want to join us, Coop?"

"I'll give her a call and see."

Weber put the phone back to his mouth and said, "We'll see you there. Coop and his lady friend might be joining us, too."

"The more the merrier," Parks told him. "If you all keep Marsha distracted enough, I might even be able to eat dessert."

~***~

The Roundup Steakhouse was a Big Lake icon, popular for generations with the locals as well as all the tourists. The place was always busy on weekends, but they got there early enough to avoid the crowds and took a circular booth under a massive set of steer horns hanging on the rough cedar wall. The decor was typical Western, with old saddles and branding irons sharing wall space with mounted deer and elk heads. Several old Winchester rifles hung from hooks high up on the walls, and a large mounted black bear stood behind a small split rail wood corral in the center of the room, greeting visitors.

"Hi, Roberta, I'm glad you could make it on such short notice," Robyn said as Coop and Roberta sat down.

"Are you kidding me? I've been hearing how good the food is here since I got back to town. I remember when I was a little girl, we used to come in here sometimes for dinner on special occasions like birthdays. That was before my accident, and I still remember this giant stuffed bear they had in the middle of the room. That thing terrified me, and my older brother always told me it was going to come to life and eat me."

"It's still there," Coop told her. "But don't worry, I'm pretty sure it's dead, after standing there all these years. But if it makes a move, I'll shoot it."

"My hero," Roberta cooed.

"Aren't these two just precious?"

"Hey, you women are all precious at first," Parks said. "Then the next thing you know everything changes. I'm warning you right now, Jimmy, I love Robyn and all that, but all that lovey dovey stuff ain't gonna last. It starts out with breakfast in bed and rubbing your feet at night, and the next thing you know you're out in the backyard with a scooper picking up dog poop and she's trying to make you eat tofu!"

"Listen to him complain," Marsha said, laughing. "After all the manure he shoveled back home on the farm and the BS he spread's around here, he's got it good. And as for the tofu, I'm just trying to keep you healthy so you'll be around longer."

"The reason you want me around longer is so you'll have somebody to abuse."

Marsha laughed and jabbed him in the ribs with her thumb. "You love every minute of it, and we all know it."

"You'd better watch what you're saying, Parks. Don't forget, Robyn carries a gun, too."

"I'm not saying anything against Robyn. She's like a sister to me."

"Being from rural Oklahoma like he is, that might not be a good thing," Marsha said. "Run, Robyn, run!"

"All I'm saying is that I've been married," Parks continued. "And I know what it's like. You think you're marrying this sexy nymphomaniac, then pretty soon you wake up one morning and the nympho's gone and all you've got left is the maniac."

"You were married before? How come I never knew that?"

"I don't know, Bubba. I guess it never came up."

"Well, I knew," Marsha said primly. "We have no secrets between us."

"Really? So you know about that cross-dressing phase he went through, when he was a stripper in Des Moines and went by the name of Carmen?"

"No, Jimmy, I never did know that. But I guess that explains why he's so good at putting my makeup on."

"When you say putting your makeup on, is he putting it on you, or on himself?"

"Whatever goes on behind doors is none of your business," Marsha said, grinning.

"Seriously, you were married before, Parks?"

"Yeah. Back when I was in the Navy. It didn't last long, less than two years."

"What happened?" Robyn asked. "Or is that too personal?"

"Nothing happened. It was just a bad idea right from the start. We were both real young and it was more a case of hormones than love, I think. Then I went out on sea duty for a few months, and when I got back we both knew the whole thing was a mistake. I think we tried to fool ourselves for a little while, until the next time my ship went out. When I got back to Norfolk she was gone."

"I'm sorry."

"Not me," Parks told her. "I've had a wonderful life, and now I get to hang out up here with you and Jimmy and Coop and Roberta and everybody else. And when I go home, I get to scoop up dog poop. It just doesn't get any better than that!"

A young waitress wearing a western shirt and calico skirt, along with red boots and a cowboy hat, brought a tray of water to their table, took their drink orders, and left.

"So, what other advice do you have for a soon to be married couple, oh wise and wonderful Parks?"

"To you, Robyn? Just forget you ever heard the word tofu. A man needs red meat to get through the day. And the night," he added, leering at Marsha. "And for you, Jimmy. Just look at her mother, because that's who you're going to be married to a few years down the road."

"Oh please, don't say that," Robyn said with a sour look on her face. "Have you ever met my mother, Parks? I swear, she's like the Wicked Witch of the West in the *Wizard of Oz*."

"Ouch, sore subject. Sorry I brought that up."

"You know, we stopped on the way back home this morning, and we weren't in the door five minutes before she was letting us know that she doesn't approve of Jimmy and me being together?"

"Now, to her mother's credit, she does make a pretty good croissant," Weber said, trying to lighten the mood.

"Don't defend her, Jimmy. You know what a witch she can be."

Before he could reply, the waitress was back with their drinks and took their meal orders. Parks ignored Marsha's protests when he ordered a 20 ounce ribeye, rare, and a double order of steak fries. "And do you have tofu?"

"Tofu? I don't think so, but I can check for you," the waitress said.

"No, I was being sure you don't have it. If you do, put it in a big bag and seal it up real tight and take it outside and throw it in the trash, will you?"

Not sure how to respond, the waitress just said, "Whatever you say, sir."

She left and they laughed, then Marsha said, "I know why you come in here. It's not about the food, you just like to have pretty girls call you sir, don't you? That's just one more of your kinks that I just figured out."

"Well, keep figuring, baby," Parks told her. "Because there are a lot more kinks where that came from."

They were halfway through dinner, and Roberta was telling them about an incident that happened while she was in law school that involved a fellow student who was giving an oral report to the class and used the term justice is blind. The poor boy had fallen all over himself trying to backtrack and say something he thought would be less offensive, while the rest of the class, Roberta included, had a great laugh about it.

Just as she finished her story, a couple stopped by their table. "Hi Jimmy, sorry to interrupt, but I was wondering how Tom Cotter is doing?"

"He's having a rough time of it, Wally."

"That was such a shame about Jill. It just broke both of our hearts. We both really felt bad, especially after what happened with her before," the woman said.

"You knew Jill?"

"You didn't know?"

"Know what, Wally?"

"Jill worked for us for about two months. But we had to fire her."

"Can I ask why?"

The man looked around, then motioned Weber to follow him to a corner, away from the customer tables. He lowered his voice and said, "I really don't want to speak ill of the dead, Jimmy. And we hated to do it, because we've known Tom for as long as I can remember. But we had to fire Jill because she was a thief."

Chapter 39

Wally McKnight was a short, stout man who was missing the thumb on his left hand, the result of a steer roping accident when he had been a young man growing up on his family's ranch. He had thinning white hair, a beard of the same color, and unruly eyebrows above slightly bulging blue eyes. Weber always thought he would make an excellent Santa Claus. Well, maybe not the skydiver style the mayor had thought up.

His wife, Sharon, was a thickset woman with a generous bosom who was half a head taller than her husband. He remembered that she had been a substitute teacher for a while, working part-time when she wasn't helping Wally in the office or out showing homes.

Their small real estate business had been the only one in Big Lake for years before the out of town developers discovered the place. They had handled the sale of the family ranch after the untimely death of his parents caused Weber to take a hardship discharge from the Army to return to Big Lake to run the ranch and raise his teenaged sister. It hadn't taken him long to discover that he didn't like horses and cows any better as a young man than he had as a teenager, and he had sold off the livestock and most of the land, keeping only a small parcel and the family home when he took a job with the Sheriff's Department.

They were seated in the real estate office with Coop and Weber, who had finished their meals and then made their apologies and left, Robyn promising to get Roberta home safely.

"Business isn't what it used to be like around here, Jimmy," Wally was telling them. "Used to be, Sharon and I could run the place just fine all by ourselves. But with so many people coming in and buying property and selling property and everything, we felt like we had to expand just to keep up. So we brought in two agents to help us out."

"And Jill Cotter was one of those agents?"

"No, not Jill. We had a man named Ted Drury, and a young woman named Rachel Faust. Ted wasn't much of a salesman and didn't last long, but Rachel's still with us. We took on Jill to just be kind of a general assistant. Answering the phones when everybody had to be out of the office, or going to the houses that we have listed and doing a walk-through and making sure they look good before we showed them, going around town and making sure signs were standing up in front of the properties like they were supposed to be. You'd be surprised how many kids come along and knock over real estate signs."

"I don't think it's kids," Sharon said. "Sometimes I think some of our competitors are doing that."

"Maybe so, but we don't know that," Wally said. "At any rate, we hired Jill because we know Tom, and we figured with him being gone so much of the time with his truck, the job would fit into her schedule. We're pretty flexible around here."

"So what happened that you had to fire her?"

"At first, we didn't give it a lot of thought," Wally replied. "But a couple of small items came up missing from houses that were listed. Nothing big, one of those tablet computers from one house, and a little silver earring box from another place."

"And Jill took them?"

"I can't prove that one way or the other, Jimmy, so I don't want to say. But she had been in both places within a day or so before the items went missing. Now, keep in mind that just about everything up here is multiple listing, so there could have been other people in and out of those houses besides Jill."

"What does multiple listing mean?"

"The way it works is, when someone comes to us and lists their house for sale, if we sell it for them, we get all the commission. But it's available to all of the different real estate companies up here and if an agent from another company sells it, we split the commission."

"So how do you know when another agent is showing a house? And how do they get into it? Do they come by and pick up the key from you or what?"

"No, when a house has a multiple listing, a lockbox goes on the door. Every agent has a master key that fits all of the lockboxes, so they can show it without having to try to track us down and get a key. They are supposed to enter it in the computer program for the listing when they show a property. But I think sometimes people cut corners and don't bother."

"Okay, and how does Jill fit into all this?"

"Like I said, part of her job was to go check on houses and make sure everything looked okay and pick up any paperwork or brochures or anything that somebody else left, so she had one of the lockbox keys. One night about a month ago, Sharon went to visit her sister because she wasn't feeling good and needed some cough syrup. Driving home, she passed a house on Shiloh Way and noticed the lights on and Jill's car in the driveway. This was like at 8:30 at night and there was no reason for her to be there. In fact, there wasn't any reason for her to be there at any time. We hadn't sent her there for anything."

"What happened?"

"Well, I stopped and went in to see what was going on," Sharon said, "and Jill was there with some guy."

"Some guy? Do you know who it was?"

"No, I had never seen him before."

"What happened then?"

"I asked her what was going on and why they were there. She came up with some nonsense about how he had stopped in the office at the last minute and said he wanted to look at some properties, and since nobody else was there she decided to show him around. Well, I knew that was a lie, because the office closed at 5 o'clock and this was over three hours later. And she wasn't an agent, it wasn't her job to show anybody around. Not to mention, it was dark by then. Nobody shows a property in the dark. She should have made an appointment for one of us to meet with him the next day."

"Maybe she was overzealous, hoping to make brownie points or get ahead," Coop suggested.

"Maybe so, I don't know. But at any rate, I gave the man my card and told him to contact us the next day if he wanted to see the placc, and I got them both out of there. After they were gone, I found three empty beer bottles in the trash. Fresh beer bottles, Jimmy."

"What did you do about it?"

"We talked about it a long time that night when Sharon got home," Wally said. "And we decided that as much as we like and respect Tom, we couldn't let that go on like nothing ever happened. We decided we'd sit Jill down and have a stern talk with her and tell her that she was skating on real thin ice with us."

"How did she handle that?"

"She didn't handle it at all," Sharon said. "She didn't come in the next day, or call, or anything. By that point I was pretty fed up, so I went to their house to have it out with her. She tried to say she was sick and had turned her phone off and overslept, but by then I wasn't having any of it. I told her I needed her keys back and that we would talk about it when she felt she was well enough to return to work. She gave me the office keys, and I never noticed anything until a day or two later, when she still hadn't come back to work."

"Then you noticed something, Sharon? What was that?"

"The lockbox key was gone from the ring."

"Did you ask her about it?"

"You bet we did. We drove right to her house, and she wasn't home, but going back to the office we saw her car coming the other way. So Wally made a U-turn right there in the middle of the road and followed her. When she pulled into her driveway we got out and told her we needed the key. She swore up and down she didn't have it. She tried to say that it had been on the key ring, so it must have gotten lost or something. But we both knew she had stolen it."

"That's when we fired her," Wally said. "Hated to do it, since we know Tom and all, but she left us no choice."

Cooper looked at Weber and said, "Well, another piece of the puzzle falls into place. Now we know how she got into that house on Echo Lane."

Chapter 40

"So, now we have the connection between Jill Cotter and the house on Echo Lane, and we know how she got in there," Weber said Monday morning. "What we don't know is how she ended up dead and naked in the lake, and how she got there from the house. And we don't know who put her car in the garage."

"Obviously that was the same person," Coop said. "Now we just have to figure out who he is. And what caused Jill to have a heart attack. And why the guy didn't call 911 to get her some help or something, instead of dumping her in the lake."

"Who can be that heartless?"

"Lots of people, Robyn," Coop said. "More than I would ever care to tell you about."

"I'd say we're talking about somebody with something to hide," Weber said.

"Yeah, but what, Jimmy?"

"Besides the fact that he had a dead woman on his hands? A dead married woman? A dead married woman who had just ingested cocaine in a house they had no business being in? I think a lot of guys would want to hide that, don't you?"

"You've got a point," Robyn said. "So what's the next step? We need to wrap this up and hopefully give Tom Cotter some closure."

Weber hated that word. He always had. How do you put closure on a tragedy? Would arresting somebody for raping a woman or murdering a child, or locking up some drunk driver who had killed a family make everything go away for their victims and those left behind? He had experienced more than his share of personal tragedy, from the loss of his parents to the way his sister had ended up, and he had never been able to experience closure. To him, there was no such thing.

"You know, I'm thinking about the guys that we know that Jill was involved with. All the men we talked to. And looking at them, what have we got?"

"Beats me, Coop. What?"

"We've got Mike Sanders, at the muffler shop. A nice guy who broke it off with Jill as soon as he found out she was still married. Is he the kind of man that would dump her body in the lake?"

"I don't see that happening," Weber said.

"I don't either. So then we've got Lonnie Henderson. Old Lonnie makes no secret of the fact that he's a hound dog. What was it he said to you, if it's offered he's going to take it or something like that?"

"Yeah, something like that."

"Again, Lonnie seems pretty nonchalant about stepping out on his wife. Almost like he doesn't care if she finds out or not."

"I think she knows all about his extracurricular activities," Mary said. "This is a small town and word gets around."

"If that's the case, why does she put up with it?"

"I don't know what to tell you, Robyn," Mary said, shaking her head. "Shelly was never what you would call beautiful growing up. Always a little bit overweight, she was the girl that got stuck playing the best friend role to the pretty, popular girls. Maybe she lucked out and married a guy who goes to work every day and brings home a paycheck, and she figures that's the best she's ever going to do. So she tolerates the rest of it. She traded the best friend role for being the wife of the good-looking man the other girls missed out on."

Weber couldn't help thinking of his beautiful blonde sister, Debbie, and how she and Marsha Perry had always been best friends. Marsha had played that same role, the best friend to the pretty girl, but Marsha's self-confidence and sense of humor would never allow her to settle for just becoming someone's wife. She was her own person and made no apologies for it.

"Anyway, getting back to Lonnie," Coop said, "I don't see him going through that much effort to try to hide anything. I think the worst he would have done would be to leave Jill's body there and call 911 anonymously. And he may be a dirt bag in the way he treats his wife, but would he dump a woman's body like that?"

"I don't think so."

"Neither do I. So who does that leave us with?"

"Our favorite bartender?"

"You got it, Reggie Sosin."

"He's certainly sleazy and callous enough to do it," Coop said. "I think we need to bring him in here and have another talk with him, on our turf."

Nick Russell

Chapter 41

"I want a lawyer."

"Those are the first words out of your mouth? You want a lawyer? Why is that, Reggie?"

"Because I'm not an idiot, Sheriff. First you come by my business hassling me, then you send a deputy out to bring me in? I wasn't born yesterday."

"Okay, it's certainly your right to have an attorney present before we talk to you. Do you have somebody you want to call?"

"Yeah, his name is Tom MacArthur, and he's down in Phoenix."

"That's fine," Weber said. "Give him a call. Do you have his number or do you need us to look it up for you?"

"I've got it."

"Fine, we'll leave you alone so you can talk to him. When you're done, open the door there and the deputy will come and get me."

"How do I know the room's not bugged?"

"You watch too much television, Reggie. Would you rather we put you in a cell? Or in one of the bathrooms to make your call? Or do you think they're bugged, too?"

"I don't trust you guys."

"I can understand that. For what it's worth, I don't much trust you, either. Make your call."

Weber left the room and walked out into the main office.

"I ran his record again, just to be sure, and he's clean," Robyn said. "For what that's worth."

"Everybody who ever got into trouble with the law had to start someplace," Coop said. "But usually they do start earlier in life than this guy."

"Did you see that smug look on his face when Dan brought him in? Like he's so much smarter than everybody else. I wanted to slap him upside the head and tell him we're not the hicks he thinks we are."

"He'll find that out soon enough, Robyn," Coop said.

Again something vague, like a distant memory or a song lyric long forgotten, teased Weber's mind. It lay right on the edge of awareness, but was too ephemeral to grasp. Before he could focus and try to figure out what it was, Deputy Dan Wright came down the hall and said, "His lawyer wants to talk to you."

Weber and Coop went back to the interview room and Sosin pushed the phone across the table to him. Weber picked it up and identified himself.

"Sheriff, my name is Thomas MacArthur and I am Mr. Sosin's attorney. I want to go on the record as saying that this is outrageous. How dare you accuse a respected businessman in your community of something like this?"

"Something like what, Mr. MacArthur?"

"Of being involved in the death of that woman. My client has already told you that he had nothing to do with it."

"For the record, Mr. MacArthur, nobody is accusing your client of anything at this point. I simply want to ask him a few more questions about his relationship with a woman who died under mysterious circumstances."

"I've instructed Mr. Sosin not to answer your questions, Sheriff, and I expect you to release him immediately."

"It's been my experience that innocent people don't have a problem talking to the police. So why is it that your client has a problem doing it?"

"That's enough, Sheriff Weber. I told you already, I want Mr. Sosin released immediately."

"Well, I'm afraid that's not going to happen."

"Is Mr. Sosin under arrest?"

"He is being detained at this point, pending further investigation."

"That's outrageous, Sheriff!"

"Maybe it is, in your opinion," Weber said. "I might suggest you make a trip up here and consult with your client, then we'll take it from there."

"There is no way this will hold up in court."

"Really? Given the evidence we have, I'll take my chances."

"How many times do I have to tell you, I didn't have anything to do with whatever happened to Jill?"

"Quiet, Reggie," MacArthur said.

"I don't think he heard that, let me put it on speakerphone for you," Weber said, pushing the button to make the call public. "You might want to repeat that advice to your client again, sir."

"Reggie, I said be quiet. Don't say another word to those people."

"I don't have time to sit here until you drive all the way up here, Tom."

"As your attorney, my advice is not to say another word. I have some things on my plate today and I can't get free. But I can be there first thing in the morning."

"In the morning? Can they keep me here overnight?"

"I'm afraid so, Reggie. They can detain you for up to 24 hours, then they have to either arrest you or let you go. If they arrest you, they have to take you before a judge within 72 hours."

"That's three days! I have a business to run, I can't sit here for three days."

"Actually, it's four days," Weber said. "Like your attorney just told you, we can detain you for 24 hours before we file charges, then we have 72 hours to take you to see the judge."

"Thank you for the lesson in Arizona jurisprudence, Sheriff," MacArthur said sarcastically.

"No problem, sir. We believe in total transparency around here so your client won't have any surprises coming."

"This is an abuse of your power, Sheriff."

"If you feel that way, you are certainly welcome to file a complaint, Mr. MacArthur."

"I want to speak to my client again, in private."

"Sure," Weber said. "You know the routine, Reggie. Just let us know when you're off the phone."

They had barely made it down the hallway and out into the main office when Dan summoned them back.

The phone was out of sight, and Sosin demanded, "Why are you guys trying to put this on me?"

Weber turned on a portable digital recorder and said, "Before you say anything else, I am going to have Deputy Cooper read you your rights."

"Am I under arrest?"

"No, I just want to make sure you know all of your rights so there's no question about things later on. Go ahead, Coop."

Once Coop had informed Sosin of his legal rights under the Miranda law, Weber said, "When you first came in here, you said you wanted to talk to an attorney. You talked to him, and he advised you not to say anything to us. A wise man would follow his attorney's advice."

"No way I'm sitting in a jail cell for three or four days while you guys play games with me. I'll be out of business before you get done."

"I'd hate to see that happen," Weber said.

"What do you want to know?"

"Are you waiving your rights to talk to us without your attorney being present?"

"Yeah. Let's get this over with. I've got better things to do than sit here talking to you guys all day."

"When was the last time you saw Jill Cotter?"

"I told you before, two or three weeks ago."

"And where was that at?"

"At the bar."

"At your place of business? The Redeye Saloon?"

"Yeah. She came in a couple of hours before closing time and hung around. Once the place was closed and everybody was gone, me and her did our thing."

"You did your thing? Can you be a little more specific than that?"

"We had sex. Do you want to know the position or what?"

"I don't think that will be necessary," Weber said. "Did this happen in the bar? In the Redeye?"

"Yeah. Sometimes Jill seemed to like a little bit of danger. I think she got a thrill out of thinking that somebody might catch us. Like one of the waitresses coming back for something."

"And that's the last time you saw her?"

"Yeah, that was it."

"Did you talk to her after that?"

"No, man. I told you before, it wasn't like we were in love or anything like that. It was just sex. I know that might sound like I was using her, and I guess maybe I was. But at the same time, she was using me, too. We both knew what it was all about, and neither one of us had any expectations from the other."

"I know we've asked you this before, Reggie, but did you and Jill ever meet at a house located at 628 Echo Lane, here in Big Lake?"

"No, never."

"Did you ever drive her car?"

"No."

"Were you ever in her car?"

"I don't think so. No, wait, yes I was, one time. We met in the parking lot behind the post office. It must've been about 2 A.M., because I had already closed the bar when she called. She wanted to do it in the backseat of the car, so we did."

"Why there and not at the bar or someplace else? Anybody could have driven through there and caught you guys."

"I already told you she was a freak, man. I think the whole danger thing was part of what got her off."

"You don't much care for women, do you, Reggie?"

"What do you mean?"

"Just that. The way you talk. To you, a woman is just a piece of meat."

"Come on, Sheriff, who are you trying to fool? You've been around. We're all just a piece of meat, one way or the other."

"How tall are you, Reggie?"

"How tall am I?"

"I don't think I stuttered."

"I'm 5'9'."

"You told me you don't do coke. Is that right?"

"I don't do coke, I don't do heroin, I don't do pot, none of that stuff. I want nothing to do with it whatsoever. Or with anybody who uses."

"Let me ask you another question. Would you be willing to take a polygraph test?"

"My attorney's not going to be happy I talked to you guys at all. He'd be really pissed if I agreed to do that."

"Okay, fine. Coop, go ahead and formally arrest this man and we'll take it from there."

"Wait a minute. I've cooperated with you guys. I even did it against the advice of my attorney. What more do you want from me?"

"I want to know what happened to Jill Cotter, and how she ended up in the lake."

"I don't know," Sosin shouted. "Jesus, what's it gonna take to make you guys believe that?"

"Well, you could start by taking a polygraph test. Unless you have something to hide, that is."

"Fine, schedule the damn test. It will prove once and for all that I'm telling you the truth."

"Or, it'll prove that you're lying through your teeth."

"I'm not lying! I told you everything I know about it, which is nothing. Jill and I got together once in a while and got it on. I told you that right up front. Just because you and her old man are friends, you're trying to lay this on me. Well, I didn't have anything to do with it!"

"Coop, see when you can schedule Gordon Schmidt to come back up here, will you?"

"I'm on it," Coop said, leaving the interview room.

There was silence for a couple of minutes, then Sosin said, "Look, I was out of line the way I talked about Jill the other day. I apologize for that. She was a nice girl and I liked her. I really did. As much as I could ever like any woman. My history with them hasn't been all that great."

"Why is that?"

"I never really knew my old man, he was gone while I was still in diapers. My mother, if you want to call her that, was nothing but a drunk. I can't tell you how many "uncles" I had while I was growing up. It didn't take me long to learn that it wasn't worth the effort to get to know their names because none of them lasted very long. My sister's a junkie, and my ex-wife was a stripper who dumped me for some customer who was always sticking hundred dollar bills in her G-string. So now I just keep it casual and don't get attached. It's better that way. And that's the thing Jill wanted, too. She told me right up front that she wasn't looking for a replacement for her husband, just somebody to play with when he was out of town."

Sosin didn't say anything for a minute, then added, "For what it's worth, she didn't deserve to end up that way. I really mean that."

There was a knock on the door and Coop came back in. "The soonest he can get back up here is Thursday at noon."

"Thursday? You guys are gonna keep me locked up until Thursday?"

"No, I'm going to let you go for now," Weber said. "But I expect you back here in this room on Thursday at noon, Reggie. Got it?"

"So, I'm not under arrest?"

"Not right now. But don't leave town, and don't make me have to come looking for you on Thursday. Because if you do, we're going to have a real problem, you and me."

"I won't, I swear it."

"Okay, get out of here."

When he left, Coop asked, "What do you think?"

"I think I don't like the man very much."

"Me either."

"Every time I look at him, I want to start beating on him."

"I know the feeling, boss. Sometimes you run across a guy you want to kick the shit out of, just on general principles."

And that thought, that elusive thought that had been teasing him for a while now suddenly clarified in his mind. Weber remembered someone else he had recently wanted to beat on. Somebody else who had no respect for women. "Hang on," he said, "I want Dan to run a set of fingerprints for me."

Fifteen minutes later Dan called him over to his desk and pointed to his computer screen. "It's a match."

Weber grinned, then turned to Coop and asked, "How would you feel about a road trip?"

Chapter 42

Hurley Wholesale Hardware Supply was a big outfit, the main office and three warehouses covering most of a city block in an industrial park near the junction of Interstates 10 and 25. Tuesday morning Weber and Coop met a detective from the Albuquerque Police Department at an IHOP restaurant and followed him to the business. A receptionist with frizzy red hair and a tired look to her greeted them. When they told her they were there to see Tony Hurley, she asked if they had an appointment.

"No, but I'm pretty sure Mr. Hurley would rather talk to us here than at the police station," said Detective Madeira, the local cop.

"Excuse me, let me see if he's available."

She picked up her telephone, pushed a button, and murmured something quietly into the receiver. Two minutes later a large man wearing a shirt and tie, with a monk's bald spot on the top of his head, came down a hallway.

"I'm Anthony Hurley, Senior. How can I help you?"

"We're looking for Tony," Weber said.

"What's this about?"

"Do you want to have this conversation standing here in front of your receptionist and those other people sitting at their desks?"

He looked at them, then said, "Follow me."

He led them down the hall to a spacious corner office with two walls of windows that overlooked the Sandia Mountains on the northeast side of the city. When they were in the office he closed the door, but did not offer them seats.

"Okay, what's this about?"

"I said we need to talk to Tony."

"I'm sorry, who did you say you are, again?"

"I'm Sheriff Jim Weber from Big Lake, Arizona. And this is Deputy Cooper."

"And I'm Detective Madeira with the Albuquerque Police Department."

"You're the one that beat up my son."

"Did he tell you that?"

"Yes, he did!"

"Well, if I was in his shoes, I'd file an official complaint."

"Don't think we haven't talked about it."

"Meanwhile, you'd better trot him out here."

"And if I don't?"

"Then you'll be interfering with official police business," Detective Madeira said. "And you can go downtown, too."

"You're kidding me. Do you know who I am?"

"I don't care if you're the governor. If you don't get that son of yours out here right now, I'm going to put the cuffs on you," Madeira said.

"I'll have you know that I'm a personal friend of the police chief. *And* the mayor."

"That's nice. Maybe one of them will post bail for you. Where's Tony?"

Weber thought the man might defy them, but apparently Madeira's words had gotten through to him. He went to an intercom on his desk, pushed a button, and said, "Get Tony in here right now."

When Tony entered into his father's office and saw Weber, he did a double take. "What's he doing here?"

"We came to pick you up and take you back to Arizona so you can stand trial for sexual assault."

"I thought you said you weren't going to file those charges if we did what you told us to do."

"New information has come up since then."

"What new information?"

"Tell us about Jill Cotter, Tony. The lady you put in Big Lake."

Tony Hurley may have been a lot of things. A spoiled rich boy. Someone with no respect for women, who saw them only as toys for his pleasure. And an all-around jerk. But the one thing he wasn't was a good poker player. It showed in his face when he heard Weber's words. But he tried to deny it.

"Never heard of her."

"Yeah, you did. And every time you open your mouth and lie to us, you're just digging your grave deeper."

"Okay, maybe I knew her."

"Maybe?"

"Yeah, I knew her. I met her in a bar a few months ago when I was in town and sometimes I'd see her when I was over there."

"And now she's dead, because of you."

"I didn't kill her! She was already dead when I put her in the water."

"Shut up, Tony! Don't say another word until I get an attorney here for you."

"You're going to have to have that attorney come to Big Lake, Mr. Hurley," Weber said. "Because that's where Tony is going."

"You can't just come in here and take him away. Don't you have to extradite him or something?"

"No, sir," Weber told him. "When Tony signed the paperwork to be released after he was arrested, he agreed to come back to Big Lake when charges were filed. He agreed to waive any right to extradition then."

"Whatever you think he did, he didn't."

"You were at that house with Jill when she died, weren't you, Tony?"

"I told you, I didn't kill her."

"We've got your fingerprint from the bottom of the toilet seat, and another partial print from her car when you parked it in the garage."

"I swear, I didn't kill her. She was already dead when I dumped her body in the lake!"

"Shut up, Tony," his father shouted.

"I didn't kill her."

"No? Then how did she die?"

"We were drinking and having sex. She was really wasted, and I convinced her to try some blow. I told her it really adds to the sensation. So we did a couple of lines, and then we started back up again, and all of a sudden she said she couldn't breathe. She kind of panicked and said she needed some air and went out on the back deck."

"This was at the house on Echo Lane in Big Lake?"

"I don't know where it was. We met in a bar and I followed her there. She said it belonged to a friend of hers who was out of town."

"What happened then? After she went out on the deck?"

"Like I said, she was freaking out. She started saying all kinds of stuff that didn't make sense. Just mumbling kind of. And then she took off into the woods bare ass naked. I kept yelling for her to come back, and then went after her. When I caught up to her I tried to get her back to the house. But she kind of gasped and her whole face scrunched up and she fell down. I thought she passed out. I really did. I tried to wake her up, but she was dead."

"Why didn't you call for help?"

"She was dead. Nobody could help her."

"And you were trying to cover your own ass, right?"

"Well, yeah, I guess so. Because I knew the cops would ask me where the coke came from."

"But why put her in the lake? Why not just leave her there?"

"I don't know. I really don't. I just thought if I put her in the lake nobody would ever find her body. I didn't know if they could get DNA or something from me on her, or what. I just couldn't take that chance. And there was this river right there that emptied into the lake, and the ice was out a couple of feet from shore. There was some current there, so I dragged her into the water and waded out and pushed her under the edge of the ice. I figured the current would pull her into the middle of the lake and she'd sink to the bottom and nobody would ever find her."

"Well, you figured wrong," Weber said pulling out his handcuffs. "Turn around and put your hands behind your back."

~***~

"It burns my butt that all we can get him on is abuse of a corpse for what he did to Jill," Robyn said on Friday morning as Coop went back to the cellblock to get Tony Hurley and take him to court to enter a plea. "He deserves more than that."

"He is getting more than that," Weber said. "I talked to the prosecutor and we're also charging him with negligent homicide, since he gave Jill the coke that contributed to her heart attack."

"Will that stick?"

"I sure hope so. But just in case, it took me some talking to convince Kallie Jo we needed to file that original charge against him for assaulting her, too. But when I told her that there was always a chance he'd skate on the negligent homicide charge, and abuse of a corpse wasn't going to get him any jail time, she came around. She knows that someone like him will keep on doing the same thing to other women until somebody finally stands up and says "no more." She decided that she couldn't live with herself if she let that happen."

"Nobody ever said that girl doesn't have some backbone to her," Mary said.

"Nope, no question about that."

"Will that charge stick?"

"I saw him groping her myself when I was in her office, and I heard her telling him no. The charge will stick."

"How is Tom doing?"

"I talked to him for a long time yesterday," Weber said. "I don't know if the poor guy's ever going to get over this. He did tell me he was going to go see Greg and Kathy, and also his brother Don over in Lakeside. I know that's a reunion that's been a long time coming, and I think it's going to do all of them some good."

~***~

Anthony Hurley Junior's arraignment took just over an hour. While his attorney tried to make a case for the fact that the Big

Lake Sheriff's Department had been negligent in not filing the criminal charges against his client in a timely manner, Judge Harold Ryman had disagreed and bound him over for trial. Bail was denied because the defendant lived out of state, had no ties to the local community, and had assets at his disposal that would allow him to disappear and assume a new identity somewhere else, which made him a flight risk.

As Weber watched Coop escort the prisoner back to jail, dressed in an orange jumpsuit and wearing handcuffs and leg irons instead of the designer clothes he was used to wearing, he couldn't hide a small smile and a nod of satisfaction. At least it was something, some justice would be served. But he knew that none of it was going to bring Jill Cotter back, or to mend her husband's broken heart. Only time would do that. Time and the love of his family.

Chapter 43

Weber was in his office the next afternoon, obediently signing forms, reviewing reports, and approving overtime slips for the extra hours his deputies had put in during the investigation into the death of Jill Cotter, knowing that Mary was not going to let him leave until they were all done.

There was a knock on his door, and dispatcher Judy Troutman stuck her head inside. "Sheriff, I'm sorry to bother you, but Roberta Jensen is on the telephone and she says it's really important that she speak to you."

"No problem," Weber said, picking up the telephone on his desk and pushing the flashing button. "Hi Roberta, it's Jimmy. What's up?"

"Well I'm not sure. But I thought you needed to know something."

"What's that?"

"Tom Cotter came into my office this morning and dropped off a will. He said that with his wife gone, he wanted to make sure that his sister and brother got his house and whatever was left when he died."

"It's a little soon to be changing wills, isn't it?"

"Some people do things like that right away, so I didn't think a lot about it. But he also left an envelope here for you. I didn't know it until my paralegal came in right after lunch. It was paper-clipped to the inside of the folder with his will."

Weber felt a chill go up his spine. "Is your paralegal there?"

"Yes, she's sitting right here."

"Ask her to read it to me, please."

A moment later the paralegal came on the phone and said, "Hi, Sheriff Weber. I'm not sure what this means, but I'm going to read it to you, okay?"

"Okay, thank you."

He heard the sound of the young woman clearing her throat, and then she read Tom Cotter's message to him:

Jimmy, I'm sorry but I can't live without her. Can you see that our ashes go into the same urn so she won't be alone anymore? I kept my promise to you. My guns are still in the cabinet at the house. Tom.

Weber hung up the phone and went out into the main office. "Get somebody over to Tom Cotter's place right now."

Then he went back into his office and called Kathy Sterling. "Kathy, is Tom there?"

"Tom? No, he came by yesterday and we had a long talk, all three of us. He apologized to Greg for not believing him and to me for shutting me out, and told us never to forget that he really did love us."

"Did he seem okay to you?"

"Given all he's been through, I guess as good as he's going to be for a while. Don't worry, Jim, we'll get him through it. That's what family does."

"Thank you," Weber said. "I'll be in touch."

"Is something wrong?"

"I don't know. I'll get back to you."

Weber hung up and called Don Cotter in Lakeside.

"Yeah, Tom was here this morning, right after I opened up. We talked for a couple of hours. He seemed pretty down, but I think we've at least closed the wound between us."

"Was he in his pickup?"

"No, Sheriff, he was in his Kenworth. Said he was headed down to Phoenix. I told him to take some more time off, but he said he just couldn't handle sitting at home right now and he needed to be back on the road. What's this all about?"

"Hopefully nothing," Weber said, hanging up.

He was headed out the door to go to the Cotter house when the call from the Department of Public Safety came in. The officer told them that according to witnesses who had seen the accident, Tom and his Kenworth had come barreling down U.S. Highway 60 into the Salt River Canyon, a dramatic chasm located halfway between Show Low and the small city of Globe,

90 miles to the south. A couple from northern Utah who were headed to Apache Junction to visit family there said that the big truck never slowed down, its horn blaring, and it looked like the driver never attempted to turn the steering wheel coming into a hairpin turn. The truck had crashed into and then through the rock barrier on the left side of the highway before flying into oblivion, landing 300 feet below in a tangle of twisted metal and shattered glass.

They may not have had as much time together as she wanted in life, but now Tom Cotter and his wife would be reunited forever.

Author's Note: There is a saying among fiction authors: "You can't make this stuff up!" And it's true. Many of the things I incorporate into my stories are based on real-life events, including the exploding Santa Claus mannequin in this book.

Back during the dark days of the Great Depression, in December, 1932, the stores in Mesa, Arizona were hurting financially. Few people have money to spend on a holiday, and things look bleak. That's when a man named John McPhee, the editor of Mesa Journal-Tribune newspaper, came up with the idea of having Santa jump out of an airplane and land near Main Street in downtown Mesa.

The idea was an immediate hit. Families lined up well in advance of the announced time for Santa's arrival, storeowners and clerks hovered over their cash registers with big smiles, anticipating all the business that would come into their shops, and McPhee smiled, thinking of the increased advertising revenue the stunt would generate. What could possibly go wrong?

Quite a bit, as it turned out. When McPhee arrived prior to the designated time, he was disheartened to discover that the circus daredevil he had hired to play the role of Santa Claus was drunk as a skunk. The man could hardly crawl off his barstool, let alone jump out of an airplane. Never one to accept defeat easily, John McPhee came up with an alternative plan. He would dress up in a Santa Claus suit of his own and hide on the ground, while a mannequin in a second Santa suit would be pushed out of the airplane and parachute to the ground. As soon as it landed, McPhee would take its place and greet the throngs of excited children.

Everything went as planned except for one problem. There was no way for the mannequin to pull the ripcord to deploy the parachute. And just like it happened in Big Lake, the mannequin crashed into the street before the horrified eyes of the crowd. Children screamed in terror, there were reports of women going into labor, and the storekeepers no doubt shed a tear or two as the crowd disappeared before their very eyes. Things were so tense that McPhee had to leave town for a few days to escape the heat.

But he soon returned to his desk, put on his editor's green eyeshade, and got back to work.

John McPhee passed away in 1958. The headline announcing his death read: The Man Who Killed Santa Dies.

Here's A Sneak Preview Of Nick Russell's Next Big Lake Book, *Big Lake Fugitive,* Coming Soon!

Chapter 1

The Honda Civic was at least ten years older than the man behind the wheel, and it didn't seem like it had been given much attention in all of those years. The paint was faded to some indeterminate color, there was a crack in the windshield on the passenger side, the springs were broken down in the seats, which were almost devoid of fabric, and the engine rattled and knocked climbing up the hills, making him wonder each time if the old car would reach the top. Going downhill was an adventure as well, given the Honda's bald tires and worn out brakes. But they say beggars can't be choosers, and neither can desperate car thieves.

He nursed it along U.S. Highway 60, fearing that every mile would be its last and it would give up the ghost. Twice New Mexico Highway Patrol cars had passed going in the opposite direction, and each time he felt the panic rising within him. Both times he watched in the rearview mirror, his heart in his throat, expecting them to make a U-turn and for their roof lights to come on, then breathed a huge sigh of relief when it didn't happen.

Passing the Karl G. Jansky Very Large Array radio astronomy observatory, located on the Plains of San Agustin between Magdalena and Datil, with its large white dish antennas pointed toward the heavens, he remembered coming there on a field trip when he was in junior high school. God, how long ago was that? It seemed like forever. He would give anything to be able to roll back the hands of time and be a schoolboy again, before he made the mistakes that landed him in his present predicament.

The Low Fuel light came on somewhere near Pie Town, but a search of the car's glove compartment and under the seats had only turned up a quarter, a nickel, and three pennies. Along with three long forgotten ketchup packets from some fast food drive through window. He couldn't remember how long it had been since he had eaten and tore the ends off of them, sucking the rancid contents into his mouth. They did as much to fill his stomach as 33¢ would do to fill the Honda's gas tank.

He considered pulling into the gas station at Pie Town and trying to beg enough gas to get down the road, but he doubted that it would do him any good and was more likely to make the clerk remember him if somebody came in asking about any suspicious strangers passing through. Especially strangers with bruised faces and one eye swollen almost shut. He never even considered trying to fill the tank and driving off without paying. There was only the one road going anywhere through here and the Honda wasn't exactly a getaway car. One of the local cowboys could probably have run him down without even kicking his horse into a fast lope.

Besides, his previous attempts at a life of crime had never worked out well, from the summer cabins he and his brother had burglarized when they were teenagers to that bust for possession last year, or his latest screw-up, which had led him into the mess he was in now. He still couldn't believe something as simple as driving a car with an expired license tag had ended up this way. Damn you, Claudia! If he would have known about the baggie of pot and the bong she had forgotten about and left in her backpack in the back seat he never would have gotten behind the wheel for that quick trip to the Circle K for a six pack and cigarettes. And now he was running for his life!

The Honda gave up the ghost a few miles past Quemado, sputtering to a stop with barely enough time to allow him to pull it into a wide gravel parking area that held two wooden picnic tables and a trash barrel. It could have been worse. Maybe the first cop that passed by wouldn't notice it as quickly as he would have if the car was on the shoulder of the road.

He felt bad about stealing the car, but he had not had a choice. Still, he figured anybody who could only afford a car this beat up must be down on their luck, too, and he wrote down the owner's name and address from the registration he found in the glove box. If he survived all of this, he planned to send them some money to reimburse them for the loss of the car.

Not sure what to do, but knowing he couldn't stay there, he was debating whether to set off on foot or try to hitch a ride when a big Winnebago motorhome pulled into the parking area towing some kind of small SUV. A moment later the door opened and a small brown dog ran out, barking at him while it wiggled its rear end and wagged its tail as it approached.

"Hi there, how are you today?"

He squatted down and petted the dog, which licked his chin.

"Bosco, you leave that man alone! Come here."

The dog slurped his chin one more time, then ran back to its owner, an older man with a fringe of white hair and a friendly smile.

"Sorry about that. Bosco here has never met a stranger."

"No problem, I love dogs. She's a sweetie."

"Yeah, when she's not being a pain in the ass. Now, you go do your business Bosco. We've still got a lot of miles to get behind us."

"Where are you headed?"

"Camp Verde. Going to spend a couple of weeks at a campground there. How about you?"

"Nowhere right now. My old car just died and I'm kind of stuck."

"I'm not much of a mechanic, but I'll be happy to call a tow truck for you."

"No!" Then, realizing he may have sounded desperate, he added, "You probably couldn't even get a phone signal out here anyway. And to be honest with you, it would cost more to tow it than it's worth."

The man looked at the car and nodded. "Probably so. Can we give you a ride somewhere? I wouldn't want to leave you out in the middle of nowhere."

"Boy, if you could do that, mister, I would really appreciate it."

"Where do you need to get to, son?"

"I'm trying to get home to Big Lake, over in Arizona."

"Don't know that I've heard of it. Where's that at?"

"Most folks haven't heard of it. It's a little mountain town about 25 miles from Springerville."

"Well, I know Springerville's on our way. We can get you that far, if that helps."

"Thank you, it would sure help a lot."

"Well, hop on in. You need anything from your car?"

"No, I don't think so."

"You travel light."

"Yeah, it wasn't a trip I planned to make anytime soon. Truth is, I didn't think I'd ever be going back there."

"Is that home to you?"

"I grew up there. Been gone a while."

"Well, sometimes it's good to go back home, even if you're not looking forward to the trip."

They followed the dog into the motorhome and the man said, "Jackie, this young fella's car broke down and we're going to give him a ride to Springerville. That's my wife, Jackie. Jacqueline's her real name, just like Jackie Kennedy. But I guess that was probably before your time. And I'm Stanley."

The woman smiled and looked at him tentatively, not entirely comfortable with her husband inviting a stranger into their motorhome. Especially one who looked so bruised and battered. He was afraid she might object and tell her husband it was best to leave him where he was and call for help when they could get a phone signal, but before she could say anything, her husband continued, "I don't believe I got your name, son."

"Weber. James Weber, Junior. My father's the sheriff in Big Lake."

Big Lake Snowdaze

Made in the USA
Middletown, DE
05 June 2022

66701611R00156